Insects: The Hunted
A Novel

John Koloen

Watchfire Press

Watchfire Press
www.watchfirepress.com
www.watchfirepress.com/jk

Cover design by Kit Foster
www.kitfosterdesign.com

Insects: The Hunted/John Koloen. – 1st ed.
Print ISBN: 978-1-940708-67-6
e-ISBN: 978-1-940708-66-9

NOVELS FROM JOHN KOLOEN

Insects

Insects: The Hunted

Insects: Specimens

For more details on upcoming releases from John
Koloen, please visit watchfirepress.com/jk.

1

CORPORAL TOMÉ BARROS knew in advance that the best he could hope for from his supervisors was a formal obrigado, trabalho bom feito for his efforts at recovering bodies in the rainforest. There would be no talk of promotion, much less moving into a desk job. It didn't help that he had to contend with the endless carping of Officer Nestor Belmonte, who believed that he would never be able to afford a family as long as Barros was his boss.

At first, the assignment had promise. For several days the federal police were involved in the search for Americans trapped in floodwaters. Then, when survivors appeared of their own accord, the feds moved on, leaving the cleanup to wildlife police and the environmental agency, IBAMA. Interviews with the survivors raised questions about several deaths and led to the discovery of other bodies.

It fell to Barros, Belmonte and Hugo Martins to hike through the mud and debris, retracing the steps of the Americans based on isolated GPS coordinates and guesswork. Two of the Americans, Howard Duncan and Cody Boyd, agreed to accompany Barros to help locate the bodies of a guide, an American student and a professor.

It was a dirty, sweaty business and had all the earmarkings of busy work. Barros complained that even if they found the bodies, they would not be able to recover them since the rainforest was too muddy for vehicles and his group would be on foot.

"Why not wait for things to dry out another week or two?" he'd pleaded with his lieutenant. "Then we could use ATVs. Do the job in one day."

The lieutenant was sympathetic but insisted that the orders were coming from above and there was nothing he could do about them. His superiors wanted to see progress.

Barros would never confide in Belmonte, and Hugo Martins was new to his squad, so he simply added this disappointment to the mountain of previous disappointments that seemed to be his lot in life. If only he could catch a break.

And then there was the business of the killer bugs that the Americans kept bringing up. Even though he'd seen several eviscerated and skeletal remains, he wasn't buying that the victims were killed by insects. Where was the evidence? People die all the time in the forest and all that's left of them are bones, and the big shots in the agency never gave them a thought. He knew their interest stemmed from the simple fact that one of the victims was an American. It was news in Brazil and the States.

What credit did he get for locating the bodies? None, just the "thank you for a job well done," and now he was trudging through the mud looking for the bodies of a bunch of nobodies. Oh, and if it worked out, would you find the insects that supposedly killed them? And, by the way, would you mind recovering the decomposing American so we can get the embassy off our backs?

That's how things really worked, he fumed.

2

DUNCAN AND BOYD kept to themselves, partly because none of the wildlife officers were fluent in English and partly because Corporal Barros, with his limited command of English, had made it known that he thought they were wasting their time.

"If we wait a week or two," he harped in English mixed with Portuguese, "we could do this the right way. Ride in on vehicles, recover the bodies instead of just marking them so that we can come back to pick them up. What sense does what we're doing make? I ask you."

Duncan shrugged, explaining that he and his assistant wanted to help but weren't able to spend additional time in Brazil.

"I need to get back to my lab," Duncan said slowly, in English.

Were it not for the language barrier, he would have explained that though his expedition was a catastrophic failure, it was important to locate living specimens of *Reptilus blaberus* to study and that he hoped they would come across remnants of the colony that had attacked them, though with every step they took his hope faded.

The forest floor was a junkyard of debris. The trails

they had followed during the expedition were obliterated or covered over with mounds of tree branches, silt, leaves, logs, dead stinking fish and other wildlife. However, they were making good time since the flooding had subsided and Duncan was hopeful that even if they found no insects, they'd be on a plane to America in a day or two. Using Boyd's coordinates, they located the remains of a dog and a portion of the skeleton of its owner. Coming to the place where they'd buried the guide, Javier Costa, they found a ribcage protruding from the earth.

On the second day, after a fitful night in tents, they reached the end of the road where Carlos Johnson and Fernando Azevedo had died. Barros took great interest in the clearing made by illegal loggers, scribbling detailed notes about the extent of the operation, the partially intact road the loggers had built and the tools that lay about. Belmonte and Martins circled the area, looking for bodies while Barros and the Americans gathered around an old truck that lay half buried in mud and debris.

"Carlos was over there somewhere, wasn't he?" Boyd said, pointing toward an area near the truck.

"I thought so," Duncan said, cautiously approaching a pile of debris between two trees.

"I don't see him," Boyd said.

"You're sure that's the right place?" Duncan said.

"Definitely. The truck was right across from where he died."

"But he's not there now."

"Maybe he is. Maybe he's covered up."

Duncan explained to Corporal Barros that they were looking for the body of the American.

"He died right there," Boyd said.

"You know, a flood changes things. Maybe the body, you know, floated away," Barros said, sounding his words carefully.

"Maybe he's under the debris," Duncan suggested.

3

BOYD COULD NOT bring himself to look at Johnson's body, which the wildlife officers found wedged between trees. He was glad that they were tasked only with locating bodies and that removal would be done later when vehicles could be used. He watched as Duncan briefly looked at the mangled, stinking corpse and nodded that it was Carlos Johnson. As far as Boyd was concerned, they had accomplished their goal and should return to Manaus and from there fly home.

Belmonte and Martins counted five skeletal remains around the clearing, none of them with identification. As intent on leaving as Boyd was, Duncan felt torn at not having accomplished his goal of capturing specimens. Everywhere he looked he saw the remnants of a devastating flood and no sign of *Reptilus blaberus*.

Nobody wanted to spend another night camping so the party hurriedly retraced their steps to the cabin where they'd tied up the boat that had brought them from Manaus. On the hike, Duncan suggested to Boyd that they organize another expedition to capture specimens.

"You can't be serious," Boyd said.

"Without specimens I've accomplished nothing. This whole trip might just as well not have happened," Duncan said.

"Don't say that. Carlos is dead."

"I know," Duncan sighed. "Do you think they'd want us to quit? For chrissakes, they died trying to…"

"No, they didn't," Boyd said angrily. "They died because we got caught up in a flood. They died because we were someplace we shouldn't have been. I'm not saying it's anybody's fault, but they did not expect to die when we started out. This was one big fuck up and the only way to deal with it is to walk away from it."

"You're right, of course. I was just thinking out loud."

BARROS HAD SET a brisk pace. Duncan and Boyd fell behind while Martins and Belmonte stayed just out of earshot of their leader so they could discuss their plans for retrieving and selling the gear the Americans had left behind.

The two officers had rummaged through the discarded equipment while searching for bodies. Belmonte pocketed a small video camera that he snatched from the mud. On the march back to the cabin, they talked in whispers as their boss and the Americans led the way.

"We might be able to sell this stuff on Mercado-Livre," Belmonte whispered to Martins. "Those Americans bought first class stuff. Those tents, if they're not torn up and we can find the poles, are worth hundreds of reals."

Martins shrugged.

"We could come back, you know, on the weekend. Might be dry enough to get out here on an ATV or something. Would be worth it. If we had an ATV," Belmonte said.

Martins shook his head.

"Think about it what it would cost. We'd need a boat, an ATV and a trailer to haul stuff. And we'd need a trailer for the ATV, otherwise we couldn't get it to the boat. We're talking hundreds of reals just to get started, maybe thousands."

"I got a cousin who's got one. I could ask him," Belmonte said excitedly, then frowned. "Course he'd want a cut, which would only be fair."

Martins grimaced.

"It's gonna cost so much we'll end up losing money. I mean, do you have a pot of gold somewhere to pay for this?"

Belmonte shook his head.

"You're right. It sounded good in my head but we could lose our shirts."

"Not only that, but if we got caught we might lose our jobs. It's a crime scene, you know."

"Well, at least I got the camera," Belmonte said. "It might be worth something."

5

BECAUSE OF HIS previous involvement with the Barbosa case, and the presence of corpses, it fell to State of Amazonas civil police investigator Eduardo Dias to determine whether any crimes occurred as a result of the ill-fated Duncan expedition.

"It's unfortunate they can't be charged with gross stupidity," he told his colleagues.

All that remained was to interview the surviving guide, Antonio Suarez. Dias did not have a high opinion of guides. All one needed to be a fishing guide was a boat. Most sport fishermen brought their own equipment and paid deposits for fuel, bait, food and other expenses. Dias understood that Suarez was an employee of Javier Costa, one of the victims. Although he knew nothing of Suarez, he expected him to lead an itinerant lifestyle with no permanent, full-time vocation or address. Locating him, especially given his common name, would be difficult, assuming he lived in Manaus. So he would focus on Costa. But first he would go over materials recovered by the wildlife officers who located the bodies. Because of the possibility of criminal charges, evidence that had been recovered was forwarded to the civil police. This included an iPhone that had belonged to one of the victims but had been underwater for several days. The computer jocks in his office told him to forget about recovering data from the phone.

"The wildlife officers found an illegal lumber operation," Dias told his supervisor.

"If that's all you've got, then it's an environmental crime. Throw that back to them."

"I still need to find this guide, and what about all the corpses?"

"Any evidence of homicide?"

"Well, the bodies were mostly just bones. You know, the Americans kept saying it was insects that killed them," Dias said.

"I know, that's what you said about that first body."

"I'm still waiting for the pathologist's report."

"Good luck with that."

"I'll just keep looking for the guide, see where it goes."

"OK, but don't waste time on it."

Looking over the list of names that were part of the expedition, he typed "Fernando Azevedo, Manaus" into a Google search window. In seconds a list of citations popped up, including his phone number at the Federal University of Amazonas. That was easy, he thought, while leaving a message on the professor's answering machine.

HOWARD DUNCAN WASN'T expecting a hero's welcome when he entered his office for the first time since leaving for Brazil. And he didn't get one, having arrived on campus in the evening. Unable to have his phone replaced until tomorrow, he was dismayed to find hundreds of emails waiting for him on his desktop computer. He scanned through several pages of them and decided to have Cody Boyd, his graduate assistant, read them or assign one of the entomology department's work-study undergrads to do it. But that couldn't happen until tomorrow, and he was worn out from the flight from Manaus to Houston Intercontinental, followed by the two-hour drive in a rental car to his apartment just off campus.

Though he was exhausted, he'd driven straight to his office with a vague notion that sitting at his desk in familiar surroundings would somehow put every unfortunate thing that happened in Brazil behind him. Not ready to deal with his colleagues, he found comfort in leaning back in his black Aeron and staring at the acoustic tile ceiling. He wondered whether his colleagues were aware of what had happened in Brazil.

At Boyd's urging, he'd called Carlos Johnson's parents

from the U.S. consular agency in Manaus. They already knew their son had died in the rainforest and were curt and short in their brief conversation. Duncan sensed their anger, listened politely and offered condolences multiple times. Although he didn't discuss it with the parents, during the flight to Houston he thought about sponsoring a scholarship in Johnson's name.

"The family might like that," Boyd said wistfully, sitting alongside Duncan. "But I wouldn't bring it up yet."

"Too soon, I agree. But it's something to think about. Maybe you could check it out for me. You know, find out if we have to work through the dean's office or through the administration. Whatever."

Boyd smiled. *It's "we" when he wants me to do something and it's "me" when he gets credit for something*, he thought.

"Sure, tomorrow," Boyd said.

EDUARDO DIAS HAD no problem locating Professor Azevedo's office. The door was locked and Dias meandered through the halls in search of an administrator who could have it unlocked. By chance, in a small lounge, he asked a woman wearing a lab coat where he could go for help. A young man sitting at a nearby table looked up upon hearing the detective mention the professor's name.

"Excuse me, sir," the young man said, "Are you looking for Professor Azevedo?"

Dias smiled at the woman as she turned away.

"I'm looking for his office. I'm with the civil police and I'm conducting an investigation into his death."

"It's a sad thing. My name is Daniel Rocha and I am, or was, the professor's assistant. I can take you to his office."

"So you know about his death?" Dias asked.

"Oh, yeah, everybody knows. I went down there to find him."

"Really! That's interesting. Were you part of the expedition?"

"Oh, no, no, no. The professor left a message on the answering machine that he was in trouble and I tried to help, but as it turned out…"

While Rocha spoke, Dias paged through his notes, looking for a mention of the assistant.

"Were you interviewed by anyone while you were down there?"

"You mean the press?" Rocha asked.

"No. Someone from my office or, perhaps, wildlife officers?"

"No. Nobody talked to me. I was kinda depressed and stuck to myself. They mostly talked to the Americans and the boat captain. All I did was try to find the professor."

Dias sat across from Rocha and started asking questions and scribbling in his notebook. Rocha explained what he did in the rainforest, what his job involved, what he knew about the professor and especially what he knew of the expedition and the Americans.

"I still don't know a whole lot about it," Rocha said, sipping from his drink. "You know, I'm not an entomology major so I can't tell you anything about the research the professor did except that he'd discovered some sort of cockroach on steroids and that the team was going to gather specimens. I can take you to his office. Maybe you can go through his papers or something."

"That would be very helpful, if you don't mind," Dias said, closing his notebook.

8

His first full day back at the office did not work out the way that Duncan had planned. Boyd emailed in sick for starters. Getting his university-issued phone replaced was more difficult than he'd expected. He had to convince a clerk that he shouldn't be charged for its loss. Eventually, with the help of an administrator, he got a new phone but couldn't pick it up until the next day.

This was frustrating because his expectation was that he would simply have it handed it to him and all of his email, voice messages, bookmarks and contacts would automatically reappear. He was not happy with the explanation that there were others ahead of him whose phones were being prepared. He was tempted to pull rank but thought better of it, insisting that it be ready in the morning.

Sitting at his desk, staring at endless pages of emails on his desktop computer, he felt helpless without an assistant. Scanning the emails, he wished he'd had a better filter, because there seemed to be an inordinate number from people whose names he didn't recognize. Normally he would delete them but, for the most part, they weren't spam. They were requests for interviews from media.

"What the fuck," he said aloud.

It hadn't occurred to him that what happened in Brazil would be newsworthy and now, more than ever, he wished that Boyd was in the office to help him out. So he called him using his office phone, which he virtually never used since he relied almost exclusively on his cell phone.

Boyd didn't even try to fake it when he answered his boss's call.

"I'm just tired and worn out," Boyd said.

"Me, too," Duncan said unsympathetically. "But I need help."

Frustrated, Duncan pressed Boyd, insisting that he come to work. Realizing he couldn't win the argument, Boyd said, "I'll be there before noon," and ended the conversation.

Minutes later, a knock came on Duncan's door. A middle-aged woman in a dark blue skirt and white blouse stepped inside.

"Dr. Duncan," she said firmly. "The dean wants to see you. You know, we've been calling you for days. Don't you ever check your messages?"

INVESTIGATOR DIAS FOLLOWED Daniel Rocha into the late Fernando Azevedo's office. After surveying the small, cluttered space, Dias studied the desktop, which was covered with notes, scientific journals and papers. The bookcases that lined the walls were filled with books, specimen cases, mementos, framed photos and other items. Everything was covered with dust.

"Has anyone been in here since the professor left?" Dias asked.

"Just me, as far as I know," Rocha replied.

"It looks like it's never been cleaned."

"The professor had a thing about custodians cleaning up."

"A thing?"

"He was afraid he'd never be able to find anything, though you would think a little cleaning wouldn't hurt," Rocha said.

Looking at his notes, the detective asked, "What about this boat captain? What do you know about him?"

Rocha explained how he'd contacted the captain in an effort to rescue the professor.

"It was Javier something," Rocha said. "Ahh, no, it was Gonzalo Juarez. I have his number on my phone."

Dias smiled. Using Bluetooth, Rocha sent the contact information to Dias's phone.

"One more thing," Dias said as he looked at his phone to confirm the data transfer, "Do you know anything about this insect they were looking for?"

"Oh, not me. I just did routine filing and mostly surfed the web."

"Sounds like the perfect job."

"Except that I'll probably be out of a job until next semester."

Reaching to a specimen box with a glass top from one of the bookcases, Rocha handed it to Dias. In it were a pair of dissected *Reptilus blaberii*.

"Wow, those are big *baratas*," Dias said with amazement.

"Yeah, I don't know much about them."

"I'd like to take this with me," Dias said.

Rocha looked conflicted. He was uncertain whether it was appropriate to remove the professor's belongings.

"Maybe you should ask the department head," Rocha said weakly. "I don't think I'm authorized to…"

"Nonsense," Dias countered. "This is an investigation. I'll tell you what, I'll write a receipt acknowledging that I have this, this specimen. Here's my card. I doubt anyone will even know that I have it, judging from the condition of this office."

The detective left the campus with a lively step. In less than thirty minutes he had the boat captain's phone number as well as a specimen that he could present to the state entomologist for examination. He felt he was close to concluding his investigation, though he hoped he'd be able to locate the surviving guide to get his story. Looking at the blue, clear sky, he felt the sort of elation that came with closing a case. He hoped it would last through the rest of the day.

MEDIA COVERAGE OF the expedition first emerged when a blogger in Manaus known for his gossipy content reported that wildlife officers had discovered a large number of bodies in the rainforest. Commenters speculated that landowners, revolutionaries, drug cartels, lumber thieves, wildlife officers themselves, and the Brazilian army were in one way or another responsible for the deaths and that the government was trying to cover it up. Since the initial coverage was in Portuguese, other media in South and North America had not picked it up and local media didn't follow up because the blog had been called out for fabricating some of its coverage, which was largely anti-authoritarian.

Nestor Belmonte was not aware of the blog as he sat at his kitchen table, holding the silt-covered camera he'd found in the forest. Yes, it could be construed as stolen property, but at the time he thought vaguely that the camera had some value, that it might be possible to dry it out, clean it up and sell it. But it was clear that the camera was in a hopeless condition. Nonetheless, he pulled out the memory card. After cleaning it, he inserted it into the card reader on his laptop and prepared to be disappointed. He was thrilled when the flash card's icon appeared on the screen.

The card contained multiple mpeg files. Would they run? He opened the first one using a media app. None of the files were longer than several minutes. Some of the files could be loaded but didn't run. Some couldn't be loaded. And some worked perfectly. The camera microphone was sensitive enough to pick up conversations and background noises, but it didn't get interesting until the images of animal carcasses and a human skeleton appeared.

"*Que porra?*" he whispered to himself as the choppy video played out on his laptop.

Fast-forwarding through the remaining files he could hardly believe what he was seeing. His pulse quickened as each scene played out. He was elated and felt a rush of energy. *This is an incredible find*, he thought as he struggled to keep up with the rapid pace of possibilities deluging his mind. Within moments one thought rose to the top.

"I'm going to be rich!" he said loudly, and quickly covered his mouth. It would not be good for others in the apartment building to know of this. He was now focused on what it would take to make money from the videos and for that he needed to talk to someone. He and Hugo Martins had planned to scavenge the site at some point. It wasn't like they would be stealing, though their boss might not see it that way. For a moment he wondered whether he could really trust Martins, but he couldn't resist the urge to confide in someone. So he called him.

DUNCAN WASN'T SURE what to expect when he was ushered into his dean's spacious office. The walls were covered with certificates and photographs of the dean shaking hands with politicians and academic superstars. He took a seat in a dark brown, tufted leather chair with padded arms. Dean Chester Dearborn nodded at Duncan as he finished a phone call.

"Ah, alumni," he said, smiling. "You can't live with 'em and you can't live without 'em."

"No, Chet, I suppose not."

Dearborn pulled a manila folder from a small pile on his massive, glass-topped executive desk.

"Have you replaced your phone yet?" the dean asked.

"I'm supposed to get one tomorrow. Why?"

"Public affairs has been trying to reach you for days."

"I'm sorry, I don't quite understand. I just got back."

"I understand that. Have you tried to contact Carlos Johnson's parents?"

"Yes, I did. From the consular office in Manaus. I tried to tell them what happened, but I guess they're still trying to come to grips with his death. I think they may have hung up on me."

"I'm glad to hear that you called them."

Duncan smiled sheepishly. If it hadn't been for Boyd's urging, he would have put the call off. Good for Cody, he thought.

Pulling up the university's daily summary of news coverage on his computer, the dean turned his monitor so that Duncan could see it. The entire screen was filled with two-sentence summaries from local, state and national media, all of them referencing the death of Carlos Johnson. One headline leaped out at him: Parents of dead student want answers.

"What did you say to them?" Deanborn said.

"I already told you I offered my condolences several times. I didn't tell them much about it because they didn't ask me anything other than how could it have happened. I tried to explain, but they kept cutting me off. I know they were upset. I thought it best just to listen. I don't know, I hope I did the right thing."

Dearborn rubbed his forehead as if massaging a headache and swept his hands through his hair. His chair swiveled slightly as he leaned forward, sighing.

"You know, I read the article and I don't know what to say to the parents. I know Johnson signed a release and all that, but things are probably going to get worse."

"How so?"

"There's a blogger in Brazil who's posted information that hasn't made it to the mainstream media yet. One of our public affairs people learned about it from a Brazilian student. He translated it."

The dean laid a printout of the post in front of Duncan. It read like a dispatch from a foreign correspondent.

"He's exaggerating," Duncan protested as he finished reading. "Where is this information coming from?"

"He doesn't say, but as you may have noticed, he says the police are investigating and that his source says you should've known better than to go where you did given the weather."

Duncan tilted his head against the back of his chair and stared at the ceiling. He thought back to the meeting with the group at Maggie Cross's rental in Manaus. Not much was said about the weather. The conversation was mostly about how to gear up, how to pay for it and how quickly they could start.

"Yeah, we didn't spend much time talking about the weather," he stammered.

"Apparently, you should have," Dearborn said harshly. "And this doesn't even touch on all the bodies that the police found. I mean, were you in a war zone and didn't know it, or what? I really want to understand this because I have a meeting coming up with the president and he wants answers yesterday."

"What do you want me to do?"

Dearborn sighed heavily.

"You're on thin ice here, OK? I want you to understand this. I want a full report on my desk by close of business today. And I don't want anything left out. I'm afraid this is just the beginning, and once the American media picks up on what's being said in Brazil, all hell will break loose. Public affairs is already working up talking points but they don't have much to go on, so I'll forward your report to them after I've read it."

The two looked at one another as the conversation abruptly ended. Duncan rose awkwardly as if on cue, stepped away from the chair and pointed himself to the door.

"Under no circumstances are you to talk to the press," the dean commanded. "If someone calls, refer them to public affairs. Is that understood?"

Duncan nodded timidly.

"And about your phone, I'll have my secretary get a new one today. Make sure you have it with you at all times."

Duncan walked slowly to his office, overwhelmed by self-doubt over the decisions he had made and fearful of what was yet to come.

12

EDUARDO DIAS ARRANGED to meet Captain Gonzalo Juarez on the dock where he kept his boat. Dias had tried to get the captain to meet at his office but Juarez insisted that the detective come to him—for good reason. One, Juarez didn't want his wife to find out that he was involved in a police matter, and two, he had a friend who once went to be interviewed at the police department and ended up in jail for three months. He felt more secure at his boat, though he didn't say that to Dias.

The meeting was brief and not as informative as Dias had hoped. The detective had a copy of the report filed by wildlife police but was hoping to flesh it out. He sensed that Juarez had held back information but couldn't put his finger on it. The man smiled a lot and was pleasant, but nervously moved about his boat while being questioned. At first Dias thought Juarez was hiding something from him but then it became clear that Juarez couldn't express himself very well in Portuguese and sometimes lapsed into Spanish, which Dias didn't speak.

Five minutes into the interview and Dias stopped taking notes as Juarez moved about the small boat. He didn't seem to know much. When he asked if he knew the guide Antonio Suarez, the captain shrugged.

"I knew the professor a little but none of the others," Juarez said. He feared that the more he talked, the more likely he would get into trouble. Holding up his finger, he retreated to the tiny wheelhouse and emerged with several flyers.

"One of the guides gave them to me. He wanted me to hand them out to passengers," Juarez said.

The flyers promoted Javier Costa's guide service and included two phone numbers.

The detective thanked Juarez and stepped off the boat.

"Looks like a nice day," Dias said.

Juarez smiled and waved as the detective left the dock. He'd been worried that he could be prosecuted for being two days late picking up the Americans and felt relieved that the detective hadn't brought it up.

NESTOR BELMONTE COULD hardly contain himself when he welcomed Hugo Martins into his apartment. He shook hands extravagantly and spoke nonstop and *rapidamente*, so much so that when Martins took a seat at the kitchen table he asked Belmonte if he had taken drugs. Belmonte laughed, grabbed two Brahmas from the fridge, popped the tops, set one in front of his guest, and slid into a facing chair. He leaned back and took a long, leisurely swallow before gently setting the bottle on the table and breaking into a wide, can't-hide-it smile.

"What?" Martins asked. "You said you wanted to show me something. By the way, thanks for the beer."

"You remember that camera I found in the forest?"

"The one you stole?"

"Stole? How can picking up something after a flood be called stealing? I thought we were friends."

"We are," Martins said, sipping his beer.

"You didn't tell anyone, did you?" Belmonte asked with mock suspicion.

"No, why would I do that?"

"Good. But as I told you on the phone..."

"Something about the camera, right. You thought you could sell it online?"

"No. It don't work. There are videos on the memory card that you gotta see. I think we can make money off them, only I don't know how and I know you do stuff online a lot more than me and—well, first watch the videos and then we'll talk."

Belmonte was too anxious to stay in the tiny kitchen with Martins while he viewed the videos. But he was also too nervous to stay out of the kitchen as he studied his friend's face for reactions, pacing back and forth like a crazy person.

"Would you please stop that," Martins barked.

"I'm just excited. Sorry."

Belmonte took his seat and sipped his beer, emptying the bottle by the time Martins had finished watching the videos.

"You want one?" He asked as he reached in his fridge for another beer. Martins held up his bottle and shook his head. "Not yet."

"So, what do you think?" Belmonte asked expectantly.

"What do I think? You mean about the videos?"

"No, about the weather. Of course, man, about the videos. Get serious."

"Gruesome," Martins started, "and really interesting. It almost looks like someone was trying to shoot a reality show only they had trouble keeping the camera steady."

"It wasn't too bad, was it?"

"I've seen worse, where you'd get nauseated watching them."

"No, I mean the content. What do you think?"

"Man," Martins said, "they're kinda sick."

"Is that in a good way or a bad way?"

"Both."

This wasn't going the way Belmonte had imagined. His friend wasn't as excited as he was. He had called Martins not just because he could trust him, but also because he knew a lot about the internet. His first week on the job, Martins told Belmonte that he'd worked as a production assistant in a video marketing firm and learned not only how to shoot videos but how to get the most attention for them when posting them online. Belmonte had no experience posting videos and hoped that Martins would help him.

"OK, so what do you mean both?"

"I don't know," Martins said. "There's some ugly stuff there."

"Yeah, isn't that what counts on the internet? You know, there's videos of beheadings and stuff."

"Yeah, but you won't find those on YouTube."

"No?" Belmonte said, disappointed. "Why not?"

"YouTube has rules about what you can post and gruesome stuff like this they don't allow."

"Really?"

Belmonte rose and moved behind Martins's shoulder, looking at the laptop's blank screen.

"So, I can't put this on YouTube?"

"No way."

"You're sure?"

"Absolutely. Those are the rules."

"Fucking rules!" Belmonte growled. "I'm always getting hung up on rules. I was hoping I, we, could make money off this, you know, put it online, get millions of views, go viral, get advertising and make a bundle. But you're saying that can't happen?"

"Not on the major sites but you might be able to sell

it to one of those blogger news sites, you know, the ones with the gossip and political bullshit. They might pay for this. It's news, you know."

"You can help me with that, right?" Belmonte asked, grinning. "We'll split whatever we get for it."

"Works for me."

THE MEETING WITH the university president left Howard Duncan chagrined and wondering whether he had a future in academia. With his dean sitting alongside him, the president had said, barely concealing his anger, that the state attorney general had opened an investigation into the matter and that the parents were "breathing down our necks." The local paper was preparing a front page article for the Sunday edition and TV affiliates were preparing their own stories. Duncan tried to explain what happened and why, but the president wasn't satisfied.

"For me, it all goes back to the decision to do this when you should have known that flooding was possible. Did you even check the weather reports?"

"Of course," Duncan said in his defense. The storms were north of their location and he felt they would avoid them. Postponing the expedition would have jeopardized their goal of finding specimens of a newly discovered insect species.

The president gave the dean a frustrated look.

"You don't get it, do you, Dr. Duncan? A student has died on your watch as a result of a possibly reckless act on your part. That is how it is going to be portrayed."

"What he's saying, Howard," Dean Dearborn said in a less strident tone, "is that it is going to be hard to demonstrate that you acted prudently. You understand? This is not about insects. This is about culpability."

Duncan realized that defending himself was pointless. The meeting wasn't to get his side of the story, as he had hoped. It was the first step taken to insulate the university and his department from what had happened and would happen.

They're cutting bait, he thought as he returned to his office.

Cody Boyd was shocked when Duncan confided in him following the meeting with the president. It was the topic of the day in the department. Everyone knew about it. Duncan had a reputation among faculty and staff. Most office staff thought him brusque and indifferent, a haughty person who didn't bother to learn their names. Faculty found him to be a professional who was always prepared for meetings and who, whenever asked, would provide advice on obtaining research grants. He taught several classes. Though he was cordial, he often seemed to be too busy for conversations. Because of his status as a highly regarded entomologist, he was often invited to social gatherings, where he would make an appearance but rarely stay for more than a cocktail. Although he was admired for his academic success, his single-mindedness made it difficult to make friends.

Duncan smiled wryly from behind his desk and asked Boyd to close the door.

"What's up? How'd it go?"

"Well, it wasn't what I expected," Duncan confided.

"I think I was blindsided. The dean was no help. The president just unloaded on me like I was an adjunct. Absolutely no respect from that man."

"Sorry to hear that."

"Yeah, but I've gotta put that behind me. Gotta get on with it, you know."

Sitting across from Duncan, Boyd wondered whether he was talking about the meeting or the disaster in the rainforest. He wondered whether Duncan thought of it in the same way. Was it a disaster or just a speed bump in his mind? With a natural reticence against pressing a man who was nearly twenty years his senior and much more accomplished, not to mention his employer, Boyd waited for the moment he could determine whether the conversation was professional or personal.

"So, are you planning to set up a scholarship for Carlos like you were talking about?"

Duncan wasn't thinking about Johnson at the moment.

"I think it's a good idea," Boyd prompted.

"I guess I've tried to block that out of mind."

Boyd's jaw dropped slightly, stunned by the response.

"Not the scholarship—the death, and not just Carlos. Azevedo, too. I just can't get a handle on it. The president thinks I acted recklessly because of the weather, but we were on an important scientific mission and the old fart himself hasn't done any research in decades. Who is he to criticize me?"

Boyd was surprised by Duncan's sudden crescendo of anger. Was he really putting his feelings ahead of the victims?

"Ah, I don't mean that, not in that way. It's not about me. And yes, I'm going to establish a scholarship."

Boyd was relieved upon hearing this.

"Maybe you can start the ball rolling on this, Cody ol' boy. What do you say? Call the development folks and find out what we need to do."

"You already asked me to do that," Boyd said.

"Yeah, yeah, I think that's a good use of your time. Find out the details; maybe we can do a fundraiser."

16

DEAN CHESTER DEARBORN was more of a politician than an academic. His professional credentials hardly equaled those of many faculty in his department, but he knew how to schmooze and get along with people at any level. He thought of himself as a departmental peacemaker, and he was good at it. He'd been on the job since before Duncan came to campus and was always at the front of the room when faculty or students achieved success. He liked to have photographs taken with the achievers, which his secretary would then display on a bulletin board outside his office. He had outlasted several presidents, which he attributed to his innate ability to avoid confrontations. He avoided criticizing anyone in front of others and even then his tone was avuncular and nonjudgmental, as he believed that people who strayed needed only a nudge to get back on track. And Duncan had strayed.

Duncan wasn't surprised that the dean wanted to confer shortly after their meeting with the president. Prior to leaving his office, he asked Boyd if there was a way he could record the meeting with his phone. Boyd looked at it, went to the iTunes store and downloaded an app.

"I think even you can use this one," he joked as he demoed the app.

"That's encouraging," Duncan said. "All I want to have to do is press a button and forget about it."

"It's pretty much foolproof."

"I'm thinking I should do this just to protect myself, you know, from an assault on my academic freedom. I wish I'd recorded my meeting with the president. I think I'll record everything from now on until this blows over."

Boyd nodded and wished Duncan luck as he left for the dean's office.

DIAS WAS NO closer to locating Antonio Suarez, the surviving guide, than he had been at the start of his investigation, which was supposed to be perfunctory. His supervisor wanted him to close the case quickly, but reports were starting to appear in the local media that the American who died had been killed by one of his companions. He was inclined to dismiss them as rumors, since they appeared in publications and blogs known for their sensationalism.

The problem was that he couldn't find the only person in Brazil who could confirm the rumors. He knew that finding a young man with such a common surname was virtually impossible. It was unlikely Suarez would be listed in any kind of directory and he probably didn't have a permanent address, and if Dias asked around, people would become suspicious and not cooperate. The only thing he had to go on was Javier Costa's promotional flyer.

Studying the flyer, he saw that the two phone numbers had different area codes. One was assigned to phones in the state of Amazonas and the other was not. The second one was probably a cell number. He dialed the Amazonas number. A woman answered after several rings. It was

Costa's wife. She told him that Suarez had informed her of her husband's death though he didn't tell her how he had died. She asked when his body would be recovered. Dias explained that he wasn't involved with the recovery but was looking for Suarez.

"Did he commit a crime?" she asked. "He's such a good boy."

"Nothing like that. I'm just looking for information."

"He might be at our rental house. My husband sometimes stayed there when he had to work crazy hours. Unfortunately, the neighborhood is in decline and we couldn't keep it rented. You wouldn't be interested in buying it, would you? I could use the money now that Javier is gone."

"No, *Senhora*, but I could use the address."

Using the GPS on his phone, Dias arrived at Costa's rental house at mid-day. The sun was high in the sky, the temperature in the low nineties Fahrenheit but the humidity was under fifty percent. Not altogether unpleasant.

He surveyed the house from the street. It looked ordinary, identical to other stuccoed houses on both sides of the street, which only differed in color. Pressing past the gate, he approached the front door and knocked several times. Looking through a gap in the curtains on the front window, he sensed movement.

He knocked again, harder, and tried the door knob. It was locked. His curiosity piqued, he moved to the back yard. There he found a concrete patio covered by a wood awning. On the slab were two patio chairs and a small cast-iron cafe table in need of paint. The sliding back door was locked, a curtain blocking the view inside. Wasting little time, he found an unlocked window and using one of the patio chairs boosted himself into a small bedroom, landing face first on the carpeted floor. A man was hiding under the bed.

"What the fuck!" Dias said.

Scrambling to his feet, he felt for the pistol on his hip, but didn't pull it out of its holster.

"Come out of there," he commanded. "I'm with the police."

18

B<small>OYD</small> S<small>AT</small> I<small>N</small> Duncan's office, watching his boss as he replayed the recording from his meeting with Dean Dearborn.

"Can you believe that!" Duncan exclaimed at intervals, staring at the iPhone, shaking his head, not even looking at his assistant.

Boyd found himself losing interest. Duncan had placed the phone in the inside pocket of his sport jacket and the sound was muffled. Boyd struggled to follow the conversation.

"Did you hear that, Cody?" Duncan said, staring at the phone. "He wants me to take the semester off. And did you hear that part where he says I might have PTSD! Of all the nerve," he said, angrily. "Do I look like I've got PTSD? Do I?"

Boyd smiled wanly and shrugged.

"You seem agitated," Boyd said, tentatively.

"Well, who wouldn't be?" Duncan said defensively. "He's basically telling me—not in so many words, but underneath it all—that my services are no longer needed. They're abandoning me like, like, I don't know what."

"Like yesterday's news?"

"Yeah. I can't believe it. You know, I've got half a mind to resign. That'll send a message through the department," Duncan said, defiantly. "At least that's what I'd like to think. But I'd just be helping them out. I know how academia works. It's not for people with thin skins, that's for sure."

After the recording ended, Duncan paced. He was agitated and he could see he was making Boyd uncomfortable. He knew it wasn't a good state to be in and wished Boyd hadn't seen him get so angry. He'd already left a message with a member of the faculty senate to find out whether they supported him.

"Did you contact development about the scholarship?" Duncan asked abruptly.

Boyd was glad he had changed the subject. *Perhaps he is getting tired of it*, he thought.

"I did and I'm supposed to meet with someone next week. The person I talked to said it doesn't take long to set one up. He said Carlos's family should probably be involved, as it will be in his honor."

"Of course," Duncan said. "We might wait on that, though. I don't think they're ready for that just yet. They were pretty angry when I called them."

"OK. I'll just meet with development and see what they say. What about you? You must be pretty, ah, upset by what's going on, huh?"

"Upset? Hmph," Duncan said, sighing. "I wish this hadn't happened, you know. It's not as if I planned this."

"I know. I'm with you on that," Boyd said.

"But it did happen and I have to expect consequences. I was in charge, there's no denying that. I may have made mistakes, but I think I did the best I could. We lost two good men…"

"Three men died," Boyd interjected softly.

"Three men died. But the rest of us survived, right? That's something in my favor, isn't it? I mean, we could all have been killed. We're lucky to be alive. As much as I want to put it behind me, it's the most exciting, terrifying and depressing thing I've ever done. And I'll bet it's that way for everyone."

"Can't agree with you more, boss."

19

DUNCAN WAS ALONE in his apartment when he received a call from the foundation supporting his grant. The voice on the other end identified herself as Elizabeth Groton, the foundation's general counsel. She told him that they were suspending his grant temporarily.

"My grant runs through the end of the calendar year. You can't just suspend it. I've got important work to do."

She asked if he'd read the grant application he signed.

"Everything I wrote is accurate," he insisted.

"That's not what I'm referring to. There's a section in the boilerplate that relieves the foundation of its responsibilities in the event of adverse publicity. If you like, I can have it sent to you."

"No, I wasn't aware of that," he said, giving up the fight.

"This is nothing personal. The foundation can ill afford negative publicity and our board feels that it's best for the foundation that we distance ourselves at this time. It has nothing to do with the quality of your work. We are picking up on articles from Brazil that the authorities are conducting an investigation and that charges may be filed, though we don't know against whom."

"Who's filing these charges?" Duncan asked, suddenly livid.

Groton declined to provide additional information and warned Duncan that if he mentioned the foundation in any interviews he could be stripped of his grant entirely.

"So, I'm between a rock and a hard place?"

"It would seem so, sir. I'm sorry, but we are doing this in the best interest of the foundation. I hope you understand. I hope things resolve quickly and successfully in your favor, as we are otherwise quite pleased with your work."

Fuckers, he thought.

20

THIS IS MY lucky day, Detective Dias thought as he escorted Antonio Suarez into the kitchenette. With the windows closed, the house was hot and stuffy. Opening the back door, they stepped onto the patio where he directed the young man to take a seat. Concerned that Suarez might flee if he took his eyes off him, Dias reached into the kitchenette and pulled out a padded chair. Sitting across from Suarez, the cafe table between them, he asked if he was Antonio Suarez.

"Yes. What is this about?" Suarez asked.

"I'm investigating the death of an American, among others, in the forest and I understand you were one of the guides."

"Am I under arrest?"

"No, why would you think that?" Detective Dias said.

"I don't know. Police arrest people."

"Well, if you committed a crime then that would be the case, but you haven't, have you?"

"Not that I know of. What do you want to know?"

Dias started writing in his notebook.

"Well, first thing, why were you hiding under the bed? That seems suspicious."

"I was afraid."

"Afraid of what, exactly?"

"It's just that I worked for Javier and I've stayed here plenty of times when we had early morning trips, you know, guiding fishermen. They like to get out early."

"And, you know, of course, Mr. Costa is dead."

Suarez lowered his head.

"I watched him die," he said quietly, "and I didn't help him. I feel ashamed about that."

Dias asked Suarez to describe what happened on the expedition and, like a river breaching its banks, the young man poured out a narrative that defied the detective's note-taking skills, so he set aside the notebook and recorded the remaining conversation on his phone. When he finished, Suarez asked if he could get a drink.

"I've got Coke. Do you want one?" he said, rising and taking a step toward the back door.

Dias followed him into the kitchenette and accepted a Coke.

Having listened to Suarez, Dias reflected on the interview he'd done with the American survivors and the report he received from the wildlife officers who interviewed the guards. Taken together, none of the narrative was complete. There were gaps, particularly in the explanation of how the victims had died. It was clear from Suarez' guilt-ridden explanation of his boss's death that the man had died horrifically, but it was difficult to accept that he and the others had been eaten alive by insects, even though that's exactly what the Americans had said when he interviewed them.

He was skeptical because they provided no proof that these insects even existed. They had explanations for everything, such as why nobody knew about them and why all of a sudden they appeared. It just defied everything he thought he understood about the animal kingdom, but it was clear that everyone involved was basically telling the same story. And of course bodies were found, but they'd been in the water and exposed for days and scavengers had gotten to them.

After Suarez had finished his monologue and Coke, Dias gave him a puzzled look.

"You know what, with everybody carrying cellphones with cameras I have to wonder why there's no photographs."

"Everyone lost everything, especially when the truck flipped over," Suarez said. "We were just trying to stay alive. I think everyone took photos, and I had a video of my boss, but I lost my phone in the water."

"Ever think of going back?"

"No," Suarez replied adamantly. "It was the worst thing that ever happened to me. I have nightmares."

Dias nodded sympathetically, turned off his phone and prepared to leave.

"So I'm OK with you?" Suarez asked tentatively as he remained in his chair.

"Oh, yeah, I don't see a problem here. You've actually been very helpful, and here's my card if you think of anything else. You know, I think you can stay if you want, at least until Mr. Costa's wife decides what to do with the house. I don't think you have to hide under the bed, and it would be a good idea to turn the air conditioner on."

As he moved toward the side yard to leave, Dias asked if Suarez had a new phone.

Suarez took a phone out of his pocket and waved it toward the investigator.

"Give me your number, in case I have any questions, OK?"

21

EXCEPT FOR A handful of colleagues who expressed concern, Duncan received little support from academia. By Thursday, the U.S. media had picked up on the death of American Carlos Johnson in the Brazilian rainforest, with most details coming from his family, who apparently knew little—though it didn't stop them from accusing the university of stonewalling. Duncan spent a portion of the morning monitoring the story, which was limited to the who, what, when and where and a little of the why.

By lunchtime enough calls from media had come in that he met with public affairs. Unlike the chilly reception he had from the president, the public affairs staff were effusive and showed what he thought to be genuine concern. Ushered to a cubicle occupied by media relations specialist Jacob Turley, he felt relieved as he was warmly greeted.

"We've got donuts today," Turley said enthusiastically. "Would you like some coffee?"

"No thanks, I think I've had enough for the day," Duncan replied as he took a seat on an armless chrome and vinyl chair.

"Well, then, have you had any contact with the press today?"

"Absolutely not," Duncan said adamantly. "If they call, I tell them to get in touch with you folks. And then I hang up. I'm not really sure what they're looking for from me."

"Well, they smell a story, and unfortunately it involves a death, so we have to be cautious about how we respond. From now on, forward any calls you get to me, email, texts, whatever," Turley said, handing him his business card.

Duncan pocketed the card.

"Professor," Turley said, "so far the questions have been predictable. Mostly they want interviews. What I need is the full story from you, warts and all."

"You got all day? A lot happened."

"Start at the beginning, if that's OK with you."

Duncan smiled confidently, thinking that by answering questions he would free himself of additional burdens and that he would be able to move on with his life and career. Even as he started his narrative, he was thinking about returning to the rainforest.

22

INTERNET GOSSIP SITES started reporting that a Brazilian blogger was claiming that Johnson was only one of a number of victims whose bodies showed signs of having been devoured. The blogger gave no sources except to characterize them as reliable. Mainstream media in Brazil had also begun following the blogger and in some cases launched their own investigations. Before long CNN had tracked down one of the American survivors, whose observations ignited a media frenzy.

George Hamel fed the media uproar with shocking headlines of people being eaten alive by insects. Editors ditched the articles they'd prepared in favor of the reports popping up like mushrooms throughout the media ecosystem. It did not take long for the story to get out as Johnson's family raised the heat on the university and especially the expedition leader.

Public affairs moved into high gear, producing press releases and compiling a list of questions from the media that they wanted Duncan to answer.

"I've already told you most of that stuff," Duncan

said curtly when Turley visited his office that afternoon. "I don't know what good it's going to do for me to go on camera at a press conference."

"It's the only way. We need to get it all out there at the same time so you aren't a victim of death by a thousand cuts," Turley said helpfully.

"What's that mean?"

"The press will hound you if they think you are holding back. And they'll know. I don't suppose you've been watching the talk shows, have you?"

"Of course not. I don't have time for that crap."

"Well, that crap is making you look like a criminal. I can't force you to participate in the press conference, but we're going to hold it with or without you. That's not my decision. It comes from a higher pay grade."

"So the vultures are circling," Duncan mused.

"Well, yeah. Right now, you are your own best defense and offense. You go out there and tell them what you told me, and I think people will have a different opinion about you and the expedition. Right now, Johnson's family is controlling the spin and they're pissed."

Duncan raised several objections. He had never done a press conference.

"I'm afraid I'll say too much."

"I don't understand."

"Well, how much detail should I give? You know, people died horribly."

"No, definitely do not go into detail about how people died. Really, don't go there," Turley said forcefully.

"But what if they ask?"

"Yeah," Turley sighed. "That's the trick. They will ask. But, you know, the media ask police about the details of all kinds of crimes—I'm not saying what happened in the jungle was a crime—but the police don't say more than they need to. And neither should you."

"So what can I say when someone asks, what was it like watching someone die like that?"

Turley glanced at the ceiling. After first volunteering to work the assignment, he wondered if there was a way he could get out of it. But that was out of the question. He'd have to make the best of what might be an impossible situation. He could see his boss calling him into her office after a blown-to-smithereens press conference, giving him the quiet treatment at first and then making insinuations that he had suddenly lost his competence.

"I'll be there," Turley said reassuringly. "I won't be right next to you, but I'll be on the dais."

"So I'll catch the bullets and you'll bandage the wounds."

"Sort of, yeah. Just stick to the basics of what happened, why y'all got stuck out there and not get too detailed about anything. You know, you said the light was bad and y'all were preoccupied with survival. You know, talk about what you personally, actually were doing, not what was happening to the others. If we can limit the questions to that, I think we'll get through this."

"That's a promise?"

"I wish. I'm just saying, I think it's our best option."

"OK, OK," Duncan agreed resignedly.

"I'll write up talking points to help you stay on point and we'll go from there. You should wear a tie and light jacket. The lights can get pretty hot."

"When we gonna do this?"

"We've scheduled it for four p.m. That way it should

be mostly local stations, which may not ask the kind of questions you'd get from national media. Anyway, that's the theory."

As Turley left, Duncan stared at his web browser, which was set to his department's home page. He wondered whether it would be a good idea to see what people were saying. He felt exposed and vulnerable. He imagined that ninety percent of the articles and comments would be damaging or even hateful. But he found it hard to resist his curiosity. And just as he was about to run a search, Cody Boyd burst into the room,

"Boss, you've got to see this! They're interviewing that Hamel turd," he said as he leaned over Duncan's shoulder and typed CNN in the address field. "It just started."

23

HAMEL'S INTERVIEW COULD not have come at a worse time for Duncan and the university. The graphic and dramatic account of events hit the internet with the fulminating power of a block of dry ice dropped into a tub of hot water. Duncan was stunned to find the small lecture hall packed with journalists. TV cameras were lined up on tripods against the back wall, sound booms sprouting like tree limbs. Photographers and reporters milled about, greeting each other and chatting earnestly.

"What is going on?" Duncan asked as Turley greeted him on the dais. A row of metal folding chairs was lined up behind a lectern emblazoned with the university's logo. Duncan recognized several others on the dais, including his dean and the public affairs director.

"I don't know if you saw it, but CNN interviewed one of the people from your group. Did you see it?"

Duncan nodded in acknowledgement.

"What did you think of it?" Turley asked.

"To tell the truth, I thought he was overly dramatic. I didn't watch the whole thing. I got kinda angry about it."

"The worst part was his description of how Johnson died."

"He described that?!" Duncan said. "Why would he do that?"

"The reporter asked the question and the guy just responded," Turley said, leading Duncan to a corner of the room. Speaking so as not to be overheard, and leaning toward each other, Turley added, "This changes everything. The way we had it set up, we thought we'd be able to control the press but now, they're gonna want you to either contradict what was said on CNN or verify it. Which is it gonna be?"

Duncan raised his hand to his chin and pulled slightly on his lower lip. He exhaled deeply. Although he was anxious when he arrived, his anxiety rose a notch as he scanned the noisy room while listening to Turley, hearing snatches of phrases. For an instant his eyes locked with those of his dean, who smiled grimly and averted his gaze.

"All you can do," Turley advised as the media relations director stepped to the lectern to start the press conference, "is tell what you saw. Don't try to hide anything. Everything is gonna come out. And whatever you do, don't speculate, don't guess. Oh, and one other thing, don't put a death grip on the lectern. Remember, this is going to be on TV."

"What if someone asks how I'm being treated by the university, my supposed colleagues?" Duncan said, snarling.

"I can't help you there," Turley said. "Good luck."

They shook hands and took their places while the media relations director struggled to get the room's attention and finally, reading from notes, set ground rules for the interview, which she knew would be ignored once the questioning started. Using a script, she introduced Duncan as a renowned entomologist holding an endowed chair and serving as the lead investigator on several major grants. She mentioned the number of entomologists who were trained in his lab and their contributions in fields as diverse as agriculture and robotics. Everything that the director said, including what Duncan was doing in Brazil, had already been distributed to the journalists as hand-outs when they entered the room. Like the preliminaries before the main bout, only a few paid attention while the media relations director tried to establish an atmosphere more collegial than adversarial. Seeing that she was basically talking to herself, she motioned for Duncan to come forward.

Duncan instinctively wrapped his hands on the edges of the lectern and then pulled them away quickly, as if from an electrical shock. Turley's mouth went from a grimace to a grin of satisfaction. At least a small part of what he said had gotten through.

The questions came at Duncan like darts, many of them as a result of Hamel's interview, which he suddenly wished he had watched in its entirety. Only moments into the questioning he felt he was under assault and looked back several times at Turley as if for assistance. None was forthcoming as the university officials squirmed uncomfortably, waiting for Duncan to say something that would turn the conference into a disaster equal, in their own minds, to the catastrophe that occurred in Brazil.

Within minutes, Duncan showed annoyance when reporters asked similar but not identical questions. What did he think of Hamel's interview? He hadn't seen most of it so he didn't comment. Was it true, as Hamel said, that Carlos Johnson had been killed with a machete by the guide?

"I can't comment on what Hamel said, I've already told you that."

"But did the guide kill Johnson?"

"You have to understand, Carlos was being eaten alive," he said matter-of-factly.

The room exploded as reporters raised their voices to be heard over other reporters who had also raised their voices. Hamel hadn't said that Johnson was being eaten alive. This was news and the press jumped on it like a pack of coyotes bringing down a deer.

The media relations director stepped forward and asked for calm, shooting an annoyed look at Duncan.

"One at a time, please," she shouted, holding her arms up as if pushing back against the onslaught of journalists. "If we can't maintain decorum, then this press conference will end right now. Do you hear me?!"

Momentarily, the journalists stopped shouting while photographers jockeyed for position near the lectern for dramatic close-ups of Duncan's sweaty face.

"I really don't think it's appropriate for me to comment about Carlos," Duncan said. "Brazilian authorities are investigating his death and we should wait for their findings before drawing conclusions."

Duncan felt he'd parried the question well, but several reporters insisted that he describe what he saw.

"Can you at least verify for us that he was killed by your guide?" one of the coyotes barked with an air of exasperation.

Hoping for direction, Duncan glanced at Turley, who shrugged helplessly.

Recognizing that he was on his own, his anxiety flushed by anger, Duncan shouted, "Yes, the guide killed him."

Before he could say another word, the room erupted again and Duncan glanced at the media relations director, who leaped from her chair and shouted, "This press conference is over!"

24

Eduardo Dias was preparing to walk to a Picanha Mania for an early lunch. It was Saturday morning and he had the weekend off. On his way he picked up a copy of *A Crítica* from a newsstand, folding it and carrying it under his arm. He could have saved himself the walk if only he'd opened the paper to the front page before taking a seat at the restaurant.

The headline that got his attention after ordering coffee was Vítima Estudante Americano de Homicídio. It was the first article in the center column, top of the fold. Without reading the article he knew it was about the student who had died in the rainforest. The Reuters article referred to George Hamel's interview on CNN and was updated with Duncan's quote from his press conference confirming that the young man had been killed by the guide.

"*Merda*," Dias said under his breath. He had just talked to Antonio Suarez yesterday. He was skinny, barely old enough to shave, and seemed harmless. A day later and he was a suspect in a homicide. The article was short on details and as soon as he finished reading he called his boss,

Captain Emilio Santos. Dias had yet to file a report on his interview with Suarez and thought that he could help with the arrest, which he knew was mandatory.

"You saw the news, Dias," Santos said gruffly.

"That's why I'm calling. I met with him yesterday. I know where he lives."

"That's excellent news," Santos exclaimed. "We've been working on this all morning and haven't been able to find him. Just give me the address and I'll send a team to take him into custody."

Dias was aware that homicide suspects were often treated poorly by police and felt empathy for the young man. Although at the time he wasn't aware of the details of the killing, he didn't think Suarez was capable of murder. Since the guide had been cooperative during the interview, the detective felt he owed it to him to help with the arrest.

"You don't have to send a team. I can do it," he said. "I can pick him up."

"You can? Where are you? Do you have a car? You're sure he's not dangerous?"

"He's not dangerous. I found him hiding under a bed. I gave him my card. He trusts me."

"You didn't make friends with him, did you, Dias? I've told you before you should not let your personal feelings get in the way of your judgment. Who knows these days who is dangerous and who is not?"

"I know, I know. You send a team, they'll break down the door and treat him like a gangster. He's not like that, I assure you."

"Well, do you have a car?"

"No, I was taking the weekend off and didn't check one out."

"OK, how about I send someone to pick you up and he'll go with you to pick up the suspect?" the captain said.

"That's fine. I'm at the Picanha Mania on Ramos Ferreira Street. How long do you think it will take?"

"Probably thirty minutes."

"You know, maybe he should just pick me up at my apartment."

Dias left the restaurant without ordering a meal and, once at his fourth floor apartment, turned his TV to Rede Bandeirantes. Sitting in front of the TV, he used his laptop to check out CNN. Although his English wasn't bad, he was more comfortable reading English than speaking it. After viewing a video from the news conference and a written account he found himself with more questions than answers.

"I need to interview that American professor," he said as his phone played its default ringtone.

"Olá, I'm Estella Oliveira. Is this Eduardo Dias?"

"Yes, who are you?" Dias said.

"Captain Santos sent me to pick you up."

"I'll be right down."

Dias put his holster and Taurus PT 24/7 on his hip and dashed down the three flights of stairs where he found the Volkswagen Golf double-parked in front of his building.

"Hey," he said, as he settled into the front passenger seat. The pair exchanged fist bumps. He gave her the address and watched as she input it quickly into a dashboard-mounted GPS. Without waiting for the route to appear, she pulled into traffic.

"The captain didn't tell me much," she said. "We're picking someone up, I understand."

"Yes, a young man accused of homicide."

"Really! That's exciting. I've never done a murder investigation before."

"You new to the department?"

"I was with the Federal Highway Police until a few months ago. I'm still on probation here."

"So, how do you like it?"

"You mean the civil police?"

Dias nodded.

"So far, so good. But tell me about this guy? Is he dangerous?"

"Have you seen the news about the American killed in the forest?"

"I've seen some stuff. Something about being killed by bugs of some kind?"

"Yeah, that's the story. The guy we're picking up killed the American."

25

DIAS STOOD ON a small concrete slab at the front door of the house where he'd found Antonio Suarez. Estella Oliveira stood behind him, warily eyeing the nearby houses.

"Antonio, it's Eduardo Dias with the civil police. We talked yesterday."

Dias glanced at Oliveira. He knocked again, harder.

"Antonio, please answer if you're here. I need to talk to you." He tried the knob but the door was locked.

Oliveira noticed a curtain move in one of the nearby houses.

"The neighbors are watching," she said.

"I was hoping we could do this quietly. Tell you what, you stay here and I'll go around back. He was hiding under a bed yesterday. Maybe that's what he's doing now."

"What if he comes out?" Oliveira asked nervously.

"You have a gun?"

"Yes."

"Use it. Shoot him in the leg if you have to. I can't afford to let him get away, not after I told the captain I'd bring him in."

"I've never shot anyone before."

"Neither have I. Just point it at him and tell him to lie down. Anyway, if he's in the house, I don't think he'll run. He's not a criminal."

"He's charged with homicide, right?"

"Not yet. Technically, I'm bringing him in for questioning."

"Oh, all right, then. I'll wait here."

"Good girl," he said fatuously. "I'm sorry, I didn't mean to sound asinine."

"Don't worry," she smiled. "I put up with worse with the highway police. Much worse."

Dias made his way quickly to the patio. He noticed that the window-mounted air conditioner was running. The back door was unlocked and he quickly pushed past the curtains into the kitchenette and listened for movement but all that he could hear was the whirring of the air conditioner. He let Oliveira in through the front door and asked her to holster her gun.

"If he's here, we won't have to shoot him," he said. "I think he's in the bedroom, but you stay out here and scream, I mean yell, if you hear or see him."

Oliveira nodded, her eyes darting around the living room as if looking for snakes.

Approaching the bedroom, Dias said calmly, "Antonio, it's Eduardo. I just want to talk to you."

"Antonio, I know you're here," he said. "Come on out. I don't want to come in to get you. I want to help you."

"No you don't," Suarez replied forcefully. "You're here to arrest me. You think I murdered the American. I saw it on TV."

"I'm not here to arrest you," Dias said calmly. "Now

come out and we'll talk about it like human beings. OK. There's another officer with me. She's new to the department."

Dias called Estella to step forward.

"Estella, please ask *Senhor* Suarez to come out of the bedroom so we can talk."

Oliveira gave Dias a puzzled look.

"Just talk. A woman's voice is reassuring," he whispered.

"Yes, *Senhor* Suarez. I'm Estella Oliveira and I want to help you," she said, looking at Dias to make sure she was doing things correctly. He smiled.

"We just want to talk to you. We want to get your side of the story," she said in a soothing voice.

"I told you everything yesterday."

"Not quite," Dias said. "You left out the part about killing the American."

26

THIS IS THE worst day of my life, Howard Duncan thought as he sat in his darkened living room, the blinds drawn and a half-empty bottle of cabernet on the coffee table. He'd watched as much coverage as he could stand and then switched channels to a show about survivalists in Alaska. Would the media hound him to Alaska?

While he understood why colleagues at the university weren't manning barricades on behalf of academic freedom—no one wanted to be associated with supporting an activity that cost the life of a student—he was amused that the farther away from the campus the coverage developed, the more likely it was that people were taking sides. There were those who wanted him to be charged with a crime, even though no actual crime was committed, and there were those who claimed that it was a matter of survival and that in such circumstances everyone took his or her chances. Survival of the luckiest or strongest. And because of the absence of live specimens, there were those who doubted the insects existed and who believed that the government was covering up what really happened.

Cody Boyd, who was still employed as Duncan's assistant, found himself in a role he'd never intended to play

as the supportive underling. Duncan reacted angrily when
the dean had suggested he take the semester off, peremp-
torily removing Duncan's class assignments. A meeting
Monday would determine whether he would have access
to his lab. This ate at him Saturday morning as he delet-
ed messages from his cell phone and blocked persistent
callers.

Duncan was grateful that Boyd was still on his side
and agreed to meet him at a restaurant far enough from
campus that he would be safe from prying eyes and mi-
crophones. Wearing cargo shorts, a collared short-sleeved
Patagonia-shirt, ventilated hiking shoes with quarter
socks and a Panama hat, he covered the three miles in
forty-five minutes. Of course, several reporters were stationed outside his apartment building at the time and he
was proud of the way he was able to leave through the
back entrance with the reporters none the wiser. Even as
he left the neighborhood he felt that surveillance of him
would only increase and that he had to make decisions
about whether to give in to their demands for interviews
or figure out an escape plan.

"You know, maybe the dean is right," he said, as he
and Boyd sat at a small, Formica table with retro vinyl
chairs. "Maybe I should lay low for a semester, let things
blow over. Or, better yet, continue my research. More
than ever, I need to get back into the field. I need to collect live specimens, that's really the next step. Whaddya
think?"

Duncan didn't often ask advice from Boyd and the
young man was nonplussed. He wasn't certain if Duncan was speaking as his boss or his friend, or equal, the

way he had when they were in the rainforest. He worked with middle-aged guys all the time but he didn't hang with them.

"You know, you're probably right. I don't see what you've got to gain by, you know, staying the course and all that. It's not like you can hide from the media on campus."

Duncan smiled appreciatively.

"Yeah, but I've got to have something to do or I'll drive myself crazy. That's why I'm thinking about going back."

Boyd nodded and buried his head in the menu.

"You think it's too soon?" Duncan asked.

"I don't know. I mean, yeah. It's too soon. It would be like you're insensitive to the situation."

Boyd felt a tightening in his throat, as if he'd said too much. He studied Duncan's face for clues.

"I was thinking about that myself, but I can't just sit in my apartment all day watching talk shows, which by the way, suck really bad. I never realized how bad daytime TV is until this. Now, man, I'm beginning to think we're a country of idiots."

"Did you get any advice from the university on how to handle all this? I mean, I thought they were in charge of media and stuff."

"Oh, they are, when they want to. It's like everything else, when it's easy everyone wants to play, when it's hard you're on your own. I don't know why I'm surprised by that."

Duncan asked for tips on how to keep his phone from filling up with messages he didn't want to listen to or read. Boyd suggested he buy a prepaid phone.

"You could give the number to people you trust so at least you can talk to people on your terms. That's what I'd do."

"What about this phone?"

"Well, it's a target. They're not gonna stop and the beauty of a burn phone is that you can toss it anytime and get another one, all with different numbers."

"You know, I would never have thought of that myself," Duncan said admiringly. "It's almost devious."

Boyd grinned.

As they left the restaurant and approached Boyd's car, Duncan asked sheepishly, "Do you have time to help me buy this burn phone and set it up?"

27

As DUNCAN FEARED and expected, the university offered a paid sabbatical for the semester and encouraged him to spend it elsewhere, which he'd already decided to do. Boyd set up Duncan's cell phone so that calls from people on his contact list would be forwarded to his prepaid phone. For days he paged through the calls and messages on his original phone to gauge the level of interest. The volume picked up as soon as it was announced that he was taking a sabbatical, and then leveled off. It happened this way all week, with each new development resulting in a crescendo of calls that soon went pianissimo. One thing did pop up at mid-week, which appealed to his curiosity. He received several calls with the country code for Brazil. Since his voice mailbox was perpetually full, no messages were left.

Then he got a call from university public affairs that was forwarded to his burn phone. It was Jacob Turley.

"Dr. Duncan, I'm so glad I can reach you. How are you doing?"

"I'm OK. How are things in public affairs?"

"Still a madhouse, I'm sorry to say. I worked at newspapers before I came here and I gotta say I've lost respect for the media. Anyway, I'm calling because a lawyer in Brazil has been trying to reach you and I told him I'd let you know. It's up to you if you want to call him back, but he said there was a person he's representing that you may know who's been charged with killing Carlos Johnson. It's been in the news. I don't know if you're aware of it."

Duncan hesitated, his eyes on his muted TV. Glancing at the screen intermittently he wasn't certain why he kept it on. Morbid curiosity perhaps. He paged down to the calls originating in Brazil. There were three, several hours apart. Turley passed on the lawyer's name and number.

"I told him it's up to you if you want to call him back," Turley said.

28

DUNCAN DEBATED WHETHER to return the lawyer's call, but he realized he didn't have a choice; he couldn't abandon the one person who had been responsible for his survival. And there was no question that he had witnessed everything. Even so, when he reached the lawyer, Andre Montes, he was stunned to learn that Suarez was in custody. The lawyer explained that the arrest was based on news reports from the United States.

"They have no actual evidence," Montes said through a bad connection. "The authorities are simply reacting to publicity. In cases like this, they'll pick a scapegoat just to make it look like they're doing something."

"They do that here, too."

"Well, in Brazil it's, ah, ah, what's the word, its S-O-P. That's a word, right? As you can tell, I'm still working on my English."

"You speak much better English than I speak Portuguese," Duncan said.

Montes explained that he had been appointed by the court to represent Suarez and that Suarez was just one of many indigent clients that he represented.

"Usually, unless we get credible testimony, we take a

plea. After reading about what's being said in your country, someone like you could make a difference. You're a scholar, a professor. An affidavit from you would carry weight," Montes explained.

While Montes described what he needed, Duncan's mind wandered. He didn't know why, but his mind flooded with images of his stay in Manaus, the heat, the humidity, the effort he had made to plan and launch the expedition that eventually resulted in Suarez's arrest.

"Of course, you should know, with my caseload, if there's any way you can find a lawyer who can devote the time this young man deserves, I think he has a chance to avoid jail," Montes said. "I have other clients who are in worse shape, who have been in jail and can't get out. I have to make choices and what I see with this young man is that he needs someone who will be on top of his case and I'm afraid I'm not the one. Sorry, but that is the reality here."

Duncan promised to send an affidavit but after ending the conversation wondered whether it would do any good. What good was an affidavit without an attorney?

29

AT FIRST, HAVING a burn phone appealed to Duncan. It gave him a sense of control, but the more he thought about it, the more it made him feel like he was hiding, which he was. At the same time, he was looking for a way to escape the media attention. He was determined not to hole up in his apartment like a criminal. While reporters weren't camped out on the front lawn, there was always someone standing in the shade of a nearby live oak with a camera. He could see them in the opening between the curtains. Definitely, he would leave town. There was no point in remaining. The university had closed the door on that by forcing him to take a sabbatical. Perhaps he'd go to Houston and lose himself in the anonymity of a big city. That would be a start, but he could quickly see that without meaningful work to do he'd be as bored in a high-rise as he would in his apartment.

As soon as he'd resolved to leave the campus, and before he'd finished packing and rented a car, his thoughts returned to the conversation he'd had with Suarez's attorney. He could not dismiss the feeling that he was at least partially responsible for the guide's arrest and he knew that he couldn't turn his back on him.

The media had it all wrong, he thought, but it seemed whenever he tried to correct the record shouting matches erupted and the message was lost. He clearly wasn't a media expert, and he was certainly not a legal expert, but he felt that somebody had to do something to help Antonio. Who besides himself could it be?

The question lingered over him like a dark cloud. Everyone seemed quick to convict. The family wanted action. The university wanted it to go away. George Hamel was out there fanning flames. No one was helping.

30

"You know, that sounds like a good plan, getting out of Dodge," Cody Boyd said over lunch at a diner miles from campus. Boyd picked up his boss several blocks from his apartment.

"Are they stalking you, still?" Boyd asked as they drove.

"I can't tell. I'm just being careful. If I was them I'd probably put somebody in the alley."

"You'd think that. Maybe they're doing it and you don't know it. Didja ever think they got cameras in trees and they control them remotely? Or drones? Seen any drones?"

Duncan laughed.

"It wouldn't surprise me, but, you know, they're getting everything from Hamel and now with the police arresting Antonio they've got a lot more to work with. Maybe they don't need me anymore."

"As if."

"Yeah, that's why I need to get away. Get some breathing room. Get ready for the next step."

Boyd was uncertain about what the next step would be, but when Duncan had a plan he generally let his assistant know because often it involved him. Secretly, Boyd hoped his boss was going to tell him that he would continue to be paid during his sabbatical.

"So, what I'm thinking is, ah, getting back in the saddle," Duncan said, pushing his coffee cup back and forth on the table.

"Really!? This soon? I mean, wouldn't that make things worse? I really don't understand, what saddle? I thought they took it away from you."

"Not really. Yeah, my funders are, you know, backing away like rats on a sinking ship, though I don't think the ship is sinking. I've had nothing but time to think about this and there's two things that I gotta do."

Despite following the developing story online, Boyd hadn't heard about Suarez's arrest and became upset when told.

"Of all the people, that was the one guy who, I don't know, without him would any of us be alive? I can't believe it."

"Yeah, well, believe it or not, that's what's happening."

After describing his conversation with Suarez's attorney, Duncan said that he would send an affidavit. "But that's like sending a condolence card to a tornado victim. What he really needs is a lawyer who can handle his case."

"So that's one thing. What's the other?"

Duncan stopped toying with his cup and smiled broadly.

"I'm going back. To Brazil. I'm gonna get specimens, live specimens, and I'm gonna bring them back and, just maybe, I'll sell myself and my specimens to the highest bidder. If the university wants to get rid of me, if my funders won't support me, then I'll do the capitalist thing."

Boyd stared at Duncan in disbelief, astonished at his

boss' angry, defiant tone. He knew him to hold strong opinions but this was revealing a completely different side to his personality.

The remainder of their lunch was a question and answer session about how he would fund his next expedition while at the same time helping Suarez. It seemed impossible to Boyd. Perhaps one or the other would be possible, but he knew Duncan wasn't wealthy. Boyd assumed Duncan had saved money, given that he didn't own a car and didn't spend a lot on rent and when he ate out it was usually at inexpensive mom-and-pops. Duncan had a reputation of being cheap, though he had paid for the past two lunches they'd had together.

Duncan was not forthcoming about his finances, but wondered himself how he would pay for everything. His conscience wouldn't let him choose between helping the guide and collecting specimens. If only he could choose one, but the way he envisioned it, both had to be done, which he admitted to Boyd.

Boyd shook his head knowingly.

"You know, Maggie likes you and she's rich. Have you called her?"

31

Reaching out was not one of Duncan's strong suits. His self-image was that of an experienced, self-sufficient man who could handle any situation outside of the social. It was the social part of life that gave him pause. He was not big on small talk, though he could manage it with the aid of a glass of wine. Sitting in his apartment for what would be his last night in town, he deliberated over what he would say to Maggie Cross—if he called her. He hated cold calls, whether giving them or receiving them. Telephone conversations had always bugged him. You never knew who was sitting next to the person you were talking to and what they were doing. He suspected George Hamel of being at her side and making rude gestures and mouthing sarcasms while Cross was on the phone. He wanted a private conversation with her. Perhaps at a nice restaurant with a glass of chardonnay. Just the two of them talking.

He knew Boyd was right about calling Cross. She would be in a position to help Suarez, if she wanted to.

He made the call using his university phone. The number was on Cross's contact list and if she didn't answer he'd know she didn't want to talk to him. He tensed as it rang.

"Hello Howard," Cross said grandly. "How are you doing? I tried to call you, but I guess the messages didn't get through."

Duncan brightened immediately. There was so much to talk about he hardly knew where to begin.

32

DUNCAN WASN'T CERTAIN how to proceed. He wondered whether Hamel was sitting alongside Maggie Cross, hanging on every word. It was difficult for him to dismiss this since all his troubles seemed to stem from Hamel's explosive interview with numberless media outlets. It was not just what he said, which was technically accurate. It was the way he characterized Carlos Johnson's death and Antonio Suarez's role in it. But why should he be concerned whether Hamel was listening in? It infuriated him that he even had to ask himself the question. Hamel was not his friend.

"That bastard Hamel has gotten Antonio in a lot of trouble. You know, they've arrested him based only on what George said on TV. He's in jail as we speak."

"You know, George is here listening."

"I don't care. I'd punch him in the face if I could. He's not nearly the man Antonio is."

Duncan was surprised at how quickly anger poured out of him. It was as if he were relieving the built-up pressure of the past week in a single blast.

"He has that effect on people," Cross said.

"Some people," Hamel protested. "I'll have you know that CNN called me, I didn't call them."

"I've got it on speaker phone," Cross said apologetically.

"Doesn't matter. I'm not calling about what he said. I'm calling about Antonio. He needs help, he needs a lawyer."

Duncan described his conversation with Suarez's court-appointed attorney.

"You know, if it weren't for him, we might not be here."

"Oh, bosh," Hamel said. "What did he do, other than lead us into a killing field? He didn't save us, we saved ourselves."

Duncan felt hair rise on the back of his neck. He resisted the temptation to strike back.

"Can you take it off speaker phone?" he asked. "I don't want to talk to or listen to him. If it's a bad time, I can call back."

"No, no, no problem. Here, it's off. He's an ass. It's his nature. Now tell me, what can we do to help Antonio?"

"His lawyer asked me for an affidavit about Carlos's death but, really, that's a waste of time. I can't afford to hire an attorney myself but I thought you could help with that. I've been thinking of going back to Brazil, for a couple of reasons. I'm taking a sabbatical."

"I heard about that."

"Yeah, I'm too much of a hot potato. Anyway, I'm moving out of town and I'll probably spend a week or two in Houston and then fly down. I'm thinking about going back into the forest, you know, for specimens."

Cross listened intently, shaking her head as Duncan described his plans. She had followed the news more closely than he did and was well aware of his situation. She knew that Duncan had used her to partially fund the expedition but at the time she had romantic feelings toward him.

"You know what it sounds like to me?" Cross said. "It sounds like helping Antonio is your excuse to go back so you can do another expedition. Are you sure that's a wise thing to do?"

"You could be right. I'm not always good at figuring out my motives."

"Now you're just being disingenuous. You know your motives quite well. I know that from how you manipulated me, although, I let you do it. I liked the extra attention. What can I say, I'm that kinda girl."

Duncan couldn't believe he was that transparent.

"I'm sorry if I offended you," he said, sheepishly.

"Nonsense," she said. "I've been around the block. I know we're all in it for ourselves. Besides, I had my own motives and, of course, I had the money and you didn't."

The conversation turned more personal and drifted for several minutes, with fewer words and longer periods of dead air. Duncan felt a closeness with Cross, not only from the experiences they'd shared but because of her nonjudgmental attitude. He could say things to her without measuring every word, as he often had to do with colleagues. Talking to her on the phone suddenly seemed inadequate.

"You know, maybe we should get together," he said, self-consciously expecting her to reject the notion.

"That's a great idea! You want to come to Chicago?"

For an instant he was on the verge of a resounding yes, followed by a second thought.

"Not if he's there. I swear, if I see him I'm gonna punch him. I'm sorry, but that's just how I feel."

"I certainly wouldn't want that to happen," she said in a cheery, calm voice. "How about I fly to Houston? You said that's where you'll be."

"You'll come down by yourself?"

"Yes, of course. George will stay here and take care of my cats. Meanwhile, I'll talk to my attorney about getting help for poor Antonio."

33

COVERAGE OF WHAT one newspaper called "*a barata com dentes*," started slowly in Manaus and grew into a thunderhead within days, to the consternation of authorities who had tried to keep a lid on it from the start. Even when it became apparent that something horrible had occurred, that bodies had been found, local coverage was limited. Reporters could not reach the sites where the bodies were found, and even if they had seen it for themselves the authorities claimed that the bodies had been carried by the flood to the area where they were found and that their condition was the result of scavengers and decomposition.

Although no specimens of the insects had been found for forensic analysis, investigators had examined the human remains and were aware of the markings left on the bones. The specimens that Investigator Dias had taken from Professor Azevedo's office and forwarded to the state entomologist's office had yet to be examined. The supposition was that some type of animal had scavenged the bodies. Since the authorities classified the investigation as ongoing, they declined to release details.

With few facts to go on, local coverage descended

into speculation. Like mushrooms after a rain, commenters popped up by the score with each article, claiming that
the government was testing a new weapon that had gotten out of hand, or that the United States had infiltrated
the rainforest with swarms of robotic killing machines.
Others saw it as the fulfillment of Old Testament curses.
In any case, it didn't continue for long, as the blogger
who first reported on the bodies posted several videos
that he claimed had come from an anonymous source.
Despite the poor lighting, the dizzying camera work and
the absence of close-ups, the public got its first, albeit in-
conclusive sight of *Reptilus blaberus* and it was enthralled.

34

HOWARD DUNCAN HAD convinced himself that the simple act of moving would be sufficient to put his life back in order and get on with his research. He had laid out the details neatly in his mind. With Maggie Cross's money to hire a lawyer, he'd go to Manaus to testify on Antonio Suarez's behalf. The young man would be released and Duncan would turn his attention to the pursuit of *blaberus.* He hoped Cody Boyd and perhaps one other researcher would join him. The goal would be to return to the lab with living specimens. How long they would survive in captivity and whether they would breed were open questions. But even with that, he envisioned numerous journal articles, a big, public apology from the university and the reinstatement of his grants. It might have worked out that way had the public not embraced the "cockroach with teeth" meme. It was all that anyone in Manaus talked about.

Boyd was the one who kept up with the developing story, bookmarking online Brazilian media outlets that he checked daily for updates. From the very beginning he saw potential in the expedition for a reality TV show, but that was before people started dying and he lost all the video he'd shot in the flood. A friend suggested he write about it, and even though he was not a writer, the idea resonated.

"That's what people do," his friend had said. "Look at what happens after any tragedy, especially stuff like this. You remember those people who died climbing Everest? There were like a bunch of books and a movie. This is like the same. And some of them made big bucks."

It wasn't the same for Boyd but he found himself writing notes to himself about the expedition and its aftermath. He had no vision for what he would do but within several days he formalized his project by creating a journal dedicated to documenting what had happened. He was still acting as the expedition's documentarian, this time in print. But he wasn't a journalist and found it difficult to keep perspective. He knew he'd have to talk to the others at some point, that if it turned into anything someone would end up being hurt. Someone would have to be blamed.

But these concerns were blown out of the water after the images from Belmonte's camera went viral. Suddenly, the authorities were unable to control the spin as interviews with anonymous sources proliferated, speculation grew and the public embraced the concept of Brazil's new man eater.

35

DUNCAN WAS IN disbelief when he learned about the frenzy to find *blaberus* in the State of Amazonas. At first, he couldn't understand how people who knew so little about this predator could treat it so cavalierly and believe they could simply walk out into the forest, capture a few and then what? What were they thinking?

"It's like a gold rush," Boyd said over the phone.

"I don't understand."

"There are contests," Boyd said disbelievingly. "People think they're gonna make money off this."

"Fat chance," Duncan sniffed.

"Yeah, well, that's not how people think. You know. They see someone who might be on to something and they want a piece of the action."

"It just doesn't make sense. They're not researchers. They're plunderers."

"I get it," Boyd said, "but, you know, that's how the world works. I'm guessing it's gonna make what you want to do a lot harder. From what I've been reading, it's like some kind of party down there."

"That party's gonna end all of a sudden, if they don't watch out."

"Oh, absolutely. I can't imagine myself being part of it."

"You mean part of what's going on down there?"

"The whole thing, kinda," Boyd said.

Duncan felt that part of his plan to return to the forest was crumbling. He wanted Boyd to participate. He trusted him. It would be important to be there with someone who understood scientific methods and was familiar with the region. Boyd, he thought, was irreplaceable. And now it sounded like he didn't want to go.

"You're not interested in going back?" Duncan asked glumly.

"To tell you the truth, doc, I don't know. There's a part of me that wants to go back, you know, and finish what we started. But there's a part that makes me wonder if it's worth the risk. I mean, what am I gonna get out of it?"

"I can make it worth your while," Duncan blurted.

36

THINGS WERE MOVING too fast for Duncan. If you believed what some of the media were saying, ordinary Brazilians were chasing after *blaberus* like schoolchildren collecting butterflies. He'd learned of two scientific expeditions being mounted. Initially, the entomology community had been divided over Duncan's expedition, especially since he'd failed to provide specimens. There were those who condemned him as reckless and those who defended him, and those who remained skeptical at the supposed discovery of a carnivorous, predatory insect. The videos, however, provided tantalizing evidence that Duncan had uncovered something unique and potentially valuable. They also brought out the competition.

Duncan hadn't thought about Nolan Thomas for three years until he saw him on cable news just after the call from Boyd. Three years ago, Thomas had left academia to join a privately-held biotech in Texas, Biodynamism Inc. Unlike Duncan, who specialized in entomology, Thomas held multiple advanced degrees in unrelated fields, including entomology and artificial intelligence. They'd met briefly at several conferences and had never communicated beyond that.

Thomas was a proponent of convergence, which he applied across multiple disciplines. Computing and technology were rife with advocates for convergence, where various fields were heading in the same direction until, somewhere in the future, they would converge or merge into something spectacular. The true believers theorized about transhumanism based on predicted developments in the various scientific fields. Some were futurists with little intellectual weight, but Thomas was a scientist and could not be dismissed. If he was in Brazil, it wasn't for the fishing.

37

BOYD FELT GUILTY for not leveling with Duncan about the job offer he'd received from a reality TV producer. He could have done it—should have done it—before his boss practically begged him to return to Brazil. Of course, he hadn't yet decided what he was going to do, but he enjoyed working with video. It came naturally to him, more so than studying or working as a research assistant. At twenty-six he was restless and it didn't help that even though he continued to be paid, he had no work to do. The university had closed Duncan's lab and it would remain that way for at least the next semester. There were rumors that Duncan's sabbatical was the first step toward dismissal. Duncan didn't seem to believe this when they spoke, but Boyd realized that he couldn't depend on Duncan forever. Sooner or later he would have to go out on his own and this could be that time. It was his life, after all.

His friends wondered what he was waiting for. Most thought being a consultant and technical advisor on a reality film shoot was very cool, way better than lugging specimen boxes in the rainforest. The gig was in response to the furor in Brazil, and the producer told him that other companies were planning similar ventures and that the first to produce would be the first to profit. Boyd liked the idea of competition but profiting wasn't a big motivator. He said as much to his friends, some of whom told him that he wasn't being realistic. What is it you want to get out of life? That was a question that hung in the air like a balloon. He hadn't given it much thought since starting graduate school but now, for reasons he didn't quite understand, things were different. Maybe it was time he started thinking about his future. Other than working in a lab for someone else, he had no vision for what he would be doing in five years.

What he wished was that one of his friends would tell him exactly what to do, but none of them did. It all came back to what he would say to Duncan. He felt that turning him down would hit him like a brick, especially now that he had so few people he could depend on.

"Et tu, Cody?" he mused. "Et tu?"

38

THE BELL 206 Long Ranger carrying five passengers descended slowly after leveling off near the village's dirt runway. Huge clouds of red dust blossomed in the rotor wash, forcing a group of curious and excited children to shield their eyes and back away as the noisy chopper came to a rest, near a large, open-air building with a thatched roof. As the passengers emerged, the children closed in to admire the large, shiny machine.

The children were accustomed to seeing an ancient DC-7 carrying supplies and the occasional passenger who could afford it, which many of them never tired of viewing, but a helicopter in their midst was a rarity and worth a close and lengthy inspection. They ignored the khaki-clad men as they made their way to the building where the men were met by the old man who was in charge of the airfield. The men were there because the village's children could not keep a secret.

Adults in the village had heard about the *baratas antropófagas* over the radiotelephone but were not impressed. They made fun of them. They sounded small and insignificant compared to a mapinguari, the rainforest's Bigfoot. But their children knew better.

Every male child grew up in the forest, learned how to hunt and fish, learned how to climb trees, learned how to stalk and learned how to keep things hidden from the adults. One of the things they kept hidden was a body they had found, reduced to bones with a skull that looked like it was screaming. As many as a dozen of the older children had made the pilgrimage to see the skeleton that lay against a trunk on a small grassy hill. With so many having seen it, it was not surprising that the secret got out.

The airfield manager had worked out arrangements with his cousins, who owned ATVs, to rent them to the Americans. The cousins agreed but only if they would be paid to drive. They followed a well-worn trail heading in a northerly direction from the village. The trail was filled with twists and turns, large stones protruding from the surface like pointed stumps, holes large enough to swallow tires. One of the Americans, speaking Portuguese slowly, complained about the bumpiness and the drivers slowed down.

"I hope we don't have much farther to go," one of the men said to the others.

The ATVs were on the trail for about a half hour when the drivers pulled into a small open area surrounded by dense forest. A footpath led into the woods. The path was well-worn and damp. It was covered with footprints.

"*Quanto mais?*" the American who spoke Portuguese asked.

"Just around the next bend," one of the drivers replied.

"What did he say, Cody?"

"Not far, Dr. Thomas," Cody Boyd said.

39

MAGGIE CROSS'S ATTORNEY arranged for a lawyer in Manaus to handle Antonio Suarez's case. This had been done before she boarded the plane for Houston. She did it for Howard Duncan who, she hoped, would return the favor by spending a pleasant weekend in her suite at the Lancaster Hotel. She felt differently about Duncan than most men she had known. Several weeks after the catastrophe in the forest, she still saw him as a shining light—strong, intelligent, not showing fear, taking the lead. She had stayed close to him, helped him fight the swarming insects, and when it was over, followed him to safety. They'd had a couple nights of romance before and during the expedition and she hoped there would be more, despite the fact he wasn't particularly handsome. Or rich, which didn't bother her in the least since she had never met a wealthy man whom she liked. When it came to getting their way, they were as single-minded as she was.

On the other hand, Duncan was intimidated in the presence of wealth. His role had always been as a beneficiary. A wealthy foundation supported his work and, though he was grateful, he was uncomfortable rubbing

elbows with its contributors. He hated the annual conference the funders sponsored at which he and others who
received funding, mostly scientists, were required to give
presentations and updates about their work and then engage in small talk. Now that his funding had been suspended, he wouldn't have to go through that ordeal, but
he still needed money if he was going to return to the
rainforest to continue his work.

The drive to Cross's hotel took less time than finding
a parking space. Dressed in beige knee-length shorts and
a dark blue short-sleeved shirt, he shivered after leaving
the humid closeness of the street for the air-conditioned
discomfort of the hotel. He noticed immediately that hotel staff wore long sleeves and vests or jackets, a tacit rec-
ognition that the hotel was too cold to be comfortable.
Riding the elevator, he still wasn't certain what he would
say to her. Was she primarily a funding mechanism or a
romantic outlet?

Goddamn, that's cynical, he thought. At the same time,
he wondered whether he could ever let someone into his
life to the extent that she became as important to him as
his work. Were that to happen, would it mean that his
work had diminished in importance or that his feelings
for someone else had simply become more important?
The past several weeks had been nothing short of an ordeal, opening up all kinds of questions that previously
had remained hidden. He hated self-doubt. It wasn't in his
nature and he put it out of his mind as he knocked on the
door to Cross's suite.

40

THE DRIVERS LED the Americans to the human remains and then stood back as they hovered around them like well-behaved children. Cody Boyd didn't need a magnifying glass to tell what had happened.

"See these cut marks," Boyd said, holding up a tibia. "These were made by Reptilus blaberus."

"You're sure?"

"Definitely."

The men passed the bone around and one of them gently set it on top of the pile. Nolan Thomas, the oldest of the men and the leader, studied the landscape, which was dense with underbrush. Water droplets from the canopy bounced off their hats but nobody paid attention. In the windless air thick with humidity, their khakis had turned brown from sweat. The screeching of monkeys in the trees made conversation difficult.

"This doesn't seem right," Boyd said.

"What doesn't?" Thomas asked.

"When we found the first body, human body, we'd already found dozens of dead animals. In fact, they were all over the place. But I'm not seeing that here."

"Why don't you ask them if there are other bodies?"

Boyd grimaced. He knew enough phrases in Portuguese to order fast food, to find a bathroom, the basic tourist questions but beyond that he resorted to an app on his phone that translated English into other languages.

"*Existem outras instâncias?*" he said awkwardly.

The drivers looked at each other and shrugged.

"The kids found it," one of the drivers said in Portuguese.

"So, what do you think?" Thomas asked. "You think there's more?"

"There has to be. If the bugs got this guy you gotta figure they got everything else. Maybe we should spread out and look."

The two men who accompanied Thomas looked at each other quizzically.

"You think they're still around?" One of them asked tentatively.

"I don't know," Boyd said. "Could be."

"I'm not sure that's a good idea. I've read articles about what happened to you. Y'all kinda walked into it, didn't you?"

"We got caught in a flood," Boyd responded defensively. "If it hadn't been for that…"

"Maybe we should ask the children," Thomas said.

41

Having returned to the village, Boyd managed to string enough words together in Portuguese to make the ATV drivers understand that he wanted to talk to the children who had seen the body. They called out to a group of boys who were inspecting the helicopter. Two came running.

One of the men asked whether they'd found other bones or skeletons. The boys looked at each other. One whispered something to the other. They weren't certain whether they were about to get into trouble.

"*Havia outros ossos?*" one of the drivers said sternly.

"Yes, we found more," one of the boys admitted in Portuguese, looking at the ground.

"What are they saying?" Thomas asked, as he took Boyd aside.

"There are other bones," Boyd said. "That just makes sense."

"Where are they?"

"I don't know. Maybe we get one of them to take us there. The men don't seem to know anything except what the kids told them."

Boyd asked the boy if he would show them the bones. He eagerly agreed.

Conferring with Thomas, it was decided that they would use one ATV and follow the boy's directions. This time the driver insisted that in addition to paying him, the boy should be paid as a guide, which brought a smile to the youngster's face.

42

THE DRIVER WASTED no time returning to where they'd found the body. However, once on foot they were surprised to see their young guide take a different path that wound around the hill where the body was found, behind and beyond it to a field of tall grass. He pointed to what, from a distance, looked like a pile of rocks. Leaving the boy and the driver behind, Thomas and Boyd moved quickly toward what turned out to be a pile of bones. While Boyd photographed it with his cellphone, Thomas pulled a skeleton out of the pile. It was a squirrel monkey.

"This has the same marks as the others," Thomas said, examining the skeleton.

"What do you suppose happened here?" Boyd said, scanning the area.

"I'll bet the kid knows," Thomas said.

Boyd struggled to translate. As best he could determine, the boy said that he and his friends were hunting when they started finding dead animals on the forest floor. Somebody got the idea that the hides could be worth money and they removed the bones and put them in a pile to see how large it would be. Later, they found the dead man.

Thomas outlined his plan on the ride back to the village. Flesh was still attached to some of the bones but, for the most part, they'd been stripped. On the chopper, despite the constant roar of the engines, they talked, the leader and the reality TV consultant.

43

DUNCAN HAD HOPED that spending the weekend with Maggie Cross would help him make a clean break with the past and it did, but not as he had wished. Everything between them was good, from sex to conversation, and for most of the weekend he felt relaxed in a carefree way that a week earlier would have been impossible. He was surprised at how willing he was to open up to Cross, not censoring his comments, just letting thoughts tumble out. And tumble out they did—the anger, the humiliation, the anxiety, and mostly the misgivings he had about the decisions he'd made in the rainforest and how much they may have contributed to the death of Carlos Johnson and Fernando Azevedo.

Cross, on the other hand, wasn't focused on the past. Sympathetic at first, she coaxed Duncan to talk about his feelings but thought it would only last a short time and then they could get on with their weekend. She had survived and returned to her normal life, and though Duncan's experience was more complicated, she expected him to do the same. That's what middle-aged people did, she believed. Instead, she'd succeeded in opening a wound from which poured a mixture of self-pity and despondency that surprised her and made her wonder whether she had misjudged him all along. Maybe he wasn't as strong and steadfast as she had believed him to be. At least he didn't cry. That would have been too much.

Duncan could never have spoken so frankly about himself to anyone, not with lawyers waiting to file suits and calls for investigations and the rumors swirling like dust devils around him. To whom else could he confess his fears and inadequacies? He had colleagues but no friends. He was afraid that anyone else he talked to could be recording the conversation and would use it against him, but he trusted Cross and the terrible experience they had shared. Although they were of the same generation, they weren't old friends and this became apparent when he asked her what she would have done had she been the leader.

"This is pointless," she said impatiently, which took Duncan by surprise. "What's done is done. You did the best you could. It's not like there were good and bad choices. I'm sorry that you're having such a hard time with it but, you know, it's not like you caused the flood."

"But would it have been better to try to walk away instead of taking the truck?"

"How could we know? It was regrettable that people died, but as far as you or I know, more would have died had we done something else. Besides, no one had any better ideas."

"Hamel thought he did."

"Yeah, well, he thinks very highly of himself and if that's who you're comparing yourself to, then I feel sorry for you. You're better than that. You can blame yourself all you want. Maybe we shouldn't have gone. But we did. No one was coerced."

Duncan was chagrined and embarrassed. *She's right*, he thought. But it was hard for him to let go.

"The students might have felt coerced," he said.

"Damn it! That's their problem if they were. Will you just get over it? It's been weeks. You're not going to go on like this forever, are you? It's really not pleasant to watch. I hate to say this, but you really need to grow a pair."

Duncan's face reddened.

"You're right," he said, shaking his head. "I'm sorry."

"Stop apologizing," she insisted. "Let's change the subject."

"To what?"

"Lunch, if nothing else."

44

BOYD LET THE phone ring. It was the third unanswered call from Duncan. He felt guilty about not telling him he had a new job as a consultant, though it was temporary. He knew his former boss would be disappointed because they'd talked about coming back to Brazil to find specimens. He'd been noncommittal at the time because he wasn't sure he wanted to do it again, and then the job offer came. He saw it as an opportunity to make good money while combining his skills as an entomologist and amateur filmmaker. The producer put him to work immediately, scouting locations with Nolan Thomas and his research group. The friends he'd confided in all agreed that he should take the job, that it would look good on his résumé and that he'd make good money.

But he hadn't fully thought out how he would break it to Duncan. The longer he delayed taking the call, the worse he felt. The guilt piled up. He knew he couldn't avoid him forever. If his mentor had his best interests in mind, then he'd understand and congratulate him rather than making him feel bad. He'd answer the next time Duncan called. He told himself he wouldn't apologize. He had done nothing wrong.

45

"I'M SORRY, BOSS," Boyd said over the phone.

"I called you like a half-dozen times. Are you screening my calls?"

"No, I wouldn't do that," Boyd lied uncomfortably. "Anyway, this is just the fourth call from you."

"Well, there you go, you've been screening…"

"No, I haven't," Boyd insisted. "I've been out of cell range."

"Where are you?"

Boyd stared at his laptop screen, which was open on a small desk in a hotel where the film crew was staying. He was glad he was in the room when Duncan called. He needed the privacy. He didn't want the producer or anyone else to know about the call.

"I'm in Manaus."

"Really!? Already. That's amazing. I thought you hadn't decided to go."

Damn it, this is hard, Boyd thought. Toying with a ballpoint pen on the desktop, he thought about what he should say.

"Are you there?"

"Yes, I'm here. It's just that I don't know how to say this."

"Say what? Just spit it out."

Duncan made the call from Cross's suite. He and Maggie had just returned from lunch and both were in much better moods. They'd decided to move forward, which was more of a relief to Duncan than he'd expected. Cross was happy to listen as Duncan described his plans to return to Brazil, as long as he didn't get into too much detail. On the walk back from the restaurant they stopped at a liquor store and, while Duncan made his call, she made mojitos. Sitting next to her on the leather couch, he put his phone on speaker and set it on the coffee table.

"I've got a job."

"I know that. I'm paying you."

"No, I got a new job. I'm a consultant with a reality film crew. I'm sorry I didn't tell you before."

Anger quickly overwhelmed Duncan. He felt an urge to throw the phone against a wall. He reached toward it, but Cross put her hand over his, smiled, and shook her head slightly.

"When did this happen?"

"Last week. It was outta the blue. It was too good to be true."

"And the past, what has it been, two years. I guess that wasn't too good to be true?"

Boyd rolled his eyes. He didn't want to argue. He wanted to remain on Duncan's good side.

"They're paying me a lot of money, you know. I'm gonna make enough to pay off some of my student loans. Besides, it's only a three-month contract."

"That's not the point," Duncan said, tersely. "You knew I was planning to go back. If you need more money …"

"It's not about the money," Boyd said hesitantly. "OK, OK, it is about the money. It's always about the money. But it's also an opportunity. I'm not here as an assistant, I'm here as a consultant. They look up to me."

Duncan realized he was losing the battle. Who could he find to take Boyd's place? How could science compete against Hollywood? He drew a blank.

"Cody, Cody, Cody," Duncan sighed, reaching for his mojito and taking a giant gulp. "So, what kind of show are you doing? It's not about what happened to us, is it?"

"No, no, no, I wouldn't have anything to do with something like that. We're actually going to follow this really smart guy named Nolan Thomas. We went to a village yesterday, really remote place, had to fly in, and …."

"Nolan Thomas?! Really, he's out there?"

"You know him?"

"I've met him. I thought he gave up fieldwork," Duncan said, doing his best to disguise how he really felt. "So, he's going after *blaberus*?"

"Yep."

"And he's already there?"

"Oh, yeah. We're scouting locations but what we saw yesterday looks promising."

"And what's his goal?"

"Oh, I don't know. I think he wants to capture some specimens, just like…"

"Me?"

"Yeah, I guess. Just like you," Boyd grimaced. "Hey, you know, maybe he won't succeed."

Just like me, Duncan thought, as he wished Boyd well and ended the call. Downing the remainder of the mojito, he looked at Cross and held the glass up.

"Can I have another?"

DUNCAN DIDN'T LET his conversation with Boyd ruin the remainder of the weekend. Cross liked him and he knew that. She knew he liked her. They both knew he needed money. There was never a question in her mind whether she would pay for Suarez's lawyer and she knew before she came to Houston that Duncan planned to return to Brazil for another expedition. Although he didn't go into detail when he first mentioned his plans, she knew that sooner or later he would let it slip out that he needed financial help and who better to ask than someone who had provided it in the past? It was obvious to her, even though Duncan seemed to think he had kept it well hidden.

Disappointed that Boyd had taken another job, he avoided talking about it with Cross until they were having breakfast in the hotel restaurant. Cross's plane was scheduled to leave early that afternoon and he thought this would be the last time he would speak to her before returning to Brazil.

"What are you going to do without Cody?" she asked.

"I don't know, that was just totally unexpected. I

know he had some doubts about going back, and I could understand that, but to just go and take another job without telling me, that's hard to deal with."

"I'm sure it wasn't personal," Cross said. "He found a better opportunity and took it."

"Yeah, you know, I've never thought of Nolan Thomas as a competitor. I don't even know what he's been working on. He hasn't published much that I've seen. Besides, he's not really an entomologist."

"And yet, he's suddenly competing against you."

"Yeah, it kinda looks that way. I wish I knew more and maybe I can squeeze some info from Cody when I see him in Manaus. It sounds like they may be close to finding *blaberus*."

"I wouldn't be looking forward to that," Cross said, smiling.

"I get the impression he's after specimens—why else would he be there—but I'm not sure how he's gonna get them. I've been thinking a lot about that lately."

Duncan outlined what he saw as the challenges facing anyone attempting to track and capture the predatory insects. Nothing was known about how their colonies were organized, how they communicated with each other, how they orchestrated attacks. The fact that most of Duncan's experience with the insects occurred in water meant that he knew nothing about how they behaved in their normal environment of dry land. Doubtless, they were a more formidable opponent on land than they were on water.

"That's a scary thought," Cross said, comfortable with playing the sounding board.

"That's why I've been thinking about it. The only thing I keep coming up with is to use traps, you know.

But the problem is figuring out where to put them. I have no idea how to locate them except by what they leave behind."

"Surely, that person—Thomas, is it—is in the same boat."

"Unless he's been secretly studying them in his lab. I wouldn't put it past him but, you know, how likely is that?" Duncan asked rhetorically.

"I wish I could help you with that, but I will never get close to those things again, ever. Not even if they're in a zoo. I'm scared to death of them. I've even had nightmares. And, really, if you want to know, I think you're crazy to go looking for them."

"Well, let's not forget I'm going down there to help Antonio, too. It's not all about the bugs."

"Oh, yes it is," Cross countered. "And you know what? I think you're not going to let anyone get to the bugs before you do. And that worries me."

Duncan shook his head.

"That's ridiculous."

"You can deny it, but I know you. You'll take shortcuts, you'll do anything to be the first. And you know it."

Duncan grinned slightly and sipped his coffee. He'd finished his omelet and felt content enough not to be drawn into an argument, even a playful one.

"I want you to be safe," Cross said, reaching across the table to touch his hand. "I don't want anything to happen to you, but I understand why you're going to do this. So I just want you to promise that, at the very least, you won't cut corners."

Duncan started to protest, but she continued.

"I won't take no for an answer. I know you need money for your expedition and I'll pay for it, OK."

"You don't have to do that," Duncan replied, not be-lieving a word of it.

"Yes, I do. And you know it. I don't want you going into the jungle without everything you need. And that's final. I think the best way will be for you to use your credit cards while you're there and I'll have George make the payments."

Duncan looked at her skeptically.

"Oh, don't worry. George isn't a thief. I'd do it but I'd probably forget."

Releasing his hand, she sat back in her chair and smiled triumphantly. Duncan returned the smile. Nothing was going to stop him now.

47

THE BOYS GATHERED around when the tribe's newest and youngest guide showed off the twenty reals he'd received from the ATV driver, whom the Americans had given twenty dollars to pay the boy. Most were impressed that someone their own age from their own village had been paid to be a guide. The young man rolled the currency in his pocket while describing how he'd earned the money.

"Did you tell them about the other animals?" One of his friends asked when he'd finished.

"Of course not," the youngster replied. "I thought we decided not to tell anyone, so I didn't tell."

"That's good, because maybe we can make money off them."

"Like someone is going to pay money for a bunch of dead animals?" another boy said sardonically.

"You never know," the young guide said. "Look at me, I'm a guide now. Americans are loaded with money. Anything can happen."

48

BOYD THOUGHT HE had never felt as engaged in his work as he did since becoming a consultant for Broken Tree Productions. He liked everything about his job: the meetings where the crew sought his advice, the scouting trips, the decent accommodations and, of course, the money. But as their questions about Duncan's ill-fated expedition turned to criticisms he felt pressured to defend it. *Were they taking shots at him or at Duncan*, he wondered.

"Your problem was that you ignored the obvious," Carl Murphy, the field producer said. "After you found all those animal skeletons, and especially that guy with his dog, don't you think you should've turned back?"

"We talked about it," Boyd said. "But it wasn't really the insects. It was the flood. If the flood hadn't happened, we wouldn't be here talking about it."

"Like that guide who got killed?" videographer Joe Robinson said sarcastically.

The crew peppered Boyd with leading questions to such an extent that he pushed away from the table and left the room.

"We're not trying to put you on the spot," the producer yelled.

"Yes, you are," Boyd shouted. "You're trying to get me to say that we screwed up. Well, maybe we did, and maybe we didn't. You weren't there so whatever you say is crap." Reentering the room, he argued, "Tell me, what the fuck would you have done?"

"Take it easy," the producer said.

"Fuck you, all of you. I'm out of here. Go find someone else for your fucking expedition."

A door slammed. The men looked at each other in amazement.

"Think we pushed him too hard?" Jack Walker, the soundman, asked.

"Goddamnit," Murphy said.

"We don't need him," Robinson said.

Murphy shook his head. He was perplexed at how things had gotten out of hand so quickly. They were supposed to get more background about the insects from Boyd and then unveil the countermeasure they'd developed if they found themselves threatened by the insects.

"What's got you so pissed?" he demanded of the videographer.

"I don't know, I guess I smelt blood in the water."

"What the fuck does that mean?! He's not the enemy, for chrissakes! Dr. Thomas is not going to like this one bit. Do any of you know anything about entomology? Any of you want to take his place? Because if you don't we're fucked. Goddamn, you people make me sick."

"Joe's that way," Walker said. "He's a fucking bully, ain't that right, Joe?"

The videographer hissed.

"I don't know, I was just trying to see what he was made of. You know, how he handles pressure."

"Well, that's a goddamn stupid thing to do," the producer squawked, storming out of the room and into the fifth floor hallway and down the carpeted hall to Boyd's room. He knocked several times before the door opened a crack.

"Mind if I come in? I don't know what the hell that was about, but it's not your fault. I don't want you to quit. OK? I can get another crew tomorrow, if that'll work for you."

Boyd shrugged and moved to a window overlooking the busy street.

"Look, I didn't sign on for this."

"I know, I know. Neither did I," Murphy said. "Frankly, I'm mortified. I've worked with Joe before and he's never lashed out like that. I don't know what he was thinking. Anyway, he's sorry, if that helps."

Boyd sighed and plopped into an overstuffed chair wedged into a corner of the room. As an experienced reality producer, Murphy often had to deal with tensions between the crew and the subjects they were filming, but nothing like this. He understood that part of his job was peacemaker. He understood how little things could become big things and that it was up to him to make them go away, at least long enough to get into post-production.

"You know, we've been looking for the bugs and really haven't found them, and that's frustrating because when we're not filming we're not making any money, and there's so much misinformation going around about what happened to y'all. It's just…it's that, you know, give it a chance. Joe's sorry. Give us another chance. This afternoon we'll go over our security arrangements. You don't have to like him," Murphy said, trying to unruffle Boyd's feathers. "You just have to work with him."

"I'll tell you what, if he does that again I'm gonna punch him in the mouth. I'm not taking shit from that asshole."

"I can work with that," Murphy said and returned to the meeting room where he spelled out ground rules for working with Boyd.

"So we gotta treat him like a prima donna," the videographer snarled.

"You know, Joe," the producer began, "if you want out, there's the door. If it's a choice between him and you, you know who I'm picking."

The videographer looked for support from the soundman and the associate producer. None was forthcoming.

"Let me say in my defense."

"Shut the fuck up, Joe!" the soundman bellowed. "You're just making things worse."

DUNCAN LEFT A message on Boyd's voicemail soon after checking into his hotel in Manaus. Thanks to funding from Maggie Cross, he had two missions. The first was to attend Antonio Suarez's bail hearing and testify if necessary. The second was to capture specimens of *Reptilus blaberus*. Suarez's lawyer had emailed instructions, including the address of the court where the case would be heard the next morning. After settling into his room, Duncan checked his phone for messages. He wasn't expecting any since only a handful of people had his new number. Out of curiosity, he used web mail to check his university email account and found it stuffed with more than a thousand messages that he would never read. Scanning the subjects was enough to reinforce his opinion that the world was filled with idiots. But he wanted to talk to someone who wouldn't ask about his previous expedition.

Dressed in jeans and a dark T-shirt, he went for a walk in the vicinity of the hotel. It was situated in an updated commercial neighborhood populated by restaurants and small shops. The sidewalks were crowded and the streets busy with traffic. The noise bothered him, so he turned down a side street off the main avenue and within a block found himself at a small plaza. Taking a seat on a bench he felt his phone vibrate.

"Cody, thanks for calling me back. I just got in and wanted to see how things are going with you."

"You wouldn't believe what went on today. I almost got into a fight."

"Really!? You? A fight?"

"Yeah, I don't know, maybe I got PTSD or somethin' but, man, that guy, I don't know, he hit my buttons. I don't know if I've ever gotten that angry. I even walked out of the room and slammed the door."

"What guy?" Duncan asked. "Did you quit?"

"No, we talked about it. The old video guy was dissing us, you know, saying that we brought everything on ourselves. I just couldn't take it. I guess that's what you've been putting up with for weeks, huh?"

"Oh, yeah, except I don't listen to them anymore; I don't even read about them. They weren't there so all they can do is second-guess us."

"Yeah, that's exactly what happened today. I just couldn't believe how angry I got."

They updated each other about what they were doing and agreed to meet at a restaurant near Duncan's hotel. As it turned out, Boyd's hotel was less than a mile away. Duncan told him about going to court in the morning and how he hoped Suarez would be released.

"You know, here's something funny for you," Boyd said. "This afternoon they unveiled their plan to protect themselves from the insects."

"Protect themselves?"

"Yeah, you know how we talked about having a flame-thrower?"

"We didn't have one so …."

"Yeah, but these guys got one."

"No kidding?"

"I saw it."

Boyd told him that the producer had hired a former mercenary who had built his own flamethrower from surplus parts. If they were threatened by the bugs, he would sweep the area with a mixture of ten percent gasoline and ninety percent diesel.

"He showed us a video and it looked awesome. I was surprised how far the flames go. I mean, if we had one of those things, we could have incinerated the bugs fifty feet out. They wouldn't have gotten to us."

"You believe that?"

"Well, yeah, sorta. We used fire. It's just that we couldn't throw the gas very far. With this, man, everything goes up in smoke."

Duncan started asking prying questions about where Thomas's group was looking and what they'd found. At first Boyd was cagey and told him about his contract and its nondisclosure clause. But, even though he no longer worked for Duncan, Boyd felt loyalty toward him and, after the morning's tiff, trusted him more than the people he worked with. He was having doubts about what the crew really thought about him and what they were saying about him behind his back. He told him about the village they'd visited and the remains that they'd found and later the pile of hides and skeletons the village's children had collected.

"Of all the places we scouted, this was the only one where *blaberus* had definitely been. The bones had all the markings."

"Any idea how old it was?"

"I couldn't tell. There wasn't much flesh left."

Although it wasn't his intention, and though Duncan gave him only mild encouragement, Boyd told him everything that had gone on since he arrived in Manaus. They both realized at a certain point that of all the people they knew in the city the only ones they could trust were one another.

"You know, I really wish you were working with me on this," Duncan said.

"Yeah, I get that. I kinda wish that, too. But, I don't know, I'm stuck with it for now."

"Well, if you need an out, call me, but make it soon. I'm gonna start putting things together after tomorrow."

"You know where you're gonna look? Don't say it's the village we went to, please don't," Boyd pleaded.

"OK, I won't say that."

50

DUNCAN CHALKED IT up to language differences. Somehow the judge presiding over Suarez's bail bond hearing thought that the American professor was the guide's employer. That counted for more than his affidavit. It wasn't until after the hearing, after waiting in a lobby while the lawyer finalized paperwork and paid the bond, that Duncan realized there had been a miscommunication. Suarez emerged with a big smile and a bounce in his step. Approaching Duncan, he hugged him gratefully.

"Thank you so much Mister Howard," he said, "Thank you for helping me and giving me a job."

Duncan gave a puzzled look to Suarez's lawyer, who smiled.

"That's what the judge said," the lawyer said in an aside. "I think there was confusion on his part. I'm sorry I didn't catch it at the time, but I was focused more on the amount of the bond. It's not a big deal. You can fire him, if you want to, and he'll still be free on bond. It's just that he thinks you're his boss. You can explain it to him. I need to be going."

Duncan was unsure what to do, whether to tell Suarez there had been a mistake and he didn't have a job, or whether to put him on his payroll. He would need a guide on the expedition he planned and, despite his age, the young man had proven his worth during the first expedition. When he explained the situation to Suarez, the guide's smile disappeared.

"You want to find the bugs?" he said, incredulously.

"Yes, I'm here to find specimens."

Suarez lowered his head and shook it slightly.

"I don't know, Mister Howard," he said, his voice barely audible so that Duncan had to lean toward him.

"It's just going to be you, me and maybe one or two others," Duncan said. "There's a village that we can fly into. We can rent ATVs. There won't be any floods. It won't be like the last time."

"I don't know, Mister Howard. I'm thankful for your help but I still have, how you say it, *pesadelos*, nightmares."

"Me too," Duncan said. "But this will be different. Besides, there's a saying in my country that if you get thrown by a horse you should get back on it."

Suarez gave him a baffled look.

"That way you overcome your fears," Duncan explained.

"Does it work, getting on the horse?"

"I don't know. It's an expression. A saying. It applies to anything you do that ends in failure. It's so you don't become a quitter."

Suarez thought about it for a moment.

"Tell you what, you think about it and I'll call you tomorrow," Duncan said.

"I don't have a phone," Suarez said apologetically.

Duncan counted out five hundred reals from his wallet, handing them to Suarez.

"This is an advance on your salary. Go buy yourself a phone and call me with the number."

Suarez brightened as he stared at the currency before shoving it into his pants pocket. Not only would he be able to afford a phone, but groceries as well. As they parted, Suarez hoped the electricity hadn't been cut off at Javier Costa's rent house. Things had a way of changing rapidly when you were in jail.

51

THE THREE OF them sat at a table in a bar near their hotel: the soundman, the producer and the consultant. It had been a long, trying day and they wanted to blow off steam. Boyd was glad to see that Joe the Asshole hadn't been invited, but he wondered whether it was because of their encounter that morning. Secretly, he hoped it wasn't. He wasn't a fragile person and didn't want special treatment or even the appearance of special treatment. He just wanted to be one of the guys.

"Oh, we never go drinking with Joe," Walker said.

"Yeah, he's a mean drunk, gets angry over nothing," Murphy added.

"Sometimes he starts fights," Walker said. "You just never know what he's thinking."

"Why do you put up with him?" Boyd asked, nursing his beer.

"Well, for one thing, he's fearless," Murphy said.

"I worked with him several years ago," Walker said. "You know how they say there's two kinds of people, those who run from the fire and those who run into the fire? Well, Joe's one of those who runs into the fire so he can video the firefighters."

"Yeah, he's worked in war zones, Serbia, the Middle East, Asia. He's even been wounded. He's got a lot of interesting stories about his assignments."

"'Course, you don't know how much of it is bullshit," Walker said.

"There's that. The other thing is that he always comes out as the good guy, you know. Like he's a saint."

"There's nobody else you can get?" Boyd asked.

"I don't know of anybody who takes the chances to get the shot that Joe takes," Murphy said. "As a producer, that's gold. I don't have to tell him anything, really. Once he gets on a shoot, he's telling me what he should be doing and, you know, most of the time he's right. The guy knows his business. I sometimes think of myself as a new second lieutenant and he's my grizzled sergeant. And you know what the Army tells second lieutenants?"

"Listen to your sergeant," Walker said.

Boyd took it all in and realized before he'd finished his second beer that he could either learn to get along with the videographer or quit. He figured there was no way Murphy would replace him, but he didn't want to continue talking about him so he asked what they knew about Nolan Thomas. Murphy and Walker looked at each other across the table and shrugged.

"The guy is, what do you call it, standoffish," Walker said.

"Aloof," Murphy agreed. "He's very smart, no question about that. But he thinks we're working for him and that gets awkward pretty quick."

"Yeah, one time, this was like two days before you came onboard and the day after we met him, we were sitting around talking, trying to explain what we were doing and what our expectations were and all that," Walker said.

"Yeah, we talked for like ten, fifteen minutes, you know. He looked like he was listening, but then he asks, 'So, who's going to carry my specimen cases?' and we look at each other like, wow, he didn't hear a word," Murphy said. "Not a word."

"I know the type," Boyd said. "Academia is filled with them. So obsessed with their work that they think the rest of the world is there to assist them."

"Is that what it was like with your former boss?" Murphy asked.

"Kinda, but not really. He's an all right guy."

"From what I've seen on TV, he's not ready for prime time," Walker sniffed, pulling on his silvery gray beard.

"I'll give you that," Boyd said. "But then, how would you react? It's like the world's taking sides and you're in the middle by yourself. You know, he's down here?"

Boyd suddenly regretted what he'd said. His companions instantly faced him, anticipating some juicy gossip.

"Look, I'm not gonna say anything bad about him."

"No, no, why would you do that?" Murphy said. "What's he down here for, if you don't mind my asking?"

I mind, Boyd thought, angry with himself for bringing it up. Certainly, he wasn't going to mention Duncan's job offer nor the fact that he'd told him about the village where they found the hides. He realized anything he said would be more than he should say. He could see the wheels turning in the field producer's bright eyes.

"You know, I'd really like to meet him," Murphy said.

"So would every reporter in the Western Hemisphere," Walker agreed.

"And that's why it's not gonna happen," Boyd said, hoping to cut the conversation short. "You know, I talked to him on the phone. Once. That's it."

"Let me pitch an idea to you," Murphy said after ordering a third round.

Carl Murphy had been a producer long enough to know a good story arc when he saw one. It was one thing to be following the secretive Nolan Thomas into the rainforest looking for predatory insects and quite another to be following the man who had actually found them and barely escaped with his life. Broken Tree Productions had contacted several of the survivors, but all of them declined to participate in a reality production. The front office hadn't told him details of their arrangement with Thomas and at the time it didn't matter, but now that he knew that Duncan was in the area, he started to wonder. The allure of getting Duncan involved was too much to resist. He knew if he could get this to happen his bosses would throw a party.

"I'll tell you what," Boyd said, "I'll ask him but only on the condition that we change the subject. I've already said too much."

52

MURPHY WAS ON the phone with his boss as soon as he stepped into his room. The drinking party broke up after the third round. Murphy could think of nothing other than that Duncan was in Brazil. Although Boyd had clammed up and wouldn't provide details, Murphy had no problem filling in the blanks. As a producer, he understood the importance of creating tension in a reality show, and what could be better than pitting Duncan and Thomas against each other without either of them actually knowing about it?

We could use two units, one with each of them, and knit the story lines together, he thought. *They could go on doing whatever they do and our man Boyd could give us the play-by-play.*

"I don't have it all figured out, but just imagine if we can get the guy who started it all into the show!"

"What are you gonna do when they find out?"

"We'll be in post by then. It won't matter."

53

ANTONIO SUAREZ SAT in the shade of the patio sipping an Antarctica Cerveja, his second, his feet propped on the small table. On the table sat his cellphone and under it a small piece of paper with the number of his American patron, Howard Duncan. The phone was an older model with a prepaid SIM card that he bought from a street vendor. It was the second purchase he made after his release from jail. The first was to seek out a *churrascaria* and chow down on barbecue. Then came the phone and the beer.

A bus took him to within several blocks of the house. His mind started to play tricks on the walk. Suddenly, he feared that someone may have moved in. Would he fight if it came to that? No, what would be the point? Eventually someone would take possession and he'd be on the street again. But he had a job and money in his wallet.

What if someone was in the house waiting to rob him? Now that he had something to lose, he approached the tiny house cautiously. To his relief, the front door was locked and the air-conditioner was off, just as he had left it. Using the key his boss had given him, he pushed the door open. The air inside was dank and stinky. The garbage hadn't been taken out since his arrest. In a burst of

energy, he removed the garbage, started the air conditioner, opened the patio door and, for the first time in more
than a week, contemplated a brighter future.

While in jail, it was all about whether he'd be released
on bail. When that happened, it was all about getting
comfortable. After that happened, he thought about how
he could tell Duncan that he didn't want to be anywhere
near the killer insects. He felt tense whenever he thought
about what had happened to his boss and the others. He
was deeply remorseful that he had ended Carlos Johnson's
life, but he had no choice. He could not let him suffer like
that. The guilt he felt for taking a life weighed on him. He
needed to confess to a priest. He would do it tomorrow,
he told himself. He would describe what happened, how
the student begged to be freed from the torture of being eaten alive. Surely, the priest would absolve him. Or
would he? What kind of penance would be required for
taking a life? He didn't understand all of the workings of
the church, but he understood how guilty he felt, and he
knew from experience that he felt better after confession.

However, he realized that by taking the money from
Duncan he had as much as agreed to work for him. He'd
spent some of it and thus couldn't simply give it back.
Staring at the phone, he wondered whether it would be
easier to not make the call. Of course, the court had
the address to the house so Duncan could find him if
he was so inclined. Which he would, Suarez knew. Why
else would he have given him five hundred reals to buy a
phone? Only wealthy people would spend that much on
a phone.

Though he'd thought he would sleep well on his first

night of freedom, he didn't. The nightmare had returned and instead of devouring the young American, the insects were feeding on him.

54

ALTHOUGH HE HAD the financial support, what Duncan really needed was a trustworthy assistant or collaborator to develop a plan and implement it. Knowing that Nolan Thomas already had a team and had located a promising site made everything seem urgent. If only Cody were working for him, he thought. If only he could convince him to work with him. But how? Unexpectedly, he found himself bumping up against his limitations. He was so accustomed to having assistants carrying out tasks that he found himself struggling with the details. In the past, he'd develop the overarching plan and others would gather the gear, the provisions, the contracts—whatever was needed to make things happen. He was a fish out of water. Should he call Boyd?

It was a relief when Suarez finally called. *I can count on Antonio*, he thought.

Suarez, on the other hand, was not nearly as excited. He hadn't slept well and he had yet to go to confession. His gratitude for what Duncan had done to help him battled with his fear of the insects. Duncan figured this out quickly when he asked the guide how he felt.

"I don't know Mister Howard, to tell the truth."

"What's wrong?"

Suarez sighed.

"I feel trapped."

"Trapped? How could you feel trapped? I just bailed you out of jail."

"Yes, yes, I know. And I am grateful. But I feel bad, you know, about what happened to Mister Carlos. And I'm afraid."

"What happened won't happen again," Duncan said. "The flooding is done."

"I know, I know. Every time I think about it, I see him."

Duncan couldn't dismiss the guide's fear. He was fearful as well and felt he'd suffered from PTSD to some extent, but thought he was over it.

"What are you trying to say, Antonio?"

"I'm, I'm very grateful for all you've done, but I don't want to die in the forest and I think that's what will happen if I go with you to look for the bugs."

Should he play hardball? If the guide were one of his students, he would, but he was uncertain at the amount of leverage he held over him.

"You know, the judge thinks you're working for me. You know that, right?"

"Yes, I know that. But the *advogado* said you could fire me if you want."

"Antonio, I'm not going to fire you," Duncan said, trying to keep his voice from rising. "But, you know, I gave you five hundred reals."

"I know. And I'm grateful."

"Stop saying you're grateful," Duncan said harshly. "It wasn't a gift. Look, I understand what you're saying.

I don't need you to find the insects, OK. I need you to keep me from getting lost. We'll do it differently this time. I already know where we're gonna go."

"You do?"

"Yes, it's a village. I haven't been there, but I've been told we can use ATVs. It won't be like last time. There won't be as many people, just you, me and maybe one or two others. And no floods."

Suarez's mood brightened.

"So, I don't have to get close to the insects?"

"No, I already have a good idea where they are, at least where they've been. And all I need to do is capture a few of them. Once I've got them, we're out of there. We'll fly in and fly out. It won't be like the last time."

Duncan knew he was making it up as he spoke. He was trying to allay the young man's fears and if it meant glossing over the reality a bit, then that's what he'd do. He knew Suarez would be a professional once they were in the field. Whether he was fooling himself was another question, which he didn't ask. He felt confident that with only three or four healthy men on the expedition, and no one to hold them back, they'd have a good chance of succeeding. Even if somehow the insects got within striking distance, they'd be in good enough shape to climb trees to avoid them, though he didn't say this to Suarez. It was one of the Plan B's floating in the back of his mind. He was sure he could come up with others.

"Mister Howard, can I ask how much I'll be paid?"

Duncan typed one hundred dollars into the currency converter on his phone.

"Four hundred reals. A day."

Suarez was speechless. Duncan thought he was hesitating.

"And there will be a bonus when we're done."

55

"How did they know I was here?" Duncan demanded after listening to Cody Boyd make his pitch. They were having dinner at a restaurant near Duncan's hotel.

"It's on the internet," Boyd said guardedly.

"You didn't tell them?"

"I didn't have to," he lied. He hadn't seen the internet article until after he'd told the producer that Duncan was in Manaus. The article was written in Portuguese and he learned of it inadvertently while reading Google translated articles from newspapers in Manaus. But it gave him cover.

"Explain how having a film crew following me around is beneficial? Not to mention that I absolutely hate people looking over my shoulder. Hate it."

"I understand, but they won't be looking over your shoulder. In fact, they won't be part of your expedition."

"Oh, c'mon. I've seen reality shows. It's like they're embedded," Duncan said.

"OK, OK, they're embedded. You know, I haven't done this before. Maybe you should talk to the producer. He's an all right guy."

"And what would I talk to him about?"

"Well, you'd have to sign an agreement."

"What?! An agreement about what?"

"Typical stuff. Nondisclosures, that sort of thing."

"You don't really know, do you?"

"Aw, fuck. I'm just a consultant."

"But you're getting paid, right? Are they going to pay me?"

"I don't know. Maybe we should just forget about it," Boyd said, dismayed.

56

"I'VE NEVER BEEN in a nice hotel like this, Mister Howard," Antonio Suarez remarked as he stood behind Howard Duncan, who pulled up Google Earth on his fifteen-inch laptop and located the village where Boyd said victims of *blaberus* had been found. Like many villages in the rainforest, it was located near a river but unlike other places he'd been, the terrain was rocky and rugged. Duncan had hoped that Suarez would be able to help him acquire equipment, but it became quickly evident that he had no notion of quality. His only suggestions were how to obtain gear cheaply from unlicensed vendors, likely of stolen goods. It was a deficiency he couldn't hold against the guide, since he was not an equipment guy like Boyd.

The way he had been planning the expedition was to explore the area near the village during the day and return at night to sleep. He wanted to avoid carrying camping gear into the forest, even though they would have access to ATVs. What preoccupied him the most was coming up with a strategy to actually capture specimens.

The preferred mechanism would be to bait traps, set them out and let them do their work. The problem was, he had no idea how to predict where the insects would be. So little was known about their behavior that he could only speculate where they might be at any given time. Since his only experience with them was during a flood, he had nothing to go on in terms of how they acted on dry land except from the video Suarez had made of his former boss's death. It was seared in Duncan's memory. He could replay it in his mind just by thinking about it.

Suarez's video showed his boss in thick, tall grass surrounded by the man-eaters. He wondered how they chose locations and he assumed that, like ants, they used scouts to forage for food. Certainly, an entire colony wouldn't travel en masse while foraging. That made no sense. The key, would be to find the scouts, which surely would not be large in number, and somehow get them to take the bait and step into a trap.

Otherwise, if there were only a handful, they might be able to grab them. They'd need gloves for that, perhaps protection for their heads. Certainly, they'd need to wear sturdy pants and shirts and gaiters or another means to secure their pants cuffs. From a safety standpoint, assuming they faced only a small number of scouts, it was plausible that they could do their jobs with a minimum of risk. The downside was that they would sweat like crazy, breathing would be more difficult because of the head-gear. And the clothing itself might make it more difficult to move freely.

There are always tradeoffs between safety and getting the job done, he thought. Nothing is one hundred percent safe, and while he believed he would have no problem going into the rainforest with heavy clothing, others might think otherwise. Duncan had never seen Suarez in more than shorts and a T-shirt. Would he, could he, wear heavy clothing and still do his job? Perhaps they could start out with light clothing and then change into the protective gear when they thought insects were in the area. That might work.

The other problem was finding at least one other person to join the expedition. He and Suarez weren't enough, unless they were very lucky. Even so, he doubted Suarez would agree to wear the clothing, much less expose himself to the bugs, which meant he would be on his own in the field with no backup in case things turned ugly.

Suarez liked the idea of hunting the insects during the day and sleeping in the village at night.

"It's safer that way," he said.

"That's the idea. It also means we don't have to carry much equipment so we can cover more ground."

When Suarez asked who else would be on the expedition, Duncan shrugged.

"Don't know yet. I'm still working on it."

"Mister Howard, I have cousins who could carry things. They don't have a job so they'll work cheap."

Duncan smiled. When it came to things he didn't enjoy doing he often reverted to what was easiest to accomplish. Suarez was making it easy for him.

MANY WHO HAD worked with Nolan Thomas thought him to be prickly and impatient with subordinates and deferential to those above him, especially those who controlled his budget. During his years in academia while working on his own grants, he was regarded as a difficult man to get along with, even by his deans. Despite his reputation, he was sought after by universities enamored with his multi-million dollar grants. Institutions competed to entice him by offering to build laboratories and provide an unending procession of graduate assistants to carry out the grunt work. His millions would make any university look that much better in annual listings of the top research institutions.

Since being recruited by a privately held company with myriad biotech projects, Thomas had become somewhat of a mystery to his former colleagues. He had published nothing over the past three years and was seen at few conferences. He shared little about the nature of his work, except that he was obviously interested in *blaberus*. His contract with Broken Tree Productions had been vetted by the company's legal department. It was an unusual move insofar as many privately held biotechs treasured confidentiality to the extent that little was known about their work. Most of Thomas's work was funded by the U.S. government. Once the agreement was signed, including blanket nondisclosure terms, Jason Gruber, an aide to Thomas, was embedded with the film crew as a liaison so that he was present for most production meetings. He had a habit of leaving when the meetings turned to purely technical issues.

"My job," he told the crew at one of the preproduction meetings, "is to keep Dr. Thomas happy, and failing that, keep him from using me as a punching bag."

Thomas attended several of the meetings to describe his plan of action and precautions they would take.

"We want to avoid the mistakes made by the previous group," Thomas said.

Boyd winced at this, and felt an urge to defend himself, but held back. He wasn't certain whether Thomas knew that he had participated in Duncan's expedition. Perhaps it was just a throwaway line.

"Jason here has studied what we have learned from the media coverage of the tragedy that befell these people," Thomas said.

"That's right, thank you, doctor. There is, of course, a lot of misinformation and speculation fanned by the media to boost its sensationalistic appeal. What I've boiled it down to is that they were ill-prepared for what they encountered and made several decisions that in retrospect may have led to greater loss of life than was necessary."

Boyd exhaled silently, struggling against the impulse to respond. Involuntarily, he shook his head several times. Gruber asked if he was upset. Boyd looked up at Gruber and shook his head once.

Gruber explained that he thought the group's leader

had underestimated the size and lethality of his quarry and that he needlessly endangered everyone as a result. Boyd wondered whether he was baiting him. Did he even know he'd been part of the expedition?

"Was it irresponsible to enter the forest at the end of the wet season? It would seem so. Did they truly understand how dangerous their situation was? Apparently not, otherwise how could you explain why, after finding a human victim, they did not turn back and alert the authorities?"

While Gruber continued his critique, which was being recorded, Boyd found himself fabricating rebuttals that he didn't share with the group. To his irritation, he found that he couldn't easily dismiss Gruber's extensive and unpleasant assessment. Mistakes had been made, that was undeniable. At the same time, nobody on earth at that time knew of the insect's lethality. When Gruber finished, he looked at Boyd.

"Do you have anything to add, Mr. Boyd?" Gruber asked.

Boyd glanced at the others sitting around the table. Everyone was looking at him. Carl Murphy grimaced, fearing an outburst. Joe Robinson watched, expecting to see fireworks. He'd noticed Boyd's discomfort as Gruber spoke and relished it like someone watching the start of a fight.

"Not really. My experience was different, but then I was there and you weren't."

Fearing discord, Murphy asked if anyone had questions for Gruber, making it clear by the tone of his voice that he didn't want to hear any questions.

"Yeah, I've got one," Robinson said, smiling at Boyd. "How again are you going to prevent what happened to Cody from happening to us?"

Murphy's expression changed quickly. It was a good question. Everyone turned their attention to Gruber.

"We're still working out the details, but I can tell you that safety is a prime consideration, unlike the previous group. Their leader let his ambition get in the way of safety, resulting in tragedy. That's not going to happen to us."

"You haven't answered my question," the videographer repeated.

"Well, you already know about the flamethrower. That was Carl's idea. I tried it. It was scary to use but effective. The insects get too close, we spray them with fire. We will also incorporate protective clothing. And we've got insecticides."

Murphy smiled and nodded approvingly after Gruber finished.

"That's very reassuring," Murphy said. "Any other questions?"

"Just one," Robinson said, raising his hand. "When do we start?"

58

BOYD WASN'T HAPPY with the way the video project was going. He didn't like the criticism from Gruber, he didn't like the deception proposed by the producer to convince Duncan to embed a film crew with his expedition. He liked the idea of a flamethrower. It was the one item he wished they'd had when they were stranded on the truck. That, more than anything else in Gruber's critique, he found to be helpful. Without testing, he had no confidence in insecticides.

Murphy took Boyd aside following the meeting to ask how things were going with Duncan.

"Is he onboard?"

"Not yet," Boyd said distractedly, still mentally reviewing what Gruber had said.

"You know, we need to make this happen. It'll make all the difference."

"I know, I know, I understand. I'm still working on him," Boyd sighed uneasily. "He wants to know what's in it for him."

"Well, it's a chance to exonerate himself, don't you think?"

"That's bullshit. He doesn't need to exonerate himself. He did as well as anybody could've done under the circumstance, I don't care what that egghead Gruber says. He wasn't there and neither were you."

"Don't get pissed at me," Murphy cautioned. "I didn't say it and, you know, that's his opinion. Maybe exonerate isn't the right word. Maybe you can just explain it better. You know, a show like this could bring him a lot of positive publicity, which I'm sure is lacking today. I mean, is he holed up in some dive hotel somewhere?"

"No, nothing like that" Boyd said. "He's getting his expedition ready, and I'm not sure I should say this, but he wants to hire me back."

"Really!? Huh," Murphy said, taken aback. But his mental wheels turned quickly. "You know, that might not be a bad idea. Do you think he'd go along with it if you're with him?"

"That might work," Boyd said.

"You still wouldn't tell him how we might end up using the footage, right? You'll still be working for us so, you know, the nondisclosures are still intact. You can't really talk about the finished product."

"Yeah, you know, I hate this part of it. It's not my nature to lie like that."

"Well, don't think of it as lying. In this business, lying isn't really lying. People expect you to hold back, if for no other reason than really, until we've finished filming, we don't actually know what we're gonna do. That's the thing about reality shows, you can't really predict outcomes. It's a lot like life that way. It's reality."

59

WHILE BOYD MET with Duncan to convince him to co-operate with the production company, promising to help outfit his group and accompany him into the rainforest, Nolan Thomas wasted little time getting into the field. Slim and tall, dressed in khaki with a kayaker's floppy hat, he looked the part of a naturalist. From the start, they shot video, capturing B-roll and supplemental footage when they weren't focusing on Thomas or one of his assistants.

In addition to his four assistants, Thomas was accompanied by field producer Carl Murphy, soundman Jack Walker and videographer Joe Robinson. Missing was the mercenary. Murphy explained that there had been a problem with his passport and that he expected him to arrive any day. "At any rate, we got his flamethrower and Jason here can handle it."

Because of the limited seating, only one villager joined the group as a driver and guide. Murphy drove the second ATV.

Using the ATVs, the group retraced the route to the human remains and then hiked to the carcasses collected by the village's youngsters. They rested on a hill from which they viewed an uneven, rugged landscape dense with palms, towering mahogany and balsam. Monkeys screeched as they moved about the trees. On the ground they heard rustling as animals made their way invisibly through the vines, understory trees and shrubs that cluttered the ground inchoately.

"What are we looking for?" Murphy asked as Thomas surveyed the shadowy forest.

"You know, it would have been so much better if the kids had just left the carcasses where they found them."

"Kids will be kids," Murphy said, drawing an annoyed grimace from Thomas.

"Not helpful," he said.

"Maybe there's more that the kids didn't find," Murphy suggested. "An airplane could've crashed here and we wouldn't know it. You can't even see the ground."

"You could be right. Too bad we didn't bring one of them with us. Maybe we should fan out and look around," Thomas said, nodding toward Murphy's crew.

"Dr. Thomas, we're not allowed to help you. Our job is to document your expedition."

"I've only got my people to help?"

"Sir, you signed the contract. It stipulates…"

"I know what it stipulates," Thomas griped.

The scientist directed his assistants to move down from the hill in different directions while he watched from higher ground. The footing was difficult as they tripped over vines and stepped over debris while the videographer and soundman moved from one to the other, recording their futile efforts. This went on for an hour as the assistants slowly moved farther and farther away, zigzagging back and forth, their eyes glued to the ground.

"Sooner or later something has to pop up, don't you think?" Thomas said.

"I hope so. That's what we're here for."

"Dr. Thomas, Dr. Thomas," Greg Covelli, one of the assistants, shouted from the distance, barely visible from his boss' hilltop perch. "I've found something."

"What is it?" Thomas shouted.

Covelli pulled something from the ground and held it in the air.

"What is it?"

"It's a monkey, I think. Nothing left but the hide and the skeleton."

Thomas directed his assistants to return and after examining the carcass he looked at the guide, who sat at the base of the hill smoking a cigarette. Looking at the mound of bones, he asked, "Where are the hides?"

"Pardon me?" Murphy said.

"The hides. We find one monkey and its hide is intact. Where are the hides for these?" Thomas asked, pointing at the bones.

"Maybe the kids took 'em?"

"I wonder why," Thomas said, examining the monkey carcass. "You see, the hide is torn up. I doubt it would have any value in this condition."

Murphy shrugged.

"Maybe he knows," one of the assistants said, nodding toward the guide.

Using an app on his phone, the producer parsed a question in Portuguese.

"*Onde estão os couros?*" Murphy said, haltingly, holding and pointing at the carcass.

"*Eu não sei,*" the guide said.

"He doesn't know," Murphy said. "I think that's what he's saying. Do you think it's important?"

"I don't know, but it's something we should check out."

"Maybe the kids could tell the hides were worthless and got into a competition to see who could find the most bones," Murphy said. "When I was their age we'd…"

"It doesn't matter," Thomas said curtly. "Let's go down there and see if we can find more carcasses. This could be a larger killing field than we imagined."

60

HOWARD DUNCAN WAS not inclined to go along with Cody Boyd's pitch about embedding a camera crew into his expedition. Meeting in his hotel room, the middle-aged entomologist shook his head.

"The last thing I want is unqualified people getting in the way," he protested.

"They're not unqualified. They've done all kinds of shoots all across the world. They've been in war zones," Boyd countered.

"What do they know about entomology?"

"They're not entomologists," Boyd said, exasperated.

"They'll get in the way."

"They won't get in the way. They've been doing this for years."

"Really?"

"That's in the contract," Boyd said, pointing to a manila folder that he'd placed on the combination dresser-TV stand when he arrived. "All they will do is shoot video."

"No makeup and stuff like that?"

"None. They aren't working for you. By the same token, they aren't going to help you either, unless it's a life or death situation."

The room consisted of a full-size bed, matching dresser, desk with chair, nightstands and an upholstered armchair. Boyd sat on the edge of the bed facing Duncan, who stood with his back to Boyd while looking out the large plate glass window. Turning to face Boyd, Duncan stepped to the dresser and grabbed the folder, leafing through it before taking a seat in the armchair, the folder in his lap.

"How many people are involved?" Duncan asked, breaking the brief silence.

"Just a camera guy and a sound guy."

"And you?"

"Of course. There could be a field producer, but I'm not sure about that," Boyd said. "Anyway, they're responsible for themselves."

"Do you know these people?"

"Some of them. I'm not sure who will be with us. The company has more people than I met. I only know the people covering Thomas."

"Oh, yeah, how's he doing?"

"He's already in the field, you know, at that village I told you about."

"Shit. He's gonna beat me to it," Duncan said uneasily.

"Not if we get rolling," Boyd said confidently. "We can get there tomorrow if we can put everything together today."

"Is that possible? We need packs, tents, traps and specimen cases. How are we gonna get all that in a day?"

"We travel light," Boyd said. "Thomas is doing day

trips. Going out in the morning and coming back to the village before dark. The place they're looking is only a few miles from the village, and they've got ATVs."

"I guess that could work. But what if *blaberus* isn't there anymore? Wouldn't we need sleeping bags and tents anyway, if we're going to spend the night in the village? They don't have a hotel, do they?"

Boyd nodded.

"So you think we might have to camp in the jungle?" Boyd said.

"It's just that it's hard to believe that a colony of voracious insects would stay in one place for long," Duncan said. "It took us, what, one or two nights to find them the last time."

Boyd knew that the more equipment they brought, the more complicated the expedition would be. Who would carry all of the gear? Where would they buy it?

"Did I tell you Antonio will come with us?" Duncan said.

"Really! That's good news."

"He said he could get one of his cousins to come, if we need him. But I'm not sure if we need him."

"Depends entirely on what we have to carry," Boyd said. "We don't want it to be like the last time. We need to travel as light as we can. But I agree with you, we need to have enough gear to spend a night in the jungle."

With Boyd sitting at the desk and Duncan pacing, they drew up a list of the essentials. Lightweight sleeping bags, a lightweight tent, backpacking stove, cook kits, headlamps and other items. Boyd agreed to contact the helicopter company that Thomas had used. They couldn't expect to find specimen cases on short notice. Instead, they'd have to settle for something jury-rigged, such as metal containers with secure lids that they could punch holes in so the specimens could breathe. They ruled out glass jars or anything that would likely break. With their limited knowledge of shopping venues, Duncan called Antonio Suarez. He filled him in on his plan to fly into the village and asked where they'd be able to find camping gear.

"At Bemol," came the immediate response.

Duncan briefly outlined his plan, to which Suarez said he was ready to go to work at any time.

"Can you go with us to Bemol?"

"Yes, of course."

Duncan said he'd rent a car and the three of them would buy what they needed. When Suarez asked if they would need his cousin, Duncan hesitated, whispered to Boyd who was on the phone with the airline. Boyd shook his head.

"We won't need him. We're gonna travel light. OK?"

"Yes, no problema."

After ending his call, Duncan watched as Boyd frowned. He was having difficulty being understood. One thing was clear, however: the helicopter business was very busy at that moment. Boyd put his phone on speaker and set it on the desk.

"I'm on hold. The guy said, as best as I could understand—his English is only a little better than my Portuguese—all their choppers are booked."

"What?! How can that be?"

"He didn't say. Look, I'm catching only a few words. If you want to talk…"

Duncan waved him off.

"Maybe we can pay more to rent one."

Another, louder voice, speaking better English, interrupted their conversation via the phone's speaker. Identifying himself as the assistant manager he confirmed no helos were available. He said that flights were booked for several days. Boyd tried to bargain but the man cut him off.

"Are there any other companies with helicopters?" Boyd asked out of desperation.

"You might try to contact one of the airlines that fly into the bush. Some of them fly on a schedule. I'm sorry that I can't be of more help."

The assistant manager disconnected the call. Boyd stared at his silent phone.

"Shit," Boyd said. "How do we even begin? I don't even know the name of the village."

"But you know where it is, right?" Duncan asked. "You can locate it on a map?"

"I've got the coordinates on my phone. But how do we find a plane? Maybe we should book a helicopter and wait a couple days?"

Duncan shook his head.

"Let's not give up so quickly. Let's call the helicopter Plan B for now. I hate the idea of wasting another day, but we're not going anywhere without equipment. You need to get Antonio and buy the gear. Maybe we can figure something out later."

As he prepared to leave, Boyd noticed the manila folder on the bed. One thing remained to be done. He handed it to Duncan, who gave him a quizzical look.

"You gotta sign the agreement," Boyd said, matter-of-factly.

Recognizing that he had no choice, Duncan agreed to let a film crew follow him as long as they didn't get in his way and as long as Boyd would serve as his assistant.

Boyd assented to this but insisted that he would continue to serve and be paid as a consultant to the production company. Duncan expressed no interest in learning anything about the videos and signed the release without reading it after Boyd told him it was the same one that was used for all the shoots.

"If push comes to shove, I'm on your side," Boyd said reassuringly.

"I'm counting on it," Duncan replied.

61

NOLAN THOMAS WAS not pleased with the progress he was making in locating the insect colony. It was evident that *Reptilus blaberus* had thoroughly cleaned the area where his group searched. The pile of bones erected by the children was proof of that. However, he could not help but notice that the trees were filled with noisy monkeys and ground-dwelling creatures had already replaced the dead, though they remained hidden for the most part, scurrying away in the underbrush as the men approached. Having returned to the village before nightfall, Thomas huddled with his assistants around a table in the village's common area, which was haphazardly lit by a string of low-wattage light bulbs powered by the village's aging diesel generator. Outside, children played while a handful of adults milled about. Their guide sat with his peers in the shadows reporting quietly on what the Americans had done during the day.

Leaning over a large topographical map spread across the table, Thomas used a pencil to outline the area they had searched. Although they had found only a handful of carcasses, there was enough flesh remaining on the freshest skeletons to estimate that they had been killed over the past several days, well after the children had found the human remains.

"You know what this means, gentlemen?" he asked. His assistants thought it was a rhetorical question and refrained from speaking for fear of being wrong. Thomas did not suffer fools. However, since Thomas didn't immediately answer his own question, Jason Gruber raised his hand.

"They're covering the same area more than once," Gruber said, tentatively.

"Exactly!" Thomas said approvingly. "Anything else?"

Gruber glanced at his three associates, who were staring at the map with great intensity, as if the answer lay hidden somewhere in its folds. Gruber had been Thomas's chief aide since he came to Biodynamism. At thirty-five, he'd earned two master's degrees, one in biomedical engineering with specialization in molecular biology and the other in laboratory management. He was also enrolled in a largely online program leading to a Doctor of Science degree. His ambition was to run his own lab.

"It's indicative of territorial behavior," he responded, hesitantly.

"Exactly, once again. Very good, Mr. Gruber," Thomas said, causing the others to release their gazes from the map.

"Can any of you tell me what this means?"

"It means they'll come back," Covelli said.

Thomas smiled. His assistants were paying attention, which pleased him.

"Tomorrow we'll expand our search area to determine their range. This will mean that we spread out and work independently. Each of you has a copy of this map and you'll mark on it wherever you find a carcass."

"What about using the wireless radios?" Gruber asked.

"Yes, of course," Thomas said. The others nodded approvingly.

Although the range of the devices would be limited by the terrain and the dense forest, they provided a psychological comfort in an unfamiliar and dangerous place. Everyone knew the insects weren't the only predators in the forest. Although many entomologists had taken sides after the revelations about Howard Duncan's ill-fated expedition, Thomas was convinced that the insects were predatory and represented a previously undocumented species, which is why he almost immediately organized his expedition after the news came out rather than waiting for a more complete accounting of what had happened. Unlike Duncan, who, having seen the horror of *blaberus* up close thereafter wanted to study the creatures in the controlled environment of a laboratory, Thomas wanted to first observe them in the field and subsequently return to his lab with specimens. Of course, Thomas knew nothing of Duncan's plans while Duncan knew only what Boyd had told him about his competition.

Thomas asked if there were any questions as he ended the meeting. Gruber raised his hand.

"What if one of us finds the insects tomorrow? What then? What should we do?"

Having risen from his bench seat, Thomas pulled his hand along his chin sagaciously and looked at his assistant thoughtfully.

"Everything we think we know about them says that

they travel in groups so, if you see one, you may see more. To tell you the truth, I don't know what to tell you except to use your best judgment and watch your step."

62

USING A RENTAL car and Duncan's credit card, Boyd and Suarez spent the better part of the day purchasing equipment. Buying or renting a satellite phone proved the most problematic purchase as Suarez had no idea where to find one. After an hour of searching, Boyd complained to his companion that they were victims of Duncan's lack of planning. Frustrated, he called Duncan.

"This sucks," Boyd whined, "I can't find any place that sells satellite phones."

"Well, hello to you, too," Duncan said.

"Sorry," Boyd said. "We've found most of what we need, but the only place I've found sat phones is online and it takes at least two days to ship. Do you think we should wait?"

"No way," Duncan said decisively. "Let's just forget the phones. They didn't do us much good the last time anyway."

"You sure?"

"Look, it would be great if we could get a phone but if we can't, then we can't. It's that simple. You think you got everything we need?"

"Mostly."

"Good, then get back here ASAP. We need to figure out a way to get there. I saw a news program on TV and it looks like the press is chasing after Thomas."

"Better him than us, right?"

63

Before Boyd returned to Duncan's hotel, he met with the Broken Tree Productions staff to deliver the signed agreement. Although he was disappointed that he hadn't been able to charter a helicopter, he took solace in the fact that he had two employers, that he was making more money than he had ever earned in his life, and that he had at least managed to purchase most of what they needed to conduct the expedition. The production company had booked several rooms—one of them cleared of its bed and organized into an office with tables, electronic and computer equipment and people he'd never seen before. The room was crowded and noisy. Field producer Carl Murphy emerged from the chaos to greet him. Boyd gave him the folder containing the agreement.

"He signed it," Boyd said happily.

"That's great," Murphy said, leafing through the contract, nodding approvingly at Duncan's signature. "So, when do we start?"

"Well, we've got the equipment we need, but we're still trying to find a way to get there. The soonest we could get a chopper is a couple days from now."

"Really? That won't do. We've had problems, too.

Seems like everyone and his brother are booking choppers. We didn't plan for two crews so we only booked the flights we needed for Dr. Thomas. Let me make some calls. We've got folks back home who work miracles. Maybe they can find something for us."

"That'd be great," Boyd said enthusiastically. "I got no idea where to look."

"When you do what we do, you improvise a lot. So, Dr. Duncan is good with this, right? He understands what we do and what we expect of him? Right? No surprises, right?"

"I told him to read the contract. He signed it. He didn't ask many questions. He's on board with it, as long as I'm part of his group."

"That's fine," Murphy said, distractedly. A staffer was trying to get his attention. "Look, I'm pretty busy here…"

"You got my number. Let me know how things turn out with the transportation," Boyd said.

Boyd was ecstatic as he and Suarez drove to Duncan's hotel, the car stuffed with camping equipment. *Why didn't I think of that in the first place*, he wondered. *Let them do the work*.

He was earning every dollar he was being paid, from both bosses.

64

OVERNIGHT, THE QUIET village of thatch-roofed huts alongside the slow-moving river was transformed into a staging ground for journalists and camera crews. Their object was to follow the exploits of Nolan Thomas and perhaps capture the first close-ups of a tiny insect that had taken on gigantic proportions. Few, if any, of those who arrived that day gave thought to how vulnerable they were should they encounter *Reptilus blaberus* in its habitat. As the headlines screamed of killer cockroaches, the widespread belief was that the insects could be easily crushed underfoot. News directors and producers armed their crews with insecticidal sprays guaranteed by the manufacturers to kill cockroaches on contact.

Thomas's group had left just after dawn, riding two ATVs from the village's small inventory, each pulling carts filled with equipment and their operators. Thomas rode in the lead vehicle, his four assistants sharing its cart filled with specimen boxes and daypacks. Field producer Carl Murphy sat behind the driver in the second vehicle with soundman Jack Walker and a young videographer named Andy Wilson, who had freshly arrived from Broken Tree

Productions' headquarters in Santa Monica, California. He had assigned the cantankerous Joe Robinson to Duncan's group. One less problem to deal with.

Silvio Santiago, the old man who managed the village's administration building, was overwhelmed by the requests for ATV rentals. A handful were known to be in operating condition. Santiago sent children to fetch the owners, most of them his relatives. Media who had arrived earliest anxiously protected their place in the imaginary queue as they negotiated prices with the manager. Prices were high and only cash was accepted. This stymied several of the crews who were accustomed to a world of credit cards and wire transfers. For extra money, the owners would drive and act as guides.

Thomas would not have cared had he known the struggles he was putting the media through, and all that Murphy cared about was that his crew had exclusive rights to Thomas's expedition.

Thomas had outlined his strategy the previous night. Assuming *blaberus* was territorial, his assistants would fan out from where the children had erected the mound of remains. The object was to determine the size of *blaberus's* territory by locating additional carcasses, which he was certain they would find. He did not expect anyone to encounter a colony during this survey.

He would remain near the mound like a commander overlooking a battlefield, along with the drivers and the field producer.

"You'll contact me periodically so I can mark your location on the map," he had told them. "I realize your observations will be imprecise unless somehow you can get a GPS coordinate, but at least this will give us a rough idea of the size of their territory."

Nudged by one of his colleagues, Thomas's chief assistant, Jason Gruber, spoke up.

"You know, Dr. Thomas, we're assuming they've moved on, right? What if they haven't? What if they're at one end or another of their hypothetical territory? What do we do then? I think we're all a little worried about it."

Thomas saw the concern on their faces.

"Maybe we should team up." Covelli said. "I think we'd feel safer."

"We could do that," Thomas said, looking at the field producer and knowing that anything he said could end up in the show. Generally regarded as an autocrat in his lab, he was not unaware of the impression that he would make on television. Instantly, the four assistants brightened. Pairing off, Gruber and his partner headed north while Covelli and his partner headed south.

Standing on a hill, Thomas had a commanding view of the forest floor, which was shaped like an elongated bowl flanked by sharply rising, loamy slopes. Brush, low-lying vegetation and vines covered much of the area with trees rising like towers blocking out much of the sunlight.

Once the assistants were out of earshot, Murphy asked, "Do you think they'll find something?"

"I hope so," Thomas said.

"I don't mean dead animals. I mean the bugs."

"I don't know," Thomas said quietly. "For all we know, they could be around us right here. Just look at the ground. How hard do you think it would be to see a dark brown, four-inch long insect in this environment?"

Murphy looked at Walker and the videographer, who

were busy preparing their equipment and carrying on their own conversation. Murphy looked at the ground under his feet nervously.

"Are you trying to scare me?"

Thomas smiled faintly.

"You know, now that I think of it, we should be recording this," Murphy said.

65

THE BROKEN TREE Productions crew that would document Duncan's expedition consisted of field producer/ soundman Bob Mitchell and videographer Joe Robinson. Mitchell called ahead to arrange to pick up Duncan at his hotel, arriving in a rental van driven by a local driver who would take them to the airport after loading equipment. It was early morning and Duncan and Cody Boyd were having their first coffee of the day, which Boyd bought at the hotel's restaurant.

The twenty-something Mitchell greeted Duncan and Boyd enthusiastically, while Robinson, the oldest man in the room and twice Mitchell's age, asked if he could have a cup of coffee. He snarled when Boyd told him the coffee came from the restaurant and left the room in a huff.

"Sorry about that. They tell me Joe's a little difficult to work with sometimes," Mitchell said apologetically. "Anyways, I'm really looking forward to this. It's my first time as a field producer and I want everything to go right."

Boyd introduced himself as the consultant on the project. Before he finished, Mitchell extended his hand to Duncan and shook it eagerly.

"And you must be Dr. Duncan. I have heard so much

about you. It's an honor to be part of your expedition. I can't tell you how happy I was when I got the call to get my ass to Manaus."

Duncan looked at Boyd skeptically but said nothing.

"So, did you get a chopper for us?" Boyd asked.

"A chopper?" Mitchell said doubtfully. "I don't think so. Let me check my phone. They've been sending me instructions ever since I left Cali."

"Columbia?" Duncan asked.

"Oh, no. Fornia," Mitchell said, as he paged through emails. "Ahh, here it is. We're flying in on Fronteira Airline. Says here they're already on the ground waiting for us. That's exciting. I've never flown into the jungle before, how about you guys?"

Boyd shook his head.

"Have you ever been in South America?" Duncan asked.

"This is my first time."

Duncan and Boyd exchanged dubious glances while Mitchell loaded a document into his phone.

"O-kay," he said. "Do you have all your equipment? I'm not sure what you're bringing, but the van should be able to hold everything. And with an airplane instead of a helicopter we shouldn't have a problem bringing it in one trip. We're actually traveling pretty light, only a hundred pounds or so. Joe will be shooting HDV on a Sony and I'm bringing a boom, wireless mics and…I can tell you aren't interested in the details so maybe you should tell me exactly what it is you'll be doing. I sorta need a heads up. All they told me was that we'd be shooting in the field in the jungle."

"You heard about our previous expedition?" Boyd asked.

"Oh, you mean where those people were killed? Yeah, but I've been so busy on another project and there seemed to be so much confusion out there that I figured I'd wait until I could get it from the horse's mouth. So to speak."

Mitchell spoke in the speedy, staccato voice of a person who had too much coffee and too little sleep. Duncan's expression turned from slightly amused to troubled as the young field producer spoke. When he was finished, Duncan wanted to parlay with Boyd in private but couldn't think of a way to do it without seeming disrespectful toward Mitchell.

"Dr. Duncan is trying to capture an insect called *Reptilus blaberus*," Boyd said. "Actually, we're not sure whether it's an insect or some kind of reptile, or a reptile-insect hybrid."

"Oh, really. Insects. I wasn't sure about that. O-kay. That's helpful. How big are they?"

Duncan, who was sitting on the edge of the bed, lifted his head toward the ceiling and sighed, shaking his head.

"Is there something wrong, Dr. Duncan?"

Duncan lowered his head and was about to respond when a knock came at the door. Boyd let the videographer in.

"You know, the coffee's really good here," Robinson said as he entered. "So, what have I missed?"

Taking turns, Duncan and Boyd gave a five-minute synopsis about *blaberus* and their plans to capture specimens. When they'd finished, Mitchell glanced at Robinson who, with his previous work on the Thomas expedition, shrugged nonchalantly.

"O-kay. So, what you're saying is that we're gonna

document you as you collect your insects." Looking at Robinson, Mitchell added, "What happens if you don't find them? Where does the story go?"

"What they're saying is that if they find too many of them we could end up dead," Robinson said, finishing his coffee. "Anybody want another cup?"

This was the excuse Duncan was looking for.

"Hey, Cody, you wanna go get the coffee with me? How do you guys like it?"

"Extra black," Robinson said.

"Cream and sugar, two packets," Mitchell said.

As soon as the door closed behind him, Duncan took several steps and stopped.

"What have you gotten me into, Cody?" he demanded.

"I don't know," Boyd said defensively. "I never met the guy."

"Jesus, if I'd known we were going into this with someone as clueless as this kid…"

"Well, I don't think we've got a choice. We've both got contracts."

"Maybe I should talk to a lawyer about that?"

"Like you'd do that. Besides, they got a plane for us. You wanna wait a few days for transportation…"

"No, no, no. We can't do that."

Before they could finish their conversation, Robinson entered the hallway, approaching them.

"I'm going out for a smoke. I can get my own coffee," he said.

Boyd and Duncan smiled nonchalantly.

"I bet you're wondering what's going on with this kid. Am I right?

"Sorta, yeah," Duncan said. "Does he realize how dangerous this could be?"

"When you were his age, did you realize how dangerous things could be? Neither did I," Robinson said. "The story I got is that he was a hotshot at UCLA. Did a student documentary using iPhones that won some awards."

"Really?" Boyd said. "He's good, huh?"

"That's what I'm told. Besides, his dad's like vice president of the company."

"You're kidding," Duncan said.

"I never kid," Robinson said, moving toward the elevator. "You guys coming?"

66

AFTER PICKING UP Antonio Suarez, Duncan's group rode the van on BR-174 toward Eduardo Gomes International Airport. As they drove past the eastern edge of the airport, the driver continued north before turning off the federal highway onto a narrower, paved road that led to another turn onto an even narrower unpaved road in a sparsely populated area, a portion of which had been cleared of trees. Duncan and Boyd exchanged bewildered looks while the others behaved as if nothing unusual was happening. As the drive got bumpier, Duncan whispered to Boyd.

"Where are we going? We passed the airport way back there."

Boyd tapped Bob Mitchell on the shoulder

"Where we going?"

"Yeah, we're not flying out of the airport. There's a strip ahead. You'll see the plane pretty soon, I think. The driver knows where we're going."

"I don't like this," Duncan whispered.

"Yeah, I kinda thought we'd be flying out of the airport. It never occurred to me to ask."

Around the next turn, they got their first glimpse of

the airplane. Sitting on the edge of what might have been a road at one time was an ancient Douglas DC-3, its silvery nose pointed toward the bright blue sky.

"What the fuck?!" Duncan said, louder than he'd intended.

"This is the best we could do on short notice, Dr. Duncan," Mitchell said, who was sitting in the front seat, looking over his shoulder. "One good thing is there's plenty of room for passengers and equipment."

"Why aren't we flying out of the airport?" Duncan asked.

"Some kind of administrative problem, I think. Anyway, look at the bright side, we won't have to check our baggage."

Duncan fumed at the flippant response. Boyd put his hand on Duncan's shoulder.

"Let's just wait and see, OK. He probably doesn't know any more than we do."

"That's what's got me concerned," Duncan whispered.

"It's either this or we wait for a chopper," Boyd said.

Everyone was looking at the plane as the driver brought the van to a halt. They were met by the co-pilot, who greeted them in Portuguese.

"Bom dia," Boyd replied. "Você fala Inglês?"

"Um pouco."

"Falo um pouco de português," Boyd said, haltingly, nodding to Suarez to translate. "Ask him how old it is."

"He says it was built in 1943 and has had many, uh, repairs, ever since. It flies good, he says."

While Suarez and the co-pilot talked, the others circled the ancient plane, pointing out riveted patches to the aluminum skin, droplets of a dark liquid pooling slowly in the dirt under one engine and other anomalies.

"I think I know why they couldn't land at the airport," Duncan said aloud.

"I've flown worse," Joe Robinson said. "We're only going like a hundred fifty miles." Looking at the cloudless sky, he added, "At least we don't have to worry about the weather. Back in the '80s I was on a DC-8 in India and we ran into a storm and ended up with what you might call a hard landing. One of the landing gear collapsed and we lost a wing tip and one of the props fell apart, but nobody got killed. Just a few injuries. Took a week to get outta there. 'Course, I was workin' for a news agency usin' my own equipment back then, shootin' sixteen millimeter. Camera got banged up and the agency wouldn't reimburse me. Never worked for them again, I'll tell you."

Duncan smiled politely and joined Boyd who, along with the co-pilot, directed the others to load their gear into the rear of the plane. Passenger seating consisted of five rows, two seats on one side of the narrow aisle and one on the opposite side. Three rows of seats had been removed to accommodate cargo. In the rear was a lavatory. The interior smelled of damp carpeting. As Duncan nervously fastened his seat belt, he gave Boyd a forlorn look.

"I don't like this one bit," he said quietly.

"Neither do I," Boyd said. "It is what it is."

"I hate that phrase."

"Me too," Boyd said, peering out the window, watching the van as it drove away trailed by clouds of dust. "Unless you want to walk back to Manaus, we're stuck with it."

"I just hope the landing gear doesn't collapse."

67

FIELD PRODUCER CARL Murphy thought of the subjects of reality TV as performers who happened to be involved in unusual or compelling activities. He coached them to sprinkle expletives into their speech so they could be bleeped when televised. It brought out emotions, which helped to connect the audience to the performers and their story. He also encouraged them to be honest in their reactions. He encouraged them to show anger when they felt it, even though there was a chance it could become personal and have lasting consequences for relationships. But he recognized quickly that he couldn't do that with Nolan Thomas's assistants. They were afraid of their autocratic boss, who could end their careers as easily as he could promote them. They complained about his bossiness behind his back, but none would dare contradict him to his face. Which is why, even though they had reservations about their vulnerability in the dense undergrowth, they didn't raise even their most serious apprehensions. They were familiar with the general outlines of what had happened to Duncan's expedition but none of them had a real appreciation for the horrible things their quarry could do to them. Even Murphy felt somewhat intimidated by Thomas, even though he'd been cooperative and affable from the start.

As soundman Jack Walker and videographer Andy Wilson joined Thomas and Murphy on the hill, the producer instructed them to capture B-roll and audio to be used when the series was edited.

"Make sure you get the guys in the frame for establishing shots," he said. "And Jack, get some of the monkey noise."

"It's pretty loud."

"We'll tone it down in post. Once you've got all that—make sure you get video of the monkeys, OK—then follow those guys down there," Murphy said, pointing toward Gruber and his partner, "before they get out of sight. Any questions?"

"Light's not great," Wilson said.

"I don't have to tell you how to do your job, do I?" Murphy said, sternly.

"Nope. Got it covered."

68

LOOKING OUT HIS window as the plane circled the village, Cody Boyd was surprised by the aggregation of tents clustered across a vacant area behind the village's housing. Some were emblazoned with logos of media companies. Several small satellite dishes sprouted like mushrooms on stalks.

"Look at that," he said, pointing out the window.

Duncan, his seat mate, grimaced.

"Goddamn," he muttered. "You don't think they're here because of me, do you?"

"How would they know we're coming?" Boyd said. "We didn't even know until this morning."

Looking across the aisle at Bob Mitchell, Duncan said loudly so he could be heard over the engine noise, "Did you know about this?"

"Know about what?"

"The media," Duncan said, pointing at Boyd's window. The young producer leaned toward the window.

"Nope."

Several crews on the ground filmed the plane as it banked and started its final descent, the pilot dropping the nose like an anchor the instant the tail cleared the surrounding forest canopy, pulling up at the last second as the wheels touched the grass and dirt runway in a plume of red dust, using most of it to slow down enough to turn around in a single, unbroken motion, coming to a stop in front of the administrative building, its nose towering above the roof.

As the pilot cut the engines, the co-pilot walked down the aisle, opened the door at the rear of the plane, dropped the short ladder, and chocked the wheels, Duncan leaned toward Mitchell with a doubtful expression. Mitchell ignored this and led the way out of the plane, his company's logo and name standing out prominently on his cap and shirt. As soon as they saw the producer emerge, the media on the ground turned away, as if to say there's no story here.

Boyd got a kick out of it and nudged Duncan.

"See that? As soon as they realized our crew is media they lost interest in us. You know, they gave me a shirt and hat."

"You oughta put it on," Duncan said. "It's like camouflage."

"I wish I'd thought of that in Manaus. I'd have gotten one for you," Boyd said. "I know what! You wear the hat and I'll wear the shirt."

While Boyd changed shirts and Duncan exchanged his floppy hat for Boyd's billed cap, Walker and Mitchell unloaded several hard cases and duffel bags, setting them under the wing.

Mitchell smiled as Duncan and Boyd emerged, followed by Antonio Suarez, who looked and dressed like a villager. The wardrobe adjustment was not lost on Joe Robinson, who had moved away from the plane to smoke.

The videographer watched with amusement as Duncan and Boyd each grabbed a hardcase plastered with Broken Tree Productions logos.

"So, you're working for us now," he said as they set the cases under the overhang of the building's thatched roof.

"We hope it looks that way," Boyd said.

Mitchell beamed.

"Brilliant, just brilliant," he said earnestly.

69

AT THE START of their first full day searching for *Reptilus blaberus,* Nolan Thomas's assistants scouted the forest floor with trepidation, fearful that they might inadvertently find themselves in the midst of a colony of the man-eaters and become their next victims. They were hyperaware of the stories of people being eaten alive and dying horrible, excruciating deaths. It didn't help that the human remains near where they parked their ATVs served as a reminder that their fears were not without foundation. But, as the day wore on and the heat and humidity increased, mosquitoes presented a more immediate threat. That and the boredom and the difficulty of making their way through vine-infested undergrowth that made it virtually impossible to see what was underfoot. Jason Gruber started thinking that the children who had thrown together the mound of small, dead mammals had done a thorough job, leaving only a couple of squirrel carcasses for him and his companions to find.

Though disappointed with his assistants' lack of success, Thomas was not discouraged. At the end of the day, his team would have done their jobs by eliminating the search area from consideration, which would allow them to widen the hunt when they returned the next day, and the next day, and the next day, however long it would take. He knew from experience that patience and persistence were the most important skills to have when doing field work. Most of his success had come not from brilliant insights and eureka moments, but from tedious, time-consuming investigation.

However, producer Carl Murphy was annoyed at the lack of opportunity to record anything but background sound and B-roll. There was only so much footage of screaming monkeys climbing trees and long shots of the gloomy forest that they would need and they had captured it. The only shot they got on film that might be even remotely useful was when one of the assistants tripped and face-planted on the forest floor. His partner laughed reflexively as he watched the man go down, but seeing the terror on his friend's face as he sprang to his feet like a gymnast, sent a shiver down his neck. It wasn't funny after all. It was a reminder that even a small mistake in the rainforest could have big consequences.

Returning to the village, Thomas and Murphy were already planning for tomorrow's activities while the others, hungry and sweaty, suffered the bruising bumps in silence, looking no farther ahead than supper.

70

AFTER UNLOADING GEAR under the overhang, the five men entered the administrative building. Silvio Santiago perched on his stool behind the high counter, watching as Robinson moved toward a large, vintage beverage cooler pushed against a wall. It was empty.

Watching Robinson, the old man spoke in Portuguese. "No drinks," Suarez translated and Robinson said, "Too bad. I was hoping for a beer." They didn't know that beer was kept in a cooler under the counter.

"Can I use your guide for a minute to translate?" Mitchell asked Boyd, who glanced at Duncan.

"He's Howard's guide."

Duncan nodded agreeably.

"Hi," Mitchell said, extending his hand to Suarez. "I'm Bob. People call me Mitch. What's your name?"

"Antonio," Suarez said, shaking limply. "I'll talk to him. What do you want to know?"

"We're gonna need ATVs in the morning."

Suarez spoke with the old man, who shook his head.

"He says they don't have any."

"Did you hear that?" Mitchell asked, moving toward Duncan, who was sitting on bench seats at a table with the others.

"Yeah, that's not good."

"That's crap. I saw some when we landed," Robinson grumbled as he lit a cigarette. "He's full of crap."

Mitchell looked at Suarez questioningly. Suarez told the old man they saw ATVs when they landed.

"Oh, sure, we have ATVs, but they're rented," the old man said.

Mitchell groaned.

"Offer to pay more," Robinson said. "Go on, ask him."

Mitchell nodded at Suarez, who asked if they could give extra money and the old man's dour expression brightened.

"He says that would be OK," Suarez said.

"Ask him how much," Robinson said, smoke billowing from his mouth.

"Four hundred," Suarez said.

"Four hundred dollars?" Mitchell said. "Goddamn it, that's a lot. And that's just for a day?"

"Reals," Suarez said, "for the day."

"O-kay," Mitchell said, trying to convert reals to dollars in his head.

"That's less than one hundred dollars," Boyd said.

"We can do that," Mitchell said. "He doesn't have a problem with, you know, doing that?"

"Don't look a gift horse in the mouth," Robinson said. "He doesn't give a shit about us or the other guys. Money talks."

"Yeah, but if he's willing to do this for us, wouldn't he do the same if someone else comes in and ups our price?" Boyd said.

"Not if we get out of here bright and early," Robinson said. "Whoever rented them isn't gonna know we stole them out from under them until we're gone."

Mitchell and the others looked at Robinson with new-found appreciation. He was not only older than everyone else, and grumpier, he was also shrewder.

"Yeah, but when they find out…" Duncan said.

"It's up to you, doc," Robinson said. "You want to walk or ride? Simple as that."

Duncan looked at Boyd and Mitchell, both of whom agreed with Robinson.

"It's a cutthroat business, doc," Robinson said. "Nothing personal."

71

While Duncan, Boyd, Suarez and Robinson erected tents, Mitchell met with Murphy in his tent. His encampment consisted of three tents, one for Mitchell and his crew, one for Thomas's four assistants and one for Thomas. Murphy sat in front of his tent on a three-legged camp stool. Light faded quickly after the sun dipped below the treetops and lanterns came to life in some of the nearby encampments. Murphy greeted Mitchell enthusiastically.

"I see you got here," Murphy said good-naturedly. "Where'd you find that plane? In a museum?"

"I didn't ask," Mitchell said. "How'd your day go?"

Although they spoke in conversational tones, Murphy noticed some of the others were trying to listen in as they stood in front of tiny, single-burner camp stoves waiting for water to boil so they could eat their dehydrated dinners. The air was heavy with the smell of mosquito repellant. Because the various camps were scattered and isolated from each other, the pair walked past the administration building and toward the river's edge where a number of boats were tied to posts. Most were dugouts; two were beamier and longer with pointed bows and thatched roofs over the rear half. Down the river's edge were houses and huts on stilts, well out of earshot. The pair sat on the remnants of a primitive dock and for a moment stared at the muddy, slow-moving water. The opposite bank was a wall of trees. It looked impenetrable.

His gaze directed at the opposite shore, Murphy summarized his uneventful day. Mitchell filled him in on his flight but avoided mentioning how they'd been able to reserve two ATVs, though he desperately wanted to do so. It had occurred to him, as they walked to the river, that they may have finagled Murphy's ATVs from the old man. He had no way of knowing, and if it turned out that it was the case, he was certain Murphy would pull rank and take the vehicles for himself. When the conversation turned to Mitchell's plans for the next day, the junior field producer looked away as if he didn't know what to say.

"ATVs are hard to find," Murphy said matter-of-factly. "Did you get any?"

"Yeah, we did. Two."

"Really. That's great. There aren't that many and I was thinking the media folks would have everything locked up. You know how they are."

Mitchell nodded.

"We haven't really worked out where we're gonna go, yet," Mitchell said. "We'll do that tonight, if we don't get eaten alive by these mosquitoes."

Mitchell furiously batted at the blood suckers. Murphy, who was dressed in a long-sleeved shirt and nylon cargo pants, smiled sympathetically as he watched Mitchell, who wore shorts and short-sleeved shirt, slap at his bare legs and arms.

"Maybe we should get outta here," Murphy suggested. "The skeeters seem to be in attack mode."

72

AFTER UNSATISFYING CUPS of dehydrated chili, Duncan, Boyd and Suarez huddled in the tent, fighting off mosquitoes. Suarez produced three roasted plantains that he had taken out of his daypack. Illuminated by Boyd's headlamp, which hung from a strap on the tent's ceiling, they ate them ravenously. Duncan asked where the guide had gotten them.

"I talked to some people I met. They offered one to me and when I told them about you they gave me more. People are very friendly."

"It helps to speak their language, huh?" Boyd said.

Suarez smiled boyishly. Unlike his companions, whose shirts were drenched with sweat, Suarez was shirtless and looked comfortable. It wasn't long before Duncan and Boyd removed their shirts. The light breeze that blew through the tent's screening refreshed them almost immediately.

"Hey, let me in," Bob Mitchell whispered urgently as he unzipped the tent's entry.

"Shut the damn door," Duncan said frantically. "You're letting mosquitoes in."

"Sorry," Mitchell said as he fumbled with the zipper, pulling on it unevenly and causing it to become stuck on the fabric.

"Here, let me do it," Boyd barked, pushing Mitchell out of the way. Though Boyd was able to make the adjustment quickly, the pests had invaded the tent and they scrambled to bat them down.

"So, Bob, what's up?" Boyd asked, the mosquitoes having been subdued. "You didn't tell anybody about our little deal for the ATVs, did you? We saw you walking with Carl."

"No, of course not," Mitchell said.

"We were just getting ready to make our plans for tomorrow," Duncan said. "Did Murphy tell you anything?"

"Yeah, he told me everything. I felt kinda bad that I kinda lied about the ATVs. I told him we got two but not how we did it."

Mitchell briefed them on what Nolan Thomas's group had done and that they planned to expand their search area in the morning.

"You know, I just hope we don't get their ATVs," he concluded. "I don't know what'll happen if they find out we did it."

"You can always blame it on us," Boyd suggested.

"I hadn't thought about that. You don't mind?"

"What's he gonna do to us? It's not like we work for him." Boyd paused.

"You do work for him, you know that, right?" Mitchell said.

"Ah, fuck. OK. So, he'll fire me. I still have a job with Howard. Besides, I haven't done much consulting."

Duncan refocused the conversation, pumping Mitchell for details. Once he'd repeated everything he remembered, Duncan looked at Suarez to see what he thought.

"Mister Howard, I heard from some kids that they found more bones, you know."

All eyes were on Suarez, who lowered his head.

"Tell us about it," Duncan said encouragingly. "You're the one who speaks Portuguese. We don't know anything."

Suarez described what he'd been told and pointed toward the rainforest, away from the route that Thomas's group had used since coming to the village.

"They say there's a trail but if you don't know where it is you can't find it."

"Do you know where it is?"

"No. But we can get one of the kids to take us there."

Duncan, Boyd and Mitchell were all smiles.

As Boyd prepared to unzip the door to let Mitchell out, he asked, "You aren't gonna tell Murphy about tomorrow, are you?"

"Not a word. Anyway, I don't think he cares."

73

THANKS TO A brief downpour, the trio in Duncan's tent spent an uncomfortable night, the rain insinuating its way through the screened openings. Tossing and turning, their bodies coated with sweat, they emerged from their partial sleep like lizards in need of life-giving sunlight. It was a good thing too, because they'd had their coffee before other campers had arisen from their troublesome sleep. They scarfed down their cups of instant oatmeal and, like men on a mission, Boyd and Suarez went directly to the administrative building to pick up their ATVs while Duncan roused Mitchell and Robinson. Everyone in the group wore a hat or shirt or carried an item emblazoned with the logo of Broken Tree Productions. Not that they would have aroused suspicion, since they would be the first to make their getaway into the forest. Though Silvio Santiago was already perching on his chair, he shrugged when asked by Suarez where the drivers were.

"He said they're still sleeping," Suarez told Boyd.

"Ask him when they'll be here."

The old man shrugged again.

"Ask him which ATVs we're supposed to use."

Santiago rose stiffly and, with a gait suggesting arthritis of the knees, waddled behind the building, pointing to a pair of vehicles, one red, one army green. Re-entering the building, Boyd and Suarez were joined by the other three members of their group. Each carried a daypack containing water, snacks, mosquito repellant, maps, wireless radios and several containers to hold specimens. Suarez carried a machete to break ground if needed.

"What's the hold up?" Duncan asked.

"The drivers," Boyd moaned.

"They're sleeping," Suarez interjected.

"What the fuck?" Mitchell said, exasperated. "We already paid for this. Tell him we need to get going."

"You tell him," Boyd said. "He doesn't speak English, you know."

"So, are you just gonna wait?" Mitchell said nervously.

"You're worried that you stole Murphy's ATVs, ain't that right?" Robinson said.

Mitchell glared at his videographer and then acknowledged his question with a nod.

"Why not just offer more money?" Robinson said. "That's the only reason we got the ATVs to begin with."

Suarez negotiated with the old man, who was reluctant at first, having noticed how anxious the Americans had become. He knew a good thing when he saw it. For an extra three hundred reals they would be able to drive themselves. His cousins, he was certain, wouldn't mind the extra money, especially if they didn't have to earn it.

"One more thing," Suarez said to Duncan. "He wants another five hundred reals as a deposit to cover damages."

Mitchell shook his head resignedly.

"I'm running out of Brazilian money," Mitchell said.

"Oh, he'll take dollars," Boyd said helpfully.

"He won't charge for the cart," Suarez said as the producer counted out currency.

Mitchell handed the money to Suarez, who set it on the counter in front of Santiago. Dropping a pair of keys on the countertop, the old man smiled broadly.

"He said thanks," Suarez said.

"He said more than that," Boyd said, whose limited understanding of Portuguese included the standard greetings and phrases.

"He also said, nice doing business with you."

74

THE ENCAMPMENT HAD come to life as Duncan's two ATVs drove slowly toward a collection of huts raised several feet above the red dirt on stilts. Nolan Thomas, surrounded by his assistants, stood in front of Murphy's tent, talking to media who crowded in front of him. Mitchell waved to Murphy as they passed.

"Boy," Mitchell said, "Carl looks pissed."

"Why?" Boyd asked.

"Look at that. Those media guys are gonna steal his show."

Robinson snorted.

"How so?" Duncan asked.

"You know what's gonna happen," Mitchell started, barely able to contain a laugh, "they're gonna follow them into the jungle. Wow. That's too funny. I'm sure if they knew who you were, they'd be all over us, too."

"Good thing they don't," Duncan said.

"I'll say," Boyd agreed.

After pausing near the huts, Suarez returned with the boy who had agreed to show them where he and his friends had found other carcasses. About five feet tall and slightly built, he was equipped with a machete and water bottle swinging from his shoulder at the end of a short rope. Shirtless and shoeless, he rode in the cart with Suarez in the lead ATV. Boyd drove and Duncan sat behind him. Mitchell drove the second ATV.

Driving away from the village, clouds of red dust rising behind them like a veil, Duncan saw that none of the media paid attention to his group. The deception was working.

75

CARL MURPHY WAS livid as he took Jason Gruber aside, out of earshot of Nolan Thomas, who was conducting an impromptu interview with an American, a Brazilian TV crew and several print journalists.

"Does he not understand that we have an exclusive contract with him?" Murphy grumbled.

"I'm sure he does," Gruber said. "He likes to lecture. He's an academic at heart."

"So why is he undermining me—us? We've accommodated you in every way."

"Don't blame me. I don't control what he does."

"So, why's he doing it? What's the deal?" Murphy said, calming slightly.

"I can't speak for him. Maybe he—look, the project he's working on is…confidential, let's say. He's not allowed to talk about it outside the lab. He can't even publish papers about it."

"I don't understand," Murphy said, baffled. "You know we're gonna put this on TV, right?"

"Oh, yeah, but this isn't directly related to our project. It could be, depending on what we find, but it's outside the scope right now. He's kinda working on a hunch. And, you know, he's a publicity hound—at least he was in academia. You knew that, didn't you?"

"Well, I don't like it. I'm afraid they're gonna steal our thunder and we'll end up with nothing."

As they talked, Murphy, who hadn't been involved in negotiations resulting in his assignment to cover Thomas's expedition, realized that either his boss hadn't been as upfront about the project as he'd thought, or that he hadn't asked enough questions. Why was Thomas's expedition a higher priority than Duncan's? Once he was assigned to the project, his producer's mind took over, completely absorbed in the process of preparation and execution. The why of it was unimportant, until now.

"So, why's he even doing it?" Murphy asked.

"Well, when he saw some of the video from what happened, he saw something that got his attention. I think he believes he can tie this into the project he's been working on. I really don't know what he's thinking, but I sure as hell can't tell you anything about his work. I'd go to jail if someone found out," Gruber said.

"Damn!" Murphy said, astonished.

"So, is he working for us or are we working for him?"

Gruber shrugged and drew his finger across his lips.

76

WITH THE YOUNG villager pointing the way, Duncan was pleased that he would be plowing new ground not yet inspected by Nolan Thomas. Early morning clouds were clearing as they motored slowly into the damp forest, following a trail that coursed like a narrow stream around rocky outcroppings and islands of forty-foot açai palms, towering Brazil nut, rubber and stilted Cashapona trees. Sunlight filtered through the canopy as if through holes in an umbrella. Ground fog appeared in thin misty clouds that evaporated as they rose. The ATV motors were loud enough to drown out all but the most determined screeches of howler monkeys. Mosquitoes swarmed all around as the Americans coated themselves with DEET. Most wore pants and long-sleeved shirts, with the notable exception of Suarez and their young guide.

Progress was slow but steady. The machines produced copious exhaust and they switched them off when they stopped to reconnoiter. As if bracing himself, the young guide pressed his hands against a tree. In seconds, his hands were covered by hundreds of ants.

"What's he doing?" Mitchell asked.

The boy rubbed his hands together, crushing the ants and wiping his hands across his arms and exposed skin. He smiled when he noticed the others watching him.

"Mosquitoes don't like the way the ants smell when you crush them," Suarez explained, though he, too, had sprayed himself with the bug spray.

"They're leaf cutters," Boyd said, having stepped off the ATV to get a closer look. "Give me a minute and I think I can tell you the species."

"We don't have time," Duncan said. "We're not here to classify Formicidae."

Although they were only three or four miles northeast of the village, the odometer showed they'd traveled more than twice that distance when the boy directed them to stop. Pointing towards the massive stump of a Brazil nut tree, he stepped into the thick underbrush, stopping when Suarez shouted, "*Pare.*"

They could see the stump but little else from where they stood.

"What's he pointing at?" Bob Mitchell asked.

"The stump," Suarez said. "He says that's where the bones are."

"Let's follow him, then," Duncan said.

"Wait, wait," Mitchell said assertively. "Let's get this on video."

While Mitchell connected a shotgun microphone to a recorder and attached it to a handheld, telescoping boom, Joe Robinson grabbed his camera and fiddled with its controls. Duncan looked at Boyd and rolled his eyes.

"Is this how it works?" he said, skeptically. "We gotta wait for them?"

"It takes time," Boyd said. "It's frustrating for us, and I think it's frustrating for them, you know, having to set things up just right before they can shoot."

Duncan sighed and leaned against his ATV, glancing idly at his watch as if timing them. It didn't take long for them to notice the noise level of monkeys watching from the trees. Several minutes passed and Duncan's impatience got the best of him.

"I'm tired of this," he complained to Boyd.

"Well, here's the deal, if you don't wait and you find something, you're gonna hafta to do it all over. Let's just wait for them to get ready. See what happens. If it's a big hassle, we can talk about it."

Duncan sighed again.

"Ohh, Kay," Mitchell said, boom in hand, followed closely by Robinson, shouldering his camera.

"Can we go now?" Duncan asked acerbically.

Following the boy through thick brush, they approached the stump. Behind it was an irregularly shaped mound of mostly mammal carcasses. It looked to have been thrown together rather than neatly stacked. Duncan and Boyd studied several carcasses closely.

"Definitely *blaberus*," Duncan said. "How long has it been here?"

"He says they did this three weeks ago," Suarez said.

The boy explained in Portuguese that, after he and his friends had found the remains scattered on the forest floor, they collected the carcasses thinking that they had value, but the adults in the village scoffed at the notion. The hides were damaged and stunk with decay and the adults ordered the children to keep them out of the village.

"There are more," Suarez said. "They found them in all directions."

"Pull some out from the bottom," Duncan said.

"What you thinking?" Boyd asked.

"Antonio," Duncan said, "Ask him if they found all of them at the same time, you know, all at once?"

"He says they found some of them and when they came back they found more."

"That explains it," Duncan said.

"Explains what?" Mitchell asked, steadying his boom above Duncan's head while Robinson focused his camera on the scientist's face.

"Some of the carcasses are old," he said, holding up the remains of a ground squirrel that he took from the top of the pile. Slicing through the hide with his knife, he held the small skeleton, which still had small strands of rotting flesh attached to it.

"That's really ripe," Duncan said, tossing it back on the pile. "Now look at the carcass that Cody's holding."

Like Duncan, Boyd sliced the hide away. The skeleton was stripped of flesh.

"Territorialism?" Boyd said tentatively.

"Exactly."

"What does that mean?" Mitchell asked.

"It means they might come back."

"Is that good?"

"I hope so, but the fact that they came through here twice in such a short time really makes me wish I had some of these guys in a lab."

"It'd be a lot safer, huh?" Boyd said knowingly.

"Not only that, but now we gotta figure out if and when they're coming back."

Duncan surveyed the forest silently while the others watched.

"What are you thinking?" Boyd asked.

"I don't know. We don't want to be anywhere near *blaberus* in huge numbers. Right?" Duncan said rhetorically. "Ideally, we want to locate a group of scouts, you know, we've got gloves, we can grab them and put as many as we can into the containers and be gone before the rest of them get to us."

"But how do you find the scouts? And how far behind is the colony? We don't know any of that," Boyd said.

"Hmm," Duncan said, turning to Suarez who stood with the boy behind the others. "When you were in that tree that night, did any of the bugs try to climb up to get you?"

Suarez shook his head.

"They jumped, Mister Howard. I don't know why they didn't climb to get me. I didn't even think about it, I was so scared."

"You thinking of going up a tree?" Boyd asked.

"Well, yeah, like that tree over there looks like a tripod or something. It looks easy to climb," Duncan said absently. "Ahh, forget it, that's not gonna work. As far as we know, they can climb trees. Just because they didn't doesn't mean they can't. We're gonna have to catch them after they've been through an area, capture the stragglers."

"What about bait?" Boyd said.

"The forest is filled with bait. Why would they take our bait?"

"Maybe so, but if we think they're gonna come through again, we can set up some kind of trap, couldn't we."

"What kind of trap?"

"What do you think Thomas is using?"

"Good question. Maybe we should ask him," Duncan said.

Duncan and Boyd discussed as many ways as they could think of to trap insects, including bottle traps, interception traps, funnel traps, sticky traps, floor traps, wing traps and bucket traps, among others, some of which they could make with the available materials. But each of them had a flaw that eliminated it from consideration. Ten minutes after they started their conversation and after they'd retraced their steps back to the ATVs, they agreed that the trap had to be sturdy enough to resist the insects' cutting surfaces, their teeth and their leaping ability. And it had to be constructed of materials available in the village.

"I got it," Boyd said. "You know how 'possum traps work, right?"

"We can't use an opossum trap, for God's sake," Duncan said disparagingly.

"No, of course not," Boyd retorted. "Just hear me out. It would be like a 'possum trap where the bug gets in but can't get out because a door or gate shuts behind it."

"Hmmm. How would that work?"

"Well," Boyd said excitedly, aware that all eyes and ears were on him, "we could get something like a plastic bottle, cut the top off and somehow attach a piece of plastic on a hinge near the spout and then glue the top back on, dump some bait into the bottle and set it out. The bugs should be able to fit through the opening, right? But if they try to get out they run into the little hinged gate. What d'ya think?"

No one said anything for several seconds.

"That's not bad," Duncan said guardedly, breaking the silence, while Robinson watched through his camera

LCD and Mitchell continued to record sound. "It's a great idea, if we can find the materials. Assuming we find what we need, we build a bunch of those and set them out and wait. It's worth a shot, assuming, of course."

Duncan patted Boyd's shoulder and smiled at the camera.

"You know, it might take a while to get results, but if the bugs come back, I think it'll work," Boyd said, grinning widely.

"Yeah, if they come back," Duncan said.

"Let's hope they do," Mitchell said.

77

As THEY DROVE, Nolan Thomas outlined his plan for the day. Able to hear only part of what Thomas said, Gruber focused on avoiding holes that pockmarked the trail and the occasional rock protruding through the surface.

Equipped with wireless radios, Gruber and one of the assistants would be dropped off near where they'd finished the day before. The others would be dropped off where they had finished. At this point, Thomas had no expectation of finding *blaberus*. The idea was to map out their territory, determine its extent as much as possible and then determine how recently the colony had been at the site.

Without carcasses to go on, he struggled to estimate the colony's size and how they sought out their prey, whether through the use of scouts or some other mechanism, and then the strategies they employed to kill. Did they crawl across the forest floor in a wave, filling up every nook and cranny? Did they surround their victims or engage in a frontal assault? Did they coordinate their activities though some unknown mechanism, such as pheromones? Were they social insects like ants? Did they have a leader? Did they have castes? How did they locate their prey? In the back of his mind he questioned whether they were accurately named. He understood from what he'd read and seen in the media that they were classified by an old professor who'd published few, if any, papers. He knew that naming the species would generate head-lines, especially if it corrected other people's mistakes. Although some of the answers would come from the lab-oratory, the broader questions about the colony itself and its behavior could occur only in the field where it could be observed in its totality. The question was how to do that without endangering their lives.

Prior to setting his assistants loose, Thomas instruct-ed them to look closely for dead *blaberus* and collect them.

"I want to see the freshest remains you find," he said in a business-like tone. "We'll agree to call them *Repti-lus blaberus* for now out of convenience." Gruber and the others exchanged surprised looks.

"You think they're misnamed?" Gruber asked ginger-ly.

"I think we have to approach this with an open mind. We have to avoid making assumptions and relying on what other people have reported."

"Right," Gruber said. "Do you think we'll need the flamethrower? It's kinda heavy."

"You didn't carry it yesterday. I don't see why you should today," Thomas said. "You've got your radios. Check in every fifteen minutes, and don't get out of radio range. I don't want to send a search party after you."

78

AFTER DROPPING OFF equipment at their campsite, and while Suarez looked for plastic bottles in the village, Duncan and his crew returned the ATVs by early afternoon. Bob Mitchell hadn't given a thought to the possibly underhanded way in which they'd obtained the ATVs until they'd dismounted at the administration building and waited for Santiago to inspect the vehicles and return their deposit. He watched several men running across the campground toward him. One of them was shouting, but he couldn't tell what he was saying.

"Here it comes," Joe Robinson whispered to Boyd.

By the time Boyd looked up, the first of the runners had reached them.

"What the fuck! You stole our ATVs, you bastard," one of the men who ran toward them said lividly. "I oughta…" he threatened, raising his fist above his head as he nearly ran into the startled Mitchell.

"You oughta what?" Robinson said with equal menace, stepping boldly alongside Mitchell. The curmudgeonly videographer had a reputation in the industry as someone not to mess with. It's why he was assigned to Mitchell's crew to begin with.

"It was my idea," Robinson said defiantly. "You got a beef with someone, it's me, not him."

Although at fifty-four Robinson was much older than the three men who confronted Mitchell, he was built like a fireplug, with thick arms, a barrel chest and an abdomen that covered his belt. Unshaven, his long-sleeve shirt saturated with sweat, he looked like someone who was ready to take the first punch and then retaliate with force.

While Duncan and Boyd watched from nearby, the three aggressors considered their options. Boyd noticed two ATVs parked in a small junk yard behind the building.

"Why didn't you take those?" one of the men said angrily, pointing toward the ATVs. "Besides, we had reservations."

"Talk to the old man," Robinson said. "He rented them to us."

Nobody wanted to upset villagers, much less the guy in charge of the ATVs.

"Well, it takes two to tango," the de facto leader of the group announced defiantly.

As they walked away, Mitchell asked what they meant.

"It means, they're gonna do to us what we did to them," Robinson said. "I kinda thought this might happen, but, what the hell, at least we got a day out of it. I got all the B-roll I'm gonna need and you got some decent sound. Didn't you, Mitch?"

Bob Mitchell was thrilled that the crusty Robinson called him by his nickname for the first time. He felt accepted.

79

SUAREZ, WHO LOOKED like the villagers and spoke their language, had no problem finding an armful of two-liter plastic bottles. The villagers collected them and found multiple uses for them and had plenty to spare. Boyd wasted no time in working on a prototype that would turn the plastic bottles into traps. It would have been easy if they were trying to catch beetles, but *blaberus* was powerful and vicious. He had little doubt that, with the appropriate bait, they would be lured inside. The question was how long it would take them to escape.

Duncan's disdain for the media bubbled into consciousness while watching the confrontation over the ATVs. He thought them arrogant for expecting to take priority over scientists whose purpose was far more important than mere coverage. At the same time, he couldn't help but notice that additional media tents had sprung up in the encampment since they'd left in the morning.

Robinson watched as Boyd sliced the top of a bottle. His instinct was to grab his camera, but he hesitated.

"You might want to do that inside the tent," he said

quietly, standing behind Boyd and nodding toward the other campers, "You're supposed to be part of our crew, remember?"

Boyd looked up, at first not certain what Robinson meant.

"Right," he said, hastily tossing the bottles and scuttling inside the tent he shared with Suarez and Duncan. "Good idea."

"Hey, Howard," Boyd said, pointing to the Broken Tree Productions logo on his shirt pocket, "we're supposed to look like we're working for them."

Duncan understood immediately, ducking into the stuffy tent. While Boyd worked on his prototype, Duncan rolled up the flaps covering the screens, letting in additional light and air.

The major problem that Boyd had to solve was how to install a flap at the opening that would allow the insects to enter but not exit.

"You know what would be great to have right now?" Boyd said. "A skewer of some kind."

"A skewer?" Duncan asked.

"Yeah, I could push it through one side and out the other and hang the flap on it. Where we gonna find a skewer?"

"OK, how about sticks?" Duncan said.

"I thought about that. They have to be thin and strong."

"You think they'll just chew through it?"

"I don't know."

"Nobody knows," Duncan said. "How about I ask Bob? They might have something."

"And then we gotta figure out how to reconnect the top with the rest of the bottle. Wish we had some glue," Boyd said.

Duncan unzipped the screen and poked his head out of the tent door. Crawling out awkwardly, he rose and felt stiffness in his back and knees. The film crew's tent was larger than Duncan's, with straight sides. He entered it by ducking his head. Inside, Mitchell and Robinson, sitting on canvas camp chairs, stared at a laptop resting on a small table, examining the day's footage.

"Hey, doc," Mitchell said. "C'mon in. Sorry we don't have another chair."

"No problem," Duncan said, looking over their shoulders at the laptop. "We're building traps and I was wondering if you all have anything like a skewer with you."

"A skewer?" Robinson asked, looking up at Duncan.

"Yeah, you know, something like that. Thin and strong and maybe six inches long. Something like that."

The two exchanged looks, as if expecting the other to have something that fit the bill.

"I can't think of anything," Mitchell said. Robinson shrugged.

"How 'bout glue?"

Again, they looked at each other as if expecting a solution.

"We got duct tape," Mitchell said.

"Yeah," Duncan said eagerly. "That might work."

Returning to his tent, Duncan handed a roll of tape to Boyd.

"That'll work," he said. "I think I figured it out. There's lots of vines in the forest. We just need to find the right size stuff. It's not as stiff as a stick but it's not brittle either. And it would be harder to chew through. What do you think?"

"Antonio can find it for us," Duncan said, smiling. "By the way, where is he?"

SILVIO SANTIAGO WAS bending Suarez's ear, complaining about how he thought Duncan's team had taken advantage of his good nature by overpaying for the ATVs.

"I shouldn't have let you talk me into it," he fretted, in Portuguese. "Tomorrow you get nothing."

Suarez had come to the building to sit under one of its working ceiling fans, but the old man was clearly upset and wouldn't let the young man sit in silence. Even though he understood little English, Santiago could tell when men were arguing in any language. Since the other film crew had flown in from Manaus, following the argument, they complained in Portuguese that he had cheated them, making him feel guilty and resulting in a promise that they would have the ATVs tomorrow. Suarez was offended that the old man blamed him.

"Don't blame me," he said, calmly. "I was just translating. It wasn't my idea. Now, will you sell me a beer?"

The old man rubbed his stubbled chin, sighed, reached under the counter, opened the cooler and pulled out a can of Brahma beer. He charged fifteen reals, which was more than double the price in Manaus. Suarez paid it without complaint, popped the top and took a deep draught. Pulling up a rickety barstool, he apologized for what Duncan's group had done and after a few moments asked if there was anything he could do to help them find transportation for tomorrow. The old man shook his head several times, insisting that all the machines had been reserved.

"And I'm not going to let anyone undercut anyone," he insisted.

Suarez didn't want to argue with him and took his beer outside to where the ATVs were parked. Someone had parked a third ATV alongside the two they'd dropped off. He couldn't help but notice the two that were parked a short distance away. They were older than the others and bore signs of misuse but seemed to have most of their parts. Beyond them, and behind the building, sat several scavenged ATVs.

"What's wrong with those two?" Suarez asked, loud enough for the old man to hear. Emerging from the building's open sides, he spit and shook his head.

"They don't work."

"Do you mind if I look at them?"

"Look all you want."

"If I get them to run, will you rent them to us?"

Santiago grew thoughtful. Nobody in the village could get them to run and that meant that they would sit there until stripped of usable parts and then pushed deeper into the junk pile.

"Are you a mechanic?"

"I worked in my brother's shop when I was growing up," the wiry Suarez said.

"Ever work on ATVs?"

"No, never."

Figuring he had nothing to lose if Suarez could get them running, he assented, watching momentarily as Duncan's guide inspected the first ATV.

"There's some tools inside if you need them," he said encouragingly. "Wrenches and hammers."

Suarez thanked him and continued to pull at wires and do what he could with his hands on both machines, turning the keys with no result. One thing was certain, the batteries were dead, though he found that they still contained low levels of acid. Topping them off with water, he asked the old man for the tools. Santiago pointed to a small, wooden crate near the cooler. Pulling out a handful of rusty wrenches, pliers and screwdrivers, Suarez asked if there were any spare batteries lying about. Santiago shook his head.

"Do you mind if I pulled one out of one of the machines that works, just to test? The batteries got no juice."

"You sure you know what you're doing?"

"Of course," Suarez replied. "I just need one. I'll put it back when I'm done."

"You won't kill it, will you?"

Suarez felt vaguely insulted but didn't respond to it.

"You know, it's to your benefit if I get them running."

The old man waved him off cavalierly. He understood that he had little to lose.

After fifteen minutes of fiddling, the first ATV sputtered to life, smoke pouring out of its exhaust in acrid, billowing clouds. The motor resonated like a tank, until he adjusted the loose muffler. The engine ran rough, coughing and spitting as if in its death throes. The noise and smoke drew Santiago outside, who watched from a distance, flapping his hat in front of him to ward off the exhaust. Suarez killed the engine. He knew that starting it was one thing, getting the ATV to move was another. He also knew that one ATV wouldn't be enough, so as the old man moved back inside, he turned his attention to the second vehicle and had it running within ten minutes.

Somehow he had to get them to run on their own batteries, and then start in the morning. He asked Santiago if he had jumper cables. The old man disappeared into a storage room behind the counter and emerged with cables. They were old and brittle and the wiring was frayed where it connected to the clamps. After replacing the working battery, Suarez started the ATV, which ran smoothly. Using the jumper cables, he took a deep breath and turned the key on the first ATV. The starter turned only slightly, but he was encouraged that it turned at all. Waiting a moment, he turned the key again and this time the engine shook and sputtered to life without filling the air with smoke. As he pressed cautiously on the accelerator, the motor revved haltingly but continued to run even after he removed the cables, which were hot. Suarez let the motor run to charge the battery and burn off old fuel, turning his attention to the second vehicle.

"You did it," Santiago said, patting him on the back.

"For now," Suarez said modestly. "We'll see what happens in the morning. For now, I want to let them run and do a little tuning, if you don't mind."

"Mind? Of course not. You obviously know what you're doing."

81

HUDDLED INSIDE THEIR tent, Duncan and Boyd became aware of the limitations of the bottle trap they were struggling to assemble. The mouth was narrow and they still hadn't determined the best way to attach flaps to prevent insects from escaping. Enlarging the entry would only make it that much more difficult to prevent escape, assuming the flap worked at all.

"Maybe we're looking at this all wrong," Boyd said.

"How so?"

"We know that *blaberus* is viviparous, right? That's what Professor Azevedo said, right?"

"As far as we know, yes."

"And, as far as we know, they're breeding like rabbits, right?"

"What is this, twenty questions?" Duncan said with slight irritation.

"There have to be a lot of juveniles that will easily fit through the opening."

"Assuming they're part of the colony and not reared in some kind of nursery."

Boyd frowned.

"Yeah, yeah, that could be. But they're not all the same size in any case. There's variation. There has to be."

"OK, I'll buy that. So we just keep the opening the way it is," Duncan said.

"Exactly. And that leaves only one problem and that's how to install the flap. The more I think about it, I'm just not sure about using vines."

"Me either. Let's talk to Antonio. He found the bottles, maybe he can help us with the flap."

"I'll find him," Boyd said as he prepared to crawl out of the tent.

"You sure that's a good idea?" Duncan said, pointing to the logo on his shirt.

"Not for you," Boyd said. "I'm a much better liar. Besides, I'm a consultant. Nobody cares about me. You're the one with a target on his back."

82

RETURNING IN THE late afternoon, Nolan Thomas's group met to review what they'd learned and to prepare tomorrow's plan. They pored over Thomas's topographical map, outlining the area they'd explored, most of it in a wide basin surrounded by steep embankments of varying heights. They did not encroach on the area that Duncan's group had visited.

They had collected several carcasses for closer inspection as well as a small number of insect specimens that turned out to be little more than husks. Little anatomical structure remained, which was not surprising to anyone given the heat and humidity. Gruber and the other assistants had stumbled through the forest with great caution, fearful of actually finding the quarry they sought. As if by agreement, they followed the path of least resistance, avoiding the more impenetrable parts of the forest floor, preferring to walk along the edge of the embankments, which were unobstructed by comparison. Thomas didn't know this, of course, since his only contact with them once they were out of sight was via wireless radio. As far as they knew, the interior of the valley could have been crawling with *blaberus*.

Whether defending a previous decision or not wanting to start over, Thomas firmly believed that they were in the right place and that it would be only a matter of time before the insects would appear.

"We don't want to be there when they're there, do we?" Gruber asked awkwardly.

"Probably not," Thomas said.

Gruber and his colleagues shared their relief with smiles.

"Tomorrow we'll set our pitfall traps," Thomas said.

"And we'll set up cameras with remotes," Mitchell said, as if it were important to the scientists.

Thomas's pitfall trap, which he had designed himself when he was a graduate student, consisted of a Teflon-coated funnel, eight inches in diameter at its widest, that emptied into a six-inch diameter polyethylene container. The device would be buried in the forest floor, and the insects would fall into it with no avenue of escape. Following the meeting, Gruber and the others would practice burying traps in the soft, grassy area around their tent.

"The great thing about these traps," Thomas said, "is that we don't need bait. My guess is that when the insects come—and I must say again that I do not like the name *Reptilus blaberus*—they'll fall in and we return the next day to collect them and be on our way back to civilization."

Gruber and the others couldn't wait to grab their stainless steel folding trowels and get busy, but Thomas wasn't finished. Using the data they provided, pinpointing the locations of carcasses, he drew a circle encompassing the approximate center of the valley extending to both embankments and several hundred yards north and south.

"I'm playing hunches on this, but from your data it

seems we found more specimens closer to where I was stationed than farther out. And so that's where we'll concentrate our efforts. Any questions?"

83

CODY BOYD HAD no trouble finding Antonio Suarez. Seconds after stepping out of his tent and getting his bearings he saw him near the administration building talking to Silvio Santiago. Knowing that the old man spoke only Portuguese, Boyd approached slowly, not wanting to interrupt the conversation.

"So how's it going?" Boyd said as Suarez reached him.

"He's still angry at us," Suarez said soberly.

Boyd didn't need an explanation.

"That mean we don't get ATVs tomorrow?" Boyd asked apprehensively. "How we gonna get the traps out?"

Suarez smiled happily.

"He has a couple that wouldn't start, so I worked on them and got them to run. I think he'll let us use them 'cause I got them to work."

Boyd gazed at Suarez in silent admiration.

"Unbelievable," he said, patting the smaller Suarez on the shoulder. "No kidding?"

"No. We can have them."

"Hot damn! Hot damn."

Suarez didn't want to dampen Boyd's enthusiasm but didn't want to mislead him either. As they returned to their tent, he explained that the batteries were in poor shape, that they might not have enough juice to start in the morning and that if they didn't start Suarez would have to jump them from one of the other machines.

"So, we have to get there early, make sure there's something to jump our machines with," Boyd said.

"To be safe. And we'll have to pay to use them."

"He knows they aren't worth much if they don't start."

Reaching the tent, Boyd followed Suarez inside. Duncan saw that both were cheerful.

"So, did you find something for the traps?"

Suarez looked at Boyd uncertainly.

"I'll explain that in a minute," Boyd said to Suarez.

"So you didn't find…"

"Better yet," Boyd said. "We've got ATVs for tomorrow."

Duncan was perplexed.

"I don't understand."

Boyd nodded to Suarez who explained the situation.

"Jeez, I didn't realize we had a problem," Duncan said, looking at Boyd. "Why didn't you tell me?"

"I didn't know either. This all happened while we were working on the traps. Antonio here saved the day."

Duncan congratulated Suarez, who smiled modestly.

"Did you ask him about the traps?" Duncan said to Boyd.

"No, I didn't. We just talked about the ATVs."

Duncan explained that he and Boyd were building bottle traps and held up the half-completed prototype. He described the problem they were having attaching the flap that would prevent the insects from escaping. Suarez listened and watched patiently. Duncan asked if he had any idea how to solve the problem.

Without a word, the guide dashed out of the tent, leaving Boyd and Duncan baffled.

"Where's he going?" Duncan asked.

They watched as Suarez ran barefoot toward the huts along the river bank.

"I don't get it," Duncan said. "Where's he going?"

"I don't know, but he must have some idea," Boyd said. "You know, really, if it weren't for him we wouldn't have these bottles to begin with, and I'm sure as hell we wouldn't have any ATVs tomorrow. I don't know what you're paying him, but it's not enough."

Moments after Boyd and Duncan had turned their attention to the prototype, Suarez returned with a handful of sharpened sticks, each about a foot long. He was panting as he held them out to Duncan.

"Will these work, Mister Howard?"

"What are they?"

"Darts, they use them with blowguns to shoot monkeys," he said, holding his hand to mouth and blowing.

Duncan held them gingerly so that the ends didn't touch his hands.

"They're not poisonous, are they?" he asked, suddenly hesitant.

"Oh, no, they've never been used," Suarez said reassuringly. "Will they work for you?"

"Yeah, no question. This is exactly what we need," Duncan said, handing them to Boyd and shaking Suarez' hand. "You're a miracle worker. I don't know how we'd get along without you."

Suarez was happy that even though he hadn't done any guide work, he was earning his pay.

84

As EVENING FELL, Gruber, Covelli and the other assistants retired to their tent. There was just enough room for four sleeping bags and personal gear, which they crammed against the polyester sides. The initial appeal of camping had worn off, replaced by carping over little things, such as letting in mosquitoes. They were also starting to express criticism about the way Thomas was using them. All of them believed they were doing work that was beneath them and their skills. Because of their fear of being over-heard by Thomas, they whispered.

Normally, Gruber defended his boss. Normally, there was a pecking order among the assistants and he was at the top. But like his colleagues, he felt that he was being misused, especially since he was doing the same work as they were. As the senior assistant, he felt he should be supervising the grunt work, not participating in it. The fact that he was now criticizing their boss made them feel they had his permission to do the same. He was no longer their superior.

"I agree with you guys," Gruber said, sympathetically. "I don't know what I expected."

With the tent illuminated by an LED headlamp dangling from the ceiling, it was difficult for them to see one another's expressions.

"I don't know about you guys, but I'm kinda scared out there," Covelli said.

"Me too," another said.

"Yeah," Gruber agreed. "We don't know much about these bugs and I really don't like it that the guy who was supposed to carry the flamethrower isn't here."

"Yeah, what's with that?"

"I heard he was on parole or something and the Brazilians wouldn't let him in."

"No kidding?" Gruber said.

"Yeah, that's what I heard."

"That thing's so heavy, I hate to wear it," Gruber said.

"A lot of good it does."

"You know what, that flamethrower would've been handy for those people who got trapped in the flood. Did you see some of that stuff online and what that one guy said? They were throwing cups of gasoline and lighting it with sticks. Man, if they had a flamethrower, shit…"

"Maybe nobody woulda died."

"Well, at least tomorrow, we're gonna lay the traps and be outta there."

"And what's with all this filming? That producer guy keeps asking me what I think and how I feel."

Everyone looked at Gruber for an explanation.

"I don't know," he said, "that's between them and the company or the doc. It's some sort of documentary or something. I'm not sure if the company hired them or what. You know how secretive they are about everything."

"Maybe they're doing a recruitment video."

"I don't know. So far, they gotta be disappointed," Covelli said. "Doesn't look like anything's happening."

"Let's hope it stays that way," Gruber said, hopefully, and abruptly changed his tone. "Whoever is farting, stop it right now or keep it in your bag."

85

SILVIO SANTIAGO WAS in a dark mood when Boyd and Suarez arrived to start the two ATVs. Villagers were fed up with the noise and presence of strangers photographing and filming their homes and boats. A youthful crew from Manaus were particularly disrespectful, laughing at the condition of some of the huts and wondering aloud if the boats would sink before reaching the opposite side of the river.

The old man barked at Suarez when he asked to use the jumper cables.

"Why are you yelling at me?" Suarez said in Portuguese, startled.

"You haven't paid me for the ATVs."

"Well, since they wouldn't start, I thought if I started them you'd let us use them."

"That was before you started them. Now they start. It's a different situation."

Suarez conferred with Boyd.

"How much?"

"Five hundred reals."

"That's what you charged us yesterday, and I didn't have to work on them."

"Five hundred for both," Santiago said. "Someone else, I rent them for five hundred reals each."

Disheartened by what he felt was unfair treatment, Suarez turned to Boyd, shaking his head.

"I don't know why he's treating us this way," Suarez said.

"Maybe he's still angry at us."

Suarez exhaled heavily. As if defending himself, he told Boyd how he managed to start the motors. Boyd was sympathetic but feared losing the vehicles, which in his mind would be the worst thing that could happen.

"He's cheating us," Suarez whispered angrily, "and he knows it."

"Tell him we'll get the money," Boyd said. "I'll go back and get it. You stay here, make sure he doesn't rent them to someone else."

While Suarez talked to the old man, Boyd ran to the campsite, bursting into the tent he shared with Duncan and Suarez. Duncan was upbeat, sipping his second cup of coffee.

"How much is five hundred reals?" Duncan asked as Boyd.

"Something like a hundred twenty-five dollars."

"That's not bad, is it, for both ATVs? I don't suppose he takes credit cards."

Boyd laughed, as Duncan inspected his wallet.

"I got maybe a hundred dollars, not reals."

"I'm sure he'll take dollars. They're good anywhere."

"What about you?" Duncan asked. "You got any money?"

"About what you got," Boyd said, holding his hand out for Duncan's dollars.

"It's all I got left, in cash. You know, we should get them to pay for it," Duncan said, nodding in the direction of Murphy's tent.

"No time," Boyd said, and hurriedly left the tent.

86

WHILE SUAREZ WAITED impatiently for Boyd to return with the cash, Gruber and one of his assistants arrived to claim their ATVs, followed by media who claimed the remaining machines. Suarez felt helpless as he watched the machines drive away, taking their batteries with them.

"Boy, it looks like everyone's in a hurry," Boyd said, as he arrived at the administration building, handing the currency to him. Santiago took the money and nodded toward the remaining ATVs.

"They're yours," he said, without asking for a deposit.

Neither of the ATVs would turn over, which is what Suarez expected. Since both had manual transmissions, he was confident they could push start them, but they needed at least one more person to do the job. While Boyd ran to Mitchell's tent, Suarez checked the fuel tanks. They were almost empty. Santiago pointed to a 55-gallon drum with a hand-operated pump near where the ATVs were parked. It stood among a dozen similar barrels. Santiago's price was double the price of gas in Manaus, but Suarez was in no position to bargain. When Boyd returned with

Mitchell and Joe Robinson in tow, Suarez delivered what he thought would be unhappy news, but the Americans paid without complaint.

"The last thing we want to do is run out of gas," Boyd said. "By the way, we're gonna need a cart or something to haul everything."

While Suarez and Robinson fueled the ATVs, Mitchell and Boyd scanned the junkyard behind the administration building. As they scavenged, they saw that Nolan Thomas and his crew were headed into the forest, each of their vehicles towing a small cart, followed closely by the remaining ATVs carrying media.

"Hey," Boyd said, pointing at Thomas's vehicles, "there goes our cart. Why the fuck would they do that?"

"Murph told me yesterday that they were gonna set traps. Looks like they needed extra room," Mitchell said. "It didn't occur to me that they'd be using ours. That sucks."

"Sucks isn't the word," Boyd lamented. "You know, Mitch, these things hold two people each and there's three of us and two of you. And we've got a bunch of traps to carry."

"I thought you were working for us," Mitchell said pointedly.

"I am," Boyd said, backtracking.

Mitchell gave Boyd a critical look.

"OK, I'm working for both of you," Boyd said.

"Look at your contract," Mitchell said censoriously. "You're supposed to work for us exclusively."

"OK, OK," Boyd said. "I don't wanna argue. We got work to do or you're not gonna get any video and we're not gonna get our traps out. And you don't wanna piss Howard off. Look at him. He's practically jogging. He's in a hurry."

"What's the hold up?" Duncan demanded as he approached Boyd and Mitchell. "Thomas is already gone."

"We're looking for a cart," Boyd said.

"Dr. Thomas took the one we used yesterday," Mitchell said.

"That's not good. What are we gonna do?"

"We're lookin'," Boyd said, agitated.

"We're already late."

"I understand that," Boyd said, barely able to conceal his frustration.

"How we gonna carry the traps?"

"I don't know, Howard," Boyd sneered. "On our heads?"

"Don't get pissed at me. You're the one who said we had ATVs. I see them over there with Antonio, but I don't see a cart."

"Sorry. I'm just frustrated. Seems like everything we do is a big hassle," Boyd said.

"It hasn't been easy, but let's focus on the problem. If we got no cart, what's Plan B?"

87

THOMAS UNFOLDED THE map on the hood of his ATV while his assistants huddled around him. Each was expected to install a half-dozen traps at precisely marked locations. None understood nor asked how he determined the locations. They speculated that his primary criterion was how difficult each location would be to reach or some kind of voodoo. Each carried his supply of traps in a canvas bag along with a trowel, water and snack bars in his day pack. Rather than working in pairs, each moved separately toward different quadrants.

Gruber thought he'd uncovered a pattern when the first two traps he set were near where the oldest carcasses were found. As he understood it, the insects had been through the area multiple times, easily determined by the scattered remains. But it was apparent that they too foraged in a somewhat predictable way insofar as their victims were laid out in relatively narrow swaths, as if avoiding areas they had recently covered. Gruber didn't think it mattered, as he placed the third trap near one of the recent kills. He assumed the others were experiencing the same thing.

What bothered him the most was how difficult it

was to step through the forest floor, which was covered with vines and roots that made it difficult to dig even the smallish holes required by the pitfall traps. Not equipped with a hatchet, he struggled to clear enough vines to more than scratch the surface with the trowel. Even then, under the vines, he found roots, which formed a nearly impenetrable subterranean web. Gruber wondered if Thomas would check their work as he battled mosquitoes and wiped sweat off his forehead. Worse for him was the presence of the young videographer flitting about like a butterfly, contorting his body in search of unusual camera angles, he and the soundman capturing Gruber's frustration as the simple act of digging a small hole proved almost too much for him.

At the same time, he worried about unwittingly stepping into a swarm of insects, which slowed him down even more. With each step he paused to stare at the ground around him, peering into the vines and debris to where, presumably, *blaberus* would travel.

Using their wireless radios, the assistants checked in with Thomas, who sat on a camp chair alongside Murphy on the hill. Behind them the half dozen, mostly Brazilian, media went in various directions, puzzled by what Thomas's group was doing. They knew he was looking for killer insects but didn't know how he was going to do it and had no idea what would happen if he found them. Murphy did his best to keep them away from Thomas, who was understood only by two Manaus reporters who spoke English. One of them had acted as translator during his impromptu press conference.

Thomas's radio crackled with static, making it difficult to carry on a conversation. Were it not for the uneven terrain, the dense growth, the towering trees, the steep embankments and bluffs to absorb and deaden the sound, they might have communicated simply by shouting. But as it was, sound didn't carry far.

Gruber was the first to finish and, along with the film crew, moved to the edge of the valley where the footing was easier and made his way back to Thomas's location. Thomas looked at his watch.

"Three hours. What took you so long?"

"I needed a chainsaw to cut through the vines. They're everywhere, not to mention roots. I've never seen anything like it. What about the others?"

"You're the first."

Gruber smiled, moved down the narrow path to the ATVs and sat in the front seat, munching on a snack bar and washing it down with bottled water. Whether his boss cared or noticed, being first was important to Gruber. He was the senior assistant and as such felt a need to be ahead of the others, if for no other reason than to retain their respect. That's the way he felt, even though it was unlikely they would ever disrespect him in such a way that he would find out. Just as Thomas controlled an important part of his future, he likewise had partial control over theirs. More than anything else, it was something he had to prove to himself—that he was faster, better than everyone else.

The second assistant finished a half hour later followed shortly by the third, all of whom checked in with Thomas before joining Gruber relaxing in the ATV. When Covelli hadn't returned, they listened as Thomas spoke loudly into his radio, almost shouting as his voice seemed to be swallowed by the static. There was something urgent about Thomas's voice, Gruber and the two assistants thought as they exchanged concerned glances.

Murphy used his compact binoculars to scan the area where Covelli was supposed to be. Thomas spoke into his radio again. No response, just static.

Wordlessly, Murphy, soundman Jack Walker and videographer Andy Wilson grabbed their equipment and started to make their way in the direction of where they thought Covelli would be. Unlike Covelli, who was supposed to be trudging through the vine-covered central part of the valley, the trio struck out for where the valley met the bluff, which was much easier to travel. Several hundred yards out they saw someone running toward them, tripping and nearly losing his balance several times. While Wilson watched through his LCD screen, the man nearly ran into Murphy. He recognized him as the translator from the press conference. He struggled to catch his breath.

"You must come," he said desperately, pulling on Murphy's sleeve. "It is terrible what is happening. He needs help."

88

HOWARD DUNCAN FRETTED as the morning wore on. He and his group had two ATVs but no way to haul the bottle traps nor the video and sound gear without leaving people behind. As it was, three men would have to crowd each other on one of the ATVs. Duncan could not afford to leave Antonio Suarez or Cody Boyd behind while Bob Mitchell and Joe Robinson were adamant about using the second ATV even though Duncan and Boyd had paid the fee from their own pockets. Mitchell claimed his company would reimburse them, but Duncan knew from experience that reimbursement required receipts and the old man didn't provide receipts.

While they waited with the ATVs at their campsite, perpetuating the deception that the two scientists were employees of Broken Tree Productions, Suarez was somewhere in the village looking for a solution. He told them that he'd seen several small wagons when he scored the bottles and was hopeful he could rent them from their owners. The wagons were used to haul items from the villagers' boats to their houses. They were little more than common children's wagons with oversized wheels and, under any other circumstance, would never have been considered as a solution to their problem. But there was nothing else available and they were desperate to get their traps out. Mitchell gave Suarez a wad of reals to pay for the wagons, which the villagers at first declined until Suarez warned them that they could suffer damage given the rough ride ahead of them. He told them the money was coming from Americans, after which they gladly accepted amounts several times greater than the wagons were worth.

When Suarez came into view, trailing a pair of wagons with crudely assembled high sides, Duncan and the others thought their worries were over and that they'd be on their way in a matter of minutes. Just as obtaining the ATVs had turned into a grueling process, figuring out how to attach and then pull the small wagons behind the hulking ATVs without capsizing them was a clockburner. Using rope, they realized that binding the handle to the ATV's attachment point would make it difficult to execute turns, while connecting it loosely so that the handle moved freely could result in the handle jabbing into the ground. No matter what they did, they would be moving very slowly. But everyone was in a hurry and, with one wagon piled with bottle traps, Mitchell and Robinson decided to leave the second one behind as neither would trust their equipment to it. Mitchell brought the minimum of sound equipment while Robinson left his heavy tripod behind. Sitting in the passenger seat, Robinson held both his camera case and Mitchell's sound gear on his lap, hoping for the best.

As they inched their way out of the village and into the forest, Duncan wondered whether there was a better, faster way to get to their destination. His frustration was getting the better of him and he felt helpless to do anything about it.

"Can we go a little faster?" he said.

"We go faster, and we lose the wagon. C'mon, Howard, we're doing the best we can," Mitchell said.

"I know, I know," Duncan said apologetically.

It didn't help that Mitchell was also frustrated by the pace and inhaling exhaust fumes and pulled ahead of Boyd's ATV.

"We're gonna move ahead of you and get some clips of you guys driving," Mitchell said, speeding down the trail, and disappearing around a bend until Boyd could no longer hear their occasionally sputtering motor.

"I wish they wouldn't do that," Duncan said.

"That's their job," Boyd said. "At least we're moving."

"We could walk faster."

Boyd ignored his boss' complaint and focused on keeping the precarious wagon from tipping over.

"You know, if there were two of us, we'd be able to carry the traps in a big bag or something," Duncan said. "We wouldn't need a wagon."

"I think we all were hoping for a regular ATV cart," Boyd said, "We're doing the best we can with what we've got to work with."

As Duncan and Boyd talked, Suarez felt vaguely hurt. Despite the noisy engine, he could hear most of what they said. He understood perfectly well that the wagons were not a great solution to their problem when he paid for them, but it was either the wagons or nothing. Listening to their back-and-forth banter, he felt that he'd made the wrong decision. Perhaps he was being overly sensitive, but their implied criticism left a bitter taste. He resisted the urge to jump off the ATV, but began to doubt his other decisions, particularly in getting the ATVs to start. The engines weren't in great shape. He wasn't certain how long the batteries would hold a charge. Their exhausts were smoky; he cringed at every misfire. He watched the wagon roll back and forth with every bump in the trail like a dugout in a storm.

Finally arriving at their destination, which they hadn't realized at the time was not far south of the valley where Nolan Thomas's assistants were placing pitfall traps, they dismounted stiffly while Robinson and Mitchell recorded. Duncan's legs were stiff and he was grouchy, which brought a smile to Mitchell's face. It was good to see emotion.

All along, since coming up with the idea for bottle traps, they'd planned on having Suarez supply them with bait, though they'd neglected to tell him.

"You should have told me in the village," Suarez said, irritated. Duncan and Boyd were surprised by the young man's tone. It was something they'd never heard before.

"What's the problem?" Duncan asked.

"I could've borrowed a bow or a blowgun. How am I going to catch bait with a machete? You should have told me."

"I'm sorry," Duncan said, unaware that Suarez had been nursing bitterness throughout the ride. "You're right. I'm sorry."

"I think we thought you're a miracle worker the way you got the ATVs and the bottles and stuff," Boyd said.

"You shouldn't think that. Only God works miracles," Suarez said, softening.

"So, what are you gonna do?" Mitchell asked after he and Robinson stopped recording.

"Find some bait," Boyd said, pointing toward the area where they planned to set their traps. "There must be at least one dead animal out there somewhere."

"Too bad we didn't bring a dog," Robinson said.

89

FOR THE FIRST time, Suarez felt unhappy with how Duncan was treating him. Sending him out to find bait for the traps with only his bare hands and a machete seemed unreasonable. However, he was not at the point of saying it couldn't be done, nor of disagreeing with him. Duncan had done many good things for him and was paying him well. It was just that the latest task seemed futile from the start. It was possible that he might stumble upon the remnants of a predator's kill, however unlikely. But short of that, what could he do, he thought, as he scanned the trees for monkeys, all of which were too high up and too wary to become targets. But as he entered the area where Duncan planned to set his traps, Suarez could not help but notice the smell of decaying flesh. As he moved slowly over the vine and root infested forest floor, the odor grew pronounced, as if a large, decaying animal were nearby, but the odor turned out to be from the bodies of several rats and squirrels. The more he looked, the more he saw the carcasses of other small mammals. It didn't take long for him to realize he stood in the midst of a killing field.

"Mister Howard, Mister Howard," Suarez shouted as he ran toward the ATVs, "The bugs are back."

Nobody paid attention at first, as it was difficult to make out what Suarez was saying. The path he took wrapped around a rocky outcrop surrounded by dense vegetation, with a gentle, twenty-foot descent. Mitchell and Robinson had unpacked their gear while Duncan and Boyd prepped their traps, setting them on the ground ready to be baited.

"Mister Howard, Mister Howard," Suarez repeated as he reached the ATVs, nearly stepping on the traps.

"Watch out," Boyd shouted, as Suarez deftly stepped to avoid the soft drink bottles.

"The bugs are back," he stammered.

"What?" Duncan asked.

"Out there. Dead animals, just like before. Many of them."

Mitchell and Robinson looked at each other, their faces instantly registering excitement. This is what they had come for. After days of shooting B-roll and recording background sounds, finally there was something interesting to do.

"Hot damn," Mitchell said, as he started toward the path.

"Hold it," Duncan squawked.

"What? Why?"

Duncan motioned for the film crew to wait.

"Are you sure?" he asked.

"Yes, yes," Suarez said, catching his breath. "Just like before."

"Did you see the bugs?" Boyd asked.

"No, thank God," he said, crossing himself. "Just the carcasses, just like before. We should get out of here, don't you think?"

Hearing this, Mitchell responded resolutely.

"We're not leaving until we get our shots." Robinson nodded in agreement, cradling his camera like a rifle.

"Don't worry," Duncan said, "We're not leaving. Apparently, *blaberus* has already been through this area. It's probably safe, assuming there's no stragglers."

"Stragglers?" Robinson asked.

"You never know," Boyd said.

"You never know what?" Mitchell asked.

"We don't know much about their behavior other than that they eat everything and move on. We think they're territorial, but we don't know the size of their territory."

"Maybe we'll get some clues," Boyd said. "One thing's for sure, there's no point putting the traps out."

"You're right about that," Duncan agreed. "Let's head down there. Antonio, you lead the way. Show us where you found them."

Suarez did not get far in front of the others as usual, tempering his normally rapid pace. Mitchell chafed but Robinson, with his arthritic knees, didn't mind going slow, especially where the path descended. Standing at the edge of the area he'd found the carcasses, Suarez pointed. The smell of rotting flesh became apparent as they approached.

"What's that smell?" Mitchell said disgustedly.

"Over there, maybe ten meters," Suarez said.

"It's the smell of death," Robinson said.

Suarez was reluctant to enter the killing field, so he let the others pass him. For a moment, their curiosity was greater than his fear but after a cursory examination of two carcasses, Duncan and Boyd became wary. Plenty of meat remained. They stared intently at the ground around them, rotating three-hundred sixty degrees, bending at the waist to get a closer look. While Mitchell held a microphone in the air near the scientists, Robinson stepped back to get a better angle, almost tripping on vines. As he steadied himself, he saw several small carcasses.

"There's more," Robinson said.

"More what?" Mitchell asked, disappointed that Duncan and Boyd weren't talking and his microphone was capturing dead air.

"Carcasses. Whaddya think?"

Boyd and Duncan spread out, hoping to find *blaberus* remains as well as to determine the extent of the kill. As they expanded their search, they realized that the area provided slim pickings for the insects. Aside from the cluster that Suarez had found, they turned up only a handful of small mammals and reptiles. Knowing that the insects had pillaged the area several times, they wondered whether the colony had exhausted the food supply or whether it was smaller than they'd estimated.

"I got one," Boyd said, holding a dead *blaberus* in his hand.

Robinson immediately zoomed in on Boyd's hand. The insect was barely two inches long.

"Looks like a cockroach to me," Robinson said after finishing his shot.

"Yeah, it's kinda small. I was expecting something bigger."

"The size isn't important," Duncan said, as Boyd handed the specimen to him. "It's a juvenile, just the kind of specimen we wanted to capture."

"Not gonna happen now, is it Howard?"

"I think what we need to do is move in that direction and see if that's where they went."

"We're not gonna chase 'em, are we?" Boyd asked uneasily.

"Absolutely not. We may be too late. They may have depleted this entire area of food."

Mitchell gave Boyd a puzzled look.

"That means they won't be coming back. We'll have to start over."

"Are you kidding?" Mitchell blurted. "That just sucks. Are you sure?"

"You know, Thomas's group is somewhere in that direction," Boyd said. "Maybe they're having better luck. You can check them out."

"It doesn't work that way," Mitchell said. "Murphy's got him covered. We're s'posed to cover you guys."

Boyd saw the discouragement on Duncan's face as they joined Suarez on the path. Both of them knew that Thomas had gotten out much earlier and that he stood the best chance of capturing live specimens. Although neither knew much about Thomas's intentions, nor his methods, the only purpose for being in this part of the rainforest was to capture specimens, without which his expedition, as well as Duncan's, would be a complete failure. The thought that he would lose the race to Thomas gnawed at Duncan. It wasn't that he had animosity toward him. They barely knew each other. It was that he felt he'd overcome many obstacles just to get where he was, which was nowhere. But unwilling to quit, he took the lead, walking west and then north, along the bottom of a steep embankment flanked by another bluff separated by a wide hollow that seemed to go on forever. Stopping often to look for signs of *blaberus*, Mitchell was the first to notice how noisy the monkeys had become. The volume increased as they walked and it seemed the trees were filled with millions of howlers screaming at the top of their lungs.

"What the fuck is going on?" Mitchell shouted in Boyd's ear.

Stopping in their tracks, they scanned the forest for the cause. Listening was stressful for all of them.

"Anyone got ear plugs?" Boyd shouted.

"I really can't take much more of this," Mitchell yelled, his face revealing his discomfort. "How can you stand it?"

And then the screeching diminished. It was as if the monkeys had strained their vocal cords and couldn't keep it up. But one of them did, shrieking in the distance, the sound coming not from above but from ground level. The sound was not simply high-pitched and recurrent but painful, as if in agony.

"They must've gotten one of the monkeys," Boyd said.

"Jesus," Mitchell said. "I've never heard anything like that."

Suarez grimaced. He'd heard the tormented screams before.

Duncan broke away from the group, looking for higher ground, hoping to get a better view. As disturbing as it was to listen to or to watch the agonizing death throes of an animal, it might represent his best and perhaps only opportunity to capture live specimens. There had to be a way to get to the top of the bluff, which was only ten feet above the hollow in some places. The sides were granular and soft, giving way when he put his foot down. Fortunately, it was overgrown with vines, which he used to pull himself to the top. He ran until he found an open spot that gave him a view of the pitiful screams.

"My God," he muttered as Boyd caught up with him.

90

Jason Gruber ran ahead of everyone after pushing the slower moving soundman and videographer out of the way. He caught up to the newsman from Manaus, who had stopped to catch his breath. He was sweaty and panting and struggling to get the words out. Gruber knew only two things, that one of his people had yet to return from his field assignment and that someone was in desperate straits. The tall American felt his composure melting away.

"What's wrong? What's the matter?" Gruber shouted as he reached the Brazilian.

"*Os insetos estão atacando. Eles estão matando um homem.*"

"In English, in English."

"The insects, they are killing a man."

Although they were a hundred yards away, they could hear the screams and the Brazilian urged Gruber to follow him, but the scientist ran in the opposite direction, pushing past the film crew and other assistants, all of whom followed the Brazilian. Nolan Thomas, who remained at his post overlooking the forest valley, watched wordlessly as Gruber ran past him and to the ATVs where he grabbed the heavy flamethrower, hoisting it by the shoulder straps and rushing toward his boss and stopping to answer a question.

"What's going on?" Thomas asked.

"I think it's Greg," Gruber said, catching his breath. "The bugs are attacking."

"What?"

"I gotta go."

Thomas watched as his chief assistant rushed awkwardly down the trail, balancing the flamethrower on one shoulder, his eyes glued to the ground to avoid tripping. It seemed to him that time had slowed to a crawl and that he would never reach his destination but he arrived only a moment behind the film crew. Remaining at a distance, the Brazilian media crews watched and did their jobs, just as Murphy, Walker and Wilson did theirs. Nobody attempted to help Covelli, whose screams filled the air like falling icicles. Fifty feet off the trail, clouds of insects swarmed over their shrieking victim. Gruber confronted the other assistants who stared at their tortured colleague, shouting for him to run, as if running would cause the hundreds of *blaberus* to let go.

No one had to tell anyone not to get close to the slowly dying victim. Everyone could tell there was nothing they could do without themselves becoming a casualty. Everyone but Gruber, who was impelled to do something, though there was no time to create a strategy that would keep him safe. None of them had ever seen anything like this, and they were at once transfixed and horrified. Each could only imagine the pain and terror the victim felt as he stumbled blindly, his eyes torn open like soft-boiled eggs, aqueous humor draining down his bloody face.

Lowering the flamethrower to the ground, Gruber

turned several knobs and switched on the device's ignition system. With a single motion, his knees bent, he slipped his arms through the shoulder straps and slowly rose, shifting the uncomfortable load until he felt the straps tighten with the fuel-tank's weight. Holding the nozzle with one hand, he pressed a button to ignite the tip and frantically moved forward and back, left and right to find a position from which he could sweep the area without scorching his screaming, fallen friend.

Even though Gruber had acted in a matter of seconds, they were a lifetime to the bloodied colleague, who struggled vainly to rise from his knees, his face now wearing a mask of writhing monsters.

"Watch out!" Someone shouted. "They're everywhere!"

Frustrated beyond endurance, the insane screaming diminishing in volume but not frequency, Gruber stepped off the path, held the nozzle like a shotgun at his waist, and let out a burst of flaming liquid that arced across the open space between him and his friend. Everyone watched in horror as the leading edge of it cascaded on the flailing victim, extinguishing his shrieks in a matter of seconds, his body crackling like burning leaves. At the same time, hundreds of the insects filled the air with tiny squeals as the flames incinerated them. Horrified by what he had done, frozen where he stood, Gruber stared at his colleague's blackened, flaming body as the nozzle slipped out of his hands.

Thomas, who had finally joined the others, shouted, "Jason, get out of there. Get out of there right now. Do you hear me?"

Gruber turned his head toward Thomas, uncomprehending, unable to move. For a moment, the insects seemed to retreat, or at least cut off their attack, perhaps to regroup. Risking his own life, Thomas bolted to his assistant, grabbed his arm and pulled him roughly to the path along the bottom of the embankment. Thomas shook his assistant who appeared to be in catatonic.

"I need you, Jason!" Thomas shouted. "We need you."

91

No one had a better position than Duncan and Boyd to see what was happening. Fifteen feet above the unfolding catastrophe on the earthen bluff, they had a clear, if somewhat distant, view of a scene that was all too familiar to them.

Unable to climb the slippery and soft side of the bluff with their equipment, Bob Mitchell and Joe Robinson proceeded down the trail, led by Antonio Suarez, who felt responsible for them. The effect of distance insulated Duncan and Boyd from the horror occurring below.

"That's not the whole colony," Duncan said.

"Think it's a scouting party?"

"Too big for that, but not big enough for a colony. There's gotta be more."

"Where are they?" Boyd asked, his discomfort rising with each scream.

"I don't know. But they're there."

They watched in disbelief as Gruber approached the victim only to incinerate him.

"My God," Boyd whispered. "Jesus, fucking Christ. Did you see that?"

Duncan saw it and pointed beyond the flames, well behind Gruber.

"They're jumping," Duncan said. "Out there, a line of them."

"I see a few. What are you seeing?"

"They're surrounded."

"All of them? Can't you see?"

So much was happening, so much of it horrible, that Boyd labored to process it. But Duncan saw beyond the single attack.

"Get out of there!" he shouted, his hands cupped around his mouth. Directly below them, Suarez and the film crew watched the unfolding tragedy as if they were standing in a safe place.

"Get up here," Boyd shouted to them.

"What? Why?" Mitchell yelled.

"You'll die, get up here!"

"We've got equipment."

Hearing the urgency in Boyd's voice, and having witnessed the death of Thomas's assistant, Robinson gently set his camera on the ground and, grabbing vines and digging his feet in, climbed toward Boyd, who reached out and, with great effort, pulled the heavyset cameraman to the top of the bluff.

"What about our equipment?" Mitchell protested.

"It's your life or your equipment," Duncan shouted. "Don't be stupid!"

Facing the young producer, Suarez looked at the top of the ridge.

"Do you want to die?" he said quietly.

"Fuck," Mitchell swore, dropped his equipment and duplicated Robinson's path to safety, followed closely by Suarez.

"Look at how fast they're moving," Duncan said.

"Get out of there!" Boyd shouted at Thomas's group. "There's more."

He had gotten their attention but several leaned toward him, cupping their ears as if they couldn't hear what he'd said.

Duncan, Boyd and Robinson, shouted in unison, "Get out!"

92

WHILE ROBINSON, MITCHELL and Suarez raced to help Thomas's crew as they struggled to climb the bluff, Duncan stopped Boyd from joining them.

"What are you doing?" Boyd asked, testily.

"Look at them."

"Look at what? They need help, can't you see?"

"No, look at *blaberus*."

Boyd gave Duncan a disapproving look but obeyed.

"What am I seeing?"

"It's not the main colony."

Boyd stared at Duncan for a moment and then looked more closely at the insects below.

"There must be at least a foot between them, at least," Duncan said. "Nothing like we saw before."

"They're scout groups?"

"It looks that way."

"It didn't look that way from down there, not where that guy got killed," Boyd said.

"I think what happened is that he ran into one group of scouts and the others converged, making it look like there are a lot more of them than there are."

As much as Boyd wanted to listen to Duncan's insights, he couldn't resist the commotion created by Thomas's group and bolted toward them only to stop halfway. Out of the corner of his eye he noticed two of the Brazilian journalists who had stationed themselves off the path and on the forest floor, presumably at a safe distance from where Covelli had died. They were swinging their arms wildly and running, high-stepping as if trying to keep their feet off the ground. They had no idea what they were dealing with and it showed as vines entangled their feet. They didn't start screaming until they fell for the first time and then they didn't stop. Their colleagues, having seen what happened to the American, backed away quickly, watching from what appeared to be a safe distance.

Duncan believed he had gained some understanding of how the insects worked on the ground. Previously, he had thought *blaberus* used scout groups to detect prey but until now had no idea how they worked, the tactics they used. Apparently, many scout groups were sent out, each working independently. Duncan was astonished by the amount of territory they covered in this way. Worse for victims, he thought, was that even though nearby groups converged on prey when it was detected, the other groups continued to search for food sources and it was the scouts that subdued the prey. Originally, he'd believed the scouts reported back to the main colony and it was the main colony that killed the prey. The one thing that puzzled him was that the scout groups seemed to close in on prey without first surrounding it. Perhaps that came later, depending on the number of scouts in the vicinity.

The second insight he gained was that once a victim had been engaged, outliers used their jumping ability to join the attack. Unlike during the flood when it seemed they jumped to avoid drowning, here they jumped as a means of propulsion. Even if they were ten feet away, they could be at your feet and in your hair in seconds. You can't let them get close, he thought as he watched. What if they had enough energy to jump multiple times, covering that much more ground? That was a scary thought. Even as he watched the two writhing Brazilians, he remained mesmerized by the insects' complex behavior and the opportunity to study the predators in the wild.

But then the Brazilians' screams broke through, as if he'd removed earplugs. The others heard the screams as well, but were intent on their own survival, pushing and pulling each other up the embankment, grabbing vines and arms reaching toward them, their eyes filled with bottomless fear until one by one they reached the top, rolled across it like logs, lying on their backs, staring at the clear blue sky, their chests heaving with emotions that burst forth in tears and sobs. They had made it. All but Gruber and Thomas.

93

Jason Gruber was in a trance. That was the only explanation. Nolan Thomas slapped him several times, resulting in nothing but a blank stare. Still wearing the flamethrower, Thomas's right hand man was unresponsive.

"They're behind you," Duncan yelled, having a clear view from where he stood. The scouts that had killed one man had reorganized to kill another. Apparently, Duncan thought, they didn't feed, these scouts, they just killed or subdued in ghastly ways. The feeding would come later.

Someone lowered a rope.

"Tie it around him," someone shouted urgently. "We'll pull him up."

"Ditch the flamethrower," another shouted. "Tie the rope under his shoulders. Quickly."

Soon, everyone was shouting encouragement, giving directions, trying to be helpful from a safe distance. Thomas was focused on what he was doing and like a sprinter in a stadium filled with screaming fans heard nothing, not even his furious heartbeat. He wrestled with the larger, unyielding Gruber, whose mind had succumbed to the horror that enveloped him after incinerating his colleague. The heavy flamethrower made it impossible to tie a rope around him and no matter what Thomas did he couldn't get him to slip his arm out of the shoulder straps. It didn't help that the nozzle and hose dangled on the ground. He worried that a misstep could trigger the igniter and engulf them in liquid fire. But he was making no progress and becoming frantic. Was it time to abandon his assistant and save himself? How much more time did he have?

Clumps of earth tumbled at Thomas's feet as Cody Boyd slid down the embankment. The taller, more muscular Boyd gently pushed the smallish scientist aside and sliced through both shoulder straps with his pocket knife, allowing the flamethrower tank to fall behind Gruber. Thomas watched in awe as Duncan's assistant grabbed the rope from him and deftly wove it around Gruber's chest and shoulders, tying it off and pushing the inanimate Gruber against the embankment where the others pulled as if competing in a tug of war. It took both Boyd and Thomas pushing from the bottom to finally get Gruber off the ground and on his way, the pullers finally getting enough momentum that he nearly flew up the last several feet and on top of the bluff. Thomas and Boyd followed quickly, reaching the top just as the first scouts had emerged from the vine-encrusted forest floor and onto the soft earth below the embankment.

The men were emotionally drained by a task that had taken only minutes. Meanwhile, the insects continued to torture the unlucky Brazilians, whose companions had fled. Nobody could help them, and listening to their pitiful screams had become unbearable. Unfortunately for them, there was no coup de grace as, after incapacitating them, only a few of the insects remained, having chopped out their eyes and gaining entrance to their throats, their screams ending only after the vocal cords were mutilated.

They would lie like that, suffering, screaming in silence, until the colony arrived to finish them off. Though nothing could be done for the pair, most of the Americans felt safe.

Duncan, however, had seen enough of the insects' behavior to realize their problems had just begun.

94

EVEN THOUGH EVERYONE helped each other in their desperate escape, the group divided themselves into two tribes while resting on the bluff. The media guys huddled together, as did the science guys. While Duncan described what he'd seen and his hypothesis, Murphy took control of the Broken Tree Productions staff. As far as they could tell, the insects had no interest in their equipment, which lay on the bottom edge of the embankment but out of reach. They inventoried their belongings. Each had a smart phone. They had snack bars, water bottles and insect repellent in their daypacks. Murphy was insistent that they continue to do their work, using cell phones for videoing and recording until they could figure out a way to retrieve their equipment. Bob Mitchell nodded in agreement, but the others shook their heads.

"No way," Joe Robinson said unequivocally. "Not until we know we're safe."

Murphy expected resistance.

"It's our job," he said.

"OK, you do what you want," Robinson said. "I'm focusing on my survival. We're not out of the woods yet."

"So to speak," Jack Walker said.

"They're down there and we're up here," Murphy said. "We're safe."

"How do we know they can't crawl up here?" Andy Wilson asked nervously. This was his first big field assignment and he wanted to make a good impression on the boss but, at the same time, he struggled to keep his fear in check.

"Maybe we should ask the doc," Bob Mitchell suggested. "He's the expert."

Murphy grimaced but recognized he was losing the argument. He wanted them to focus on their work as a means of relieving their anxiety, just as he had done, but they weren't going for it. He followed his staff as they joined the scientists, who sat on the soft, grassy earth listening as Duncan explained what he'd seen and his hypothesis about the scout groups. Originally, he'd surmised scout groups were small, consisting of fewer than fifty members.

"It could be several hundred," he said, "based on what I observed. And they seem to go about their work in a very organized fashion, covering a lot of ground quickly, as you may have noticed."

The scientists let this sink in.

"What do you mean by organized, professor?" Gruber asked after raising his hand. He seemed to have recovered from his shock.

"They are never out of contact with each other. Each seems to sweep in an arc, the ends of the arc meeting at some point. They converge if one of them locates prey, but I don't know what they do if don't find anything. Anybody else notice anything?"

"Can they fly?" Mitchell asked.

"I don't think so, but they can jump."

"Can they jump up here?" Mitchell asked.

"I don't think so, not from the bottom. They'd have to find a higher platform. Anyway, there's a breeze blowing against them so I think we're safe, for now."

"I wish he hadn't said that," Wilson whispered to Robinson.

"Said what?"

"For now."

"No shit," Robinson chided.

"So, does that mean we're still in trouble?" Wilson asked hesitantly.

"Louder," someone shouted.

"He asked if we're out of trouble," Duncan said, rising to his feet, brushing dust off his bare legs. "I'd say no. I think you're never safe with these guys around."

Nobody could dispute this after watching Covelli die, not even Nolan Thomas, who had remained silent.

"Is there any way to protect ourselves?" Wilson asked.

"What about the flamethrower?" someone asked.

Gruber stared at his lap. Thomas patted him on the shoulder, concerned for his mental state.

"I know what you're thinking," Gruber erupted, jumping to his feet. "I know what you all think. I killed Greg and now, because of me, we don't have the flame, the flamethrower."

"Nobody is saying that," Thomas said, standing alongside his chief assistant.

"You didn't do it on purpose," one of the assistants volunteered.

"Fat lot of good that did for Greg," Gruber said moodily.

"He was dead no matter what," Duncan said. "That happened to us. That's how one of my students died, only he begged for us to kill him."

"What happened?" Wilson asked, who knew little about Duncan's first expedition.

"One of us stabbed him with a machete," Duncan said, "at great risk to himself."

This sank in at different rates to each, except for Gruber, who remained riddled with guilt.

"It wasn't intentional," Thomas said, looking up at Gruber's tear-streaked face. "Everyone knows that."

"Look at it this way," Duncan said, "if he hadn't died, he'd still be lying down there being slowly eaten alive, suffering pain you cannot imagine. I've seen it before. I know the horrible things these insects do. How would you feel, how would any of us feel right now if we knew that he was still lying there, alive but with no chance of survival? His screams would drive us crazy until we couldn't take it anymore."

"Greg, his name was Greg Covelli," one of the assistants said.

Duncan nodded, his attention drawn to the open field between them and the next line of trees. Boyd scanned the tree line with binoculars that he carried in his daypack. The others took interest, all standing now, looking. Thomas whispered encouragement to Gruber.

"You see," Thomas said quietly. "If he hadn't died when he did, we'd have killed him. There's only so much people can put up with. You ended his suffering sooner, and in many ways you ended ours as well."

Gruber smiled slightly.

"That's better," Thomas said in a fatherly voice. "We need you."

Boyd handed his binoculars to Duncan, who thought he'd seen something moving but it was too far away and may have been nothing more than the tall grass waving in the soft breeze.

"Shit," Duncan said.

Hearing this, several of the others clamored to look through the binoculars. Jack Walker, who got to them first, peered for a full thirty seconds.

"I don't see anything," he complained, handing them to someone else.

"What are we gonna do?" Boyd whispered to Duncan.

THERE WAS LITTLE time for planning. It wasn't as if they'd had many choices, but Duncan wanted to focus on what they needed to do. They couldn't simply stay where they were. Either they found a way around the insects, or they'd have to go through them. Peering over the ledge at the flamethrower with its slashed shoulder straps, several others thought the solution lay within reach.

Before Duncan could open his mouth, Bob Mitchell pointed to the valley below and asked loudly, "What about the flamethrower?"

"What about it?" Boyd asked loudly, as Mitchell approached. Everyone had gathered around Duncan.

"Well, wouldn't that help, if we had it?"

"It might," Duncan said, "But we don't have it. And don't even think about doing something stupid. You'll die and the only thing we'll do is throw rocks at you, if we're still here, which we won't be."

Duncan outlined what to expect and what he planned to do, namely run across the field and hope for the best. He suggested they cover their hair, keep their mouths closed and use their backpacks as shields by waving them about as they ran.

"You want to knock them down if you can, but you can't stop, not for anything or anybody. Somebody falls, keep running."

"So, it's every man for himself, is it?" Gruber interjected.

Duncan saw that most didn't like what he'd said. Robinson seemed fine with it, as were Boyd and Suarez.

"How can we just abandon people?"

"Do you think the insects are gonna call a time out? They'll disable you and then they'll take their time eating you. You'd have to be extremely lucky to stop even a few seconds without being attacked. You understand you won't see them until you're right on top of them, right? And the first thing they'll do is go for your hair and your eyes. And when the pain makes you scream, they'll scuttle down your throat. The only thing working in our favor is that this is not the main colony."

"You know for sure it's not the main colony?" one of Thomas's assistants asked guardedly.

"Yeah, that's what it looks like."

"So, you're not sure?"

"I'm seeing what you're seeing. They're still a good fifty yards away. I think we'd be seeing a lot more of them jumping if it were the colony. Obviously, I can't know for sure. All I'm saying is that if you stumble, if you let them get to your mouth or your eyes, you're done. Any questions?"

"Maybe we should vote on it," someone suggested.

"Vote on what?" Boyd argued testily. "We stay here and we're dead. You stop to help someone and you're dead. Those are your choices."

"Dr. Duncan," Nolan Thomas said, "You and your

colleagues are the only people who have dealt with these creatures, I defer to your wisdom. We should prepare to run for our lives."

Duncan nodded gratefully as Thomas pulled his staff aside, each of them swearing that if he fell they'd stop to help him, to which he shook his head and told them to save themselves and that he would do the same.

Murphy and his staff continued the debate as Duncan, Boyd and Suarez prepared themselves to run the gauntlet. Using Boyd's binoculars, Duncan scanned the field, trying to determine whether the scouts had left any gaps in their coverage. Although they didn't cover the entire field, groups on the end were already performing a flanking maneuver that in a short time would close off escape at either end. Now the question was how deep they were. Would they be able to sprint through them, or would there be more of them at the edge of the tree line? Is that where the colony was? Were these scouts associated with the scouts from the valley? Were there multiple colonies? Should they run single file or line up shoulder to shoulder? Duncan kept these questions to himself to avoid pointless bickering. If it turned out they escaped the scouts only to find themselves surrounded by the colony, then the game was over. What if they could somehow retrieve the flamethrower? He found that his resolve stood up only until the next question. But he couldn't let anyone know that. Time was running out.

96

EACH MAN DID his best to cover his face and steel himself for what lay ahead. They shook hands, embraced and wished each other success. The front line scouts were within seventy feet as the men assembled on the bluff, facing their nemesis.

Several men mouthed quiet prayers. Everyone covered his mouth with bandanas. One and then another shouted at the insects, pumping themselves up. Adrenaline had cut in and they looked at each other with courage and defiance, cheering one another like men preparing for battle. Emotions were high, tears flowed on some of their faces. Robinson held a can of insect repellant like a sword. Everyone around him laughed.

"Remember," Duncan shouted, "keep your mouths closed and run like hell and keep running until you get to the trees."

"What if that's where the colony is?" Someone asked.

"Climb a tree," Boyd shouted.

"What if someone falls?"

"Give yourself up for dead, boys," Robinson said. "Fight the good fight."

"It'll be a miracle if any of us survives."

"Thanks for reminding us," someone chirped.

"Don't look around you," Duncan commanded. "Keep your eyes focused on what's in front of you. This is the most important moment of your life, don't blow it."

"All right, you bastards," Walker shouted, shaking his fist. "It's your turn to die."

"On my mark," Duncan roared. "One. Two. Three. Run like hell."

97

THE BRAZILIAN JOURNALISTS raced to the village, having watched helplessly as their colleagues fell victim to the man-killing insects. One of them kept his camera operating on the chaotic scene until it became apparent that his friends were not going to escape. Because of their wild gesticulations, he had first thought they were putting on an act. But it was clear when they started screaming that they were not acting. He was at once ashamed for having filmed it and for not trying to intervene, though to have done so would have meant certain death. None of them was prepared for what had happened and now, having reached safe haven at the administration building, they broke down and sobbed uncontrollably.

Silvio Santiago, upon seeing the two ATVs bouncing into the village at full speed, cursed the men as they braked at the last moment, sending clouds of fine red dust into the open air building.

"What are you doing?" he bellowed. "No more rentals for you. If there's any damage…"

The three men made their way past Santiago, slumping onto bench seats under the huge, thatched roof. One of them was bawling as his companions sought to calm him.

"What's wrong with him?" Santiago asked. "Is he worried about losing his deposit? Because that could happen after I inspect the vehicles."

"Shut up, old man," one of the journalists barked.

"You can't talk to me like that."

"Listen, two of our colleagues are dying in the forest," one of them said frantically.

"What? Dying?"

"They were attacked by the bugs."

"What bugs? What kind of bugs?" Santiago said.

"Killer bugs. The forest is filled with them."

"We have to help them," the sobber muttered. "They may not be dead."

The administrator had never heard of such a thing and was skeptical. He had lived his entire life in the village and had never heard of killer bugs.

"It's what those scientists were looking for."

"Where are they?"

They described what they'd seen, the incineration of one of the Americans, their friends going down, the Americans climbing to the top of the bluff to escape. Santiago was doubtful as he peppered them with questions, suspecting a plot to steal ATVs. He asked about the other ATVs.

"Don't you get it?" one of them said angrily. "People are dying."

Santiago was not impressed after they described the insects.

"Little things like that. What are they, cockroaches? You guys are up to something. And you, young man, stop crying. You're not fooling me," Santiago said.

"We have to go back to help them."

"Not with my machines, not the way you drive them."

"Don't you get it old man? Don't you understand what we're saying?"

"I understand, but I don't believe you. Your story is preposterous."

The one who had been sobbing suddenly grew angry. His red eyes widened, his nose flared and before his companions knew what was going on he launched himself at Santiago, grabbing him by the shoulders and pushing him backward until he collided with one of the heavy posts supporting the roof. The old man slumped to the ground, his back against the post. Before he could do anything else, his companions pulled him away from Santiago.

"What the fuck are you doing?"

"I can't believe this piece of shit. My friend Alex is still out there and this shit won't lift a finger."

"What can we do to help them? We ran away, remember. We were afraid for our lives. There's nothing we can do. We have to notify the authorities."

Momentarily stunned, two of the men gently assisted Santiago to his feet. Santiago cast an angry glance at the perpetrator, who quickly apologized for his behavior, draining the emotion from the moment. Santiago nodded appreciatively, returning to his perch behind the counter.

"You want to call the cops?" he asked, rotating on his stool and reaching for the microphone to his radiotelephone. "You talk, I'll work the dials."

98

THE YOUNGEST MEN reached the tree line quickly and, with an excess of adrenaline flooding their veins, they immediately started giving themselves high fives and cheering the others as if watching a track meet. They had made it, and for them it seemed like an easy run. The insects didn't have time to react, so Carl Murphy, Andy Wilson, Antonio Suarez, Cody Boyd and Bob Mitchell, all in their twenties, arrived without a scratch. As the young men raced through them, the scouts started leaping into the air, perhaps surprised by the sudden rush of feet, perhaps a part of their strategy. In any case, when the insects descended, some of them landed on the wave of slower runners. It wasn't that the older men were far behind the younger men, it was simply bad timing and the effect of gravity. If the insects weren't in the air, the men might well have gotten through as easily as the young guys.

Thomas and his assistants ran awkwardly as a group. It was clear that none of them were athletes as they rushed across the field, waving their packs in front of them like unwieldy clubs. Beside them, his face set in grim determination, Joe Robinson limped on his painful knees while Jack Walker, who had hesitated at the start, lumbered behind him, now facing an alert and aggressive foe. Somehow, Robinson got past the last row of insects without one of them landing on him, though he was certain he had knocked several out of the air with his fists. It was not the same with Walker, who stumbled before reaching the first row of insects, his face a mask of reddish dust. As he pushed himself to his hands and knees, he could feel them landing on his back, their tiny forelimbs chopping at his shirt and drawing pinpricks of blood. While the initial assault came from the air, it was the insects on the ground that scuttled across his bare legs, forcing themselves under his khaki shorts at one end and others shimmying up his arms and from there leaping to his beard and the back of his neck. He knew he had to get to his feet and somehow move forward but specks of dirt irritated his eyes and clogged his nostrils. He could hear the others shouting but didn't know what they were saying.

The men screamed as loudly as they could. *Get up. Get up. Run. Move forward. Keep your mouth closed. Don't let them get to your eyes. Run, for God's sake, run.* Some even took steps toward him, but others held them back. Duncan put his arms around Boyd to keep him from bolting.

"There's nothing you can do for him," Duncan said.

"We can't just leave him out there," Boyd protested.

While Duncan restrained Boyd, the others, with the exception of Gruber, threw sticks and dirt at the bugs, inching closer and closer to narrow the range. Thomas joined Duncan in urging them to stay back, but they weren't listening, caught up as they were in the moment. Seconds later Thomas and Duncan joined in. They had to do something, even if it was futile. Gruber was the only one who wasn't participating as he stood by himself, watching from behind. Tall, lanky, reserved, ten years older than the young guys, he didn't fit in. He saw how pointless their actions were. There was no way they were helping the struggling soundman by throwing sticks. Even those that landed among the insects did no damage. But he understood why they were doing it. They were doing what they could, fruitless as it might be, in an effort to avoid the guilt that would come with having done nothing. Ironically, he'd done something and as a result was consumed by guilt. But if he hadn't tried, if he hadn't strapped on the flamethrower and tried to help his colleague, he knew the guilt would be equally inescapable.

It turned out to be his misfortune that he was the only one who had learned to use the flamethrower, albeit he did it only once and then the lesson lasted only several seconds. He'd thought at the time that he would never be called upon to use it and so was content that he'd learned how to turn it on and ignite the flame. He would have needed another lesson to learn how far it could reach and how to properly aim it. That didn't happen until too late. Shaking his head slowly, staring one hundred feet away at the overweight Walker blindly pushing himself to a stand, his eyes closed by dust particles, his arms outstretched as if reaching for something, Gruber burst through the line formed by his colleagues, stunning everyone. They watched in disbelief as Gruber, propelled by hormones and the notion that he could succeed where he'd failed before, dashed past them, accomplishing more in seconds than all the sticks and stones could accomplish in a lifetime. In an instant, he wrapped his long arms under Walker's shoulders and with enormous effort lifted and dragged the heavier, shorter man whose shoes barely touched the ground, toward the others who had stopped their meaningless efforts and cheered him on with an enthusiasm that left some of them hoarse. Pushing past them, Gruber continued until he and his cargo collapsed beyond the tree line.

Thomas and Duncan marveled at what Gruber had done. It had happened in a matter of seconds, before they could even form a coherent thought. And now they crowded around Walker, furiously pulling insects off his clothing and body and stomping them into the ground as he laid out on his back like a sack of rice, coughing and rubbing the dust from his eyes.

"You're safe now, old man," Joe Robinson said good-naturedly, as Walker raised himself to a sitting position, his upper body bent forward and shaking uncontrollably.

Others had surrounded Gruber, congratulating him, shaking his hand. Thomas and Duncan joined the celebrants, encircling him, their smiles beaming down on him like tiny suns. Their joy was as unrestrained as young men are capable of. For his part, Gruber, sitting in the dirt, sobbed, his emotions having caught up with him, his hands shaking. Unable to speak, he rolled over onto his hands and knees, cast a glance at Walker who was still coughing, and grinned through his tears. So much had happened to him in the past hour—he'd killed a man and saved one—that when he stood he looked dazed, as if waking from a deep sleep. Others gave him room and as the celebration wound down they discovered that their ordeal wasn't over.

"They're coming back!" someone shouted.

99

As THEY HELPED Walker—who was a complete wreck with dozens of bite marks and tiny, dripping wounds—to his feet, most of them prepared to march into the sparsely wooded forest. They were just waiting for Duncan to give the order. It was because of him that they'd escaped the insects twice. Everyone knew it, though nobody talked about it.

"Shouldn't we be going?" Bob Mitchell asked. "They're getting close."

"What do you want us to do?" Thomas asked.

Duncan didn't have time to explain everything in the nuanced manner of a professor. He wanted to remind them that they had only seen *blaberus* scouts and that their job was to locate and cripple prey in such a way that it couldn't escape. In a short time he'd learned how they scouted as individual groups, how the scout groups converged when victims were located, how they quickly covered huge areas. He'd also learned that they jumped not only for self-preservation but as a means of propulsion, which is what they were trying to do now. Only a slight breeze pushed them back as they gained height. Those scuttling on the ground were making time, relentlessly closing in on the worried men. If only he knew where the colony was. Duncan realized that whatever decision he made could lead all of them to a horrible death. There would be no way they could run through an entire colony and survive. But he didn't bring any of this up. There wasn't time. They were waiting for an order. Any order.

"Don't run," he commanded. "We're gonna cut through the trees. Keep together. Single file."

"Do we know where we're going?" Someone asked.

"Doesn't matter as long as we're outta here," some-one else responded.

100

IT WAS IMPOSSIBLE to keep the group together. There were no discernible trails, so they made their way by avoiding obstacles and following the path of least resistance, stomping through deep grass and marching through forested areas. What maps they had they'd left with the ATVs. Murphy had brought a satellite phone but lost it along with their video and sound equipment. With no cell towers, their smartphones were useless.

The young guys from Broken Tree Productions took the lead and seemed unable to maintain a slow pace, impatient at waiting for the others catch up. They joked about how much slower the old guys were, meaning anyone not walking with them. They eagerly shared observations and remembrances of their recent adventures and especially their narrow escapes.

Behind them were Thomas's group, who stuck together, followed by Duncan, Boyd and Suarez, with Robinson and Walker shuffling in the rear. All of them easily outdistanced the insects to the point that after a half hour the fear that initially drove them gave way to a false sense of security that their troubles were behind them. Duncan refrained from bursting this bubble of blossoming confidence and let them enjoy what was becoming an amiable hike. It was early afternoon, the sun was high and the morning breeze had faded as they weaved their way into the unknown.

Duncan sent Boyd ahead to get Murphy and his men to take a break anywhere they could find shade. He'd been formulating a plan since they started, conferring with Boyd and Suarez about what to do if they needed to find shelter. He'd also kept an eye on Robinson and Walker and thought they could use the rest. But he was also troubled by how unprepared he was, how for the second time he was running from *blaberus* with no way to defend himself except keeping them at a distance. He'd grown complacent about the danger, so focused had he become on capturing specimens. When they left the village that morning, the only thing on his mind was installing the traps and reaping the rewards the next day, as if that were a foregone conclusion.

He gained no comfort from putting the insects behind him because he knew that there could be multiple colonies, each of them with their own scouts, somehow sensing prey. How did they do it? Did they simply send scouts out randomly? That didn't seem like a successful strategy to him. Did they have olfactory capabilities? It was clear that they were well organized when hunting, wasting no time in locating prey and disabling it. But how did they determine where to look? Was it in their DNA?

The young men had found a shaded area formed by a house-sized boulder with bamboo and brush growing out of it. The loamy soil was cool in the shade. There was plenty of room for each to find a soft spot to sit, with their backs against the huge rock. Thomas's group sat together as did Duncan, Boyd and Suarez. The video guys made sarcastic remarks as Walker and Robinson finally arrived. Robinson snarled but Walker grimaced as he lowered himself. Duncan noticed that he was rubbing his abdomen and pressing his hand against his throat. He seemed to be in pain. Was he injured? Duncan was going to ask but Murphy interrupted his train of thought.

"What's next, Dr. Duncan? Do you know where we are?"

"No idea."

Someone asked how far they'd traveled.

"About two miles, according to my pedometer," Andy Wilson said.

"That's not very far."

"What's next?"

101

"I THINK WE should keep moving until we're sure they're not following us," Murphy said.

They were debating their next move. Duncan didn't want to participate as he was tired of making decisions. He remembered what it was like in the flood, how uncomfortable it was to have others depending on him to save their lives. It didn't matter that most of them survived. What haunted him were the ones who didn't. When Murphy suggested they split up and the others ruminated, Duncan stood and faced the men. Splitting up would increase their vulnerability, he argued. The more of us there are, the better, he told them.

"I want to get back to the village," Murphy said, "and so far we have no plan on how to do that. Couldn't we just walk a few more miles that way?" He pointed toward the north. "That's kinda parallel to where we were, right. Then we could turn that way and head back. I mean, you don't think the bugs are everywhere, right? Wouldn't we be able to get around them that way?"

The suggestion made sense to many. Everyone wanted to get back to the village and safety, Duncan included. Murphy made a strong case. They weren't equipped to spend a night in the forest. They were running out of food and water. They were fatigued. The adrenaline was long gone. They needed to make it easy on themselves. Several looked at the compass apps on their phones.

"It only took an hour or so to get here, right."

"Something like that," Mitchell said encouragingly.

"Maybe it takes two-three hours to get back. Then we find the ATVs and we're safe."

Duncan couldn't disagree. There were no signs of *blaberus* and even though he felt there could be multiple colonies, he had no proof, not even enough to convince himself. Sensing that the others would follow him, Murphy asked the group for a vote. In the absence of a better plan, hands were raised. Some abstained but there were no votes in opposition. Now that they had a plan, Murphy took the lead, rising quickly and brushing himself off as others around him did the same, all but Jack Walker who, as he tried to raise himself, fell to the ground, groaning and slowly pounding his abdomen with his fist.

Joe Robinson, who was sitting next to him savoring his last cigarette, asked uneasily, "Are you OK, Jack?"

"The bastards are inside me," Walker said, gagging and pounding his ample stomach.

102

WALKER WAS IN a bad way and no one had a clue how to help him. Blood bubbled from the corner of his mouth, which was set in a grimace, his jaw locked, his bright red face shining with sweat. He lay outstretched on the ground with Robinson sitting beside him, his back propped against the stony outcrop. Gritting his teeth until it hurt, the middle-aged soundman struggled to stifle his groans, which periodically morphed into screams that unsettled everyone. Few could remain sitting as Walker became the center of attention.

Robinson pulled back reflexively as Walker's cheeks bulged only to deflate in an eruption of blood that leaked onto his beard and chest. For a moment he seemed relieved, as if a painful boil had been lanced. He spoke hesitantly, as if choking on his words but actually fighting against his body's gag reflex.

"They're killing me," he said, barely above a whisper, his lips pursed and drawn tight, his eyes filled with terror. "Do something. Goddamn, I can feel them." Walker choked out the words.

Without warning, he screamed again and again. Robinson held Walker's trembling hand and looked up at the others as if one of them knew what to do. Nearest were Duncan, Boyd, Nolan Thomas and his group. Carl Murphy and Bob Mitchell huddled at a distance, driven away by Walker's agony.

"They're in my throat," Walker stammered, squeezing Robinson's arm, gagging like a drunk with dry heaves. "Gimme a knife," he pleaded. "Kill me." And then he screamed, a routine that repeated itself for what seemed like an eternity.

As unnerving as it was to be near him, Walker's screams penetrated the sparsely forested surroundings, inciting howler monkeys to form a chorus, creating even more tension, especially among the younger men. Murphy led his group around the huge rock outcrop, which muffled the screams and allowed himself to be heard without raising his voice. Impatient to a fault, and seeing no other way out, he outlined his escape plan.

"So, we're just going to leave Jack to die?" Mitchell asked.

"There's nothing we can do for him here," Murphy said. "If we get back to the village, at least we can call for help, send a helicopter with medical people."

"But just leaving him like this?"

"Joe's with him," Murphy said. "He's not gonna go with us anyway. This is just us, the young guys. We got the best chance of anybody."

"I don't know," Andy Wilson said. "It's starting to get dark and we don't know where the bugs are. We could be walking right into them."

"It's not that far," Murphy said. "We're only a mile or two from the ATVs. Besides, we've got headlamps and if we can't make it out tonight we'll make a fire and get some rest and find our way back in the morning."

"Assuming we don't get eaten by the bugs," Mitchell said.

"You don't have to go if you're afraid," Murphy challenged. "You want to stay here and listen to Jack scream all night, then go ahead. I'm going with or without you. It's up to you."

"Are we just gonna sneak outta here?" Mitchell asked.

"No, I'll tell everybody. We got a better chance if we split up. It's the only way we'll find help."

103

THOMAS AND DUNCAN opposed Murphy's plan.

"There's safety in numbers," Duncan said.

"There's no guarantee you're gonna make it," Thomas said. "This is a big jungle. It's easy to get lost. Hell, I don't how to get back except by going the way we came and I'm sure not going to do that."

"Nobody's saying you can't stay. That's up to you. I'm just saying we're gonna go. You know, if we get through we'll send help. I just don't see what good it does for everyone to stay put. You guys don't have a better plan, do you?" Murphy asked.

Thomas and Duncan glanced at each other.

"I think we'll stay here for the night," Duncan said. "We can't just leave Jack behind, can we?"

"No," Murphy said.

"But that's what you're doing, right?" Thomas said. "And he's your guy."

"Look, we're not running away. We're going for help. Maybe if we can get back quick enough with medical people he can be saved. But what can we do by just standing here?"

Duncan sighed and ran his hand across his forehead.

There was no point in arguing. They were free to go, if they wanted. He felt that Boyd and Suarez would remain but wondered about Thomas's team.

"They'll do what I tell them," Thomas said assuredly. "I don't think it's a good idea to go charging off into the jungle."

"But if they're lucky…"

"Yeah, if they're lucky, they might get through and, who knows," Thomas said, his voice moderating into a whisper, "maybe that poor man won't die, however un-likely that seems right now."

104

LIGHT WAS FADING as Murphy, Wilson and Mitchell prepared to leave. To a man, they felt they were doing the
right thing and that when it was over they would be he-
roes. They would be the ones to send help so that the
others would survive. It was simply a matter of covering
as much territory as they could before nightfall, spend the
night in a safe place with a big fire and then to the village
in a quick march if they couldn't find the ATVs. It would
all be over by tomorrow. That was the plan.

Each carried whatever water and snack bars they
hadn't consumed and other items, such as heat reflective
emergency blankets, ponchos, lighters, pocket knives and
headlamps. Young, fit and energized by the object of their
mission, they would travel light and with no one to hold
them back they expected to cover a lot of ground before
making camp. As they left the others behind they were
even talking about reaching the ATVs before dark and
perhaps the village. The one thing they were all happy to
leave behind was the tortured, periodic screams of their
colleague.

Robinson did what he could to comfort the unfortunate Walker. He wiped driblets of blood from his mouth

and placed a stick between Walker's teeth to keep him from biting his tongue. Although he was much closer to Walker, his screaming didn't bother Robinson as much as it did Duncan, Thomas and the others who had slowly moved away until they were at the far end of the rocky outcrop. Even so, they would have appreciated earplugs.

After Murphy left, the remaining men second-guessed his motives and calculated his chance of success. He faced the same dilemma they did, namely, avoiding *blaberus*. They speculated whether the insects foraged nocturnally. Like Murphy, they planned to build a fire large enough to detect the approach of the insects and provide them with a weapon to defend themselves. Duncan and Boyd knew from experience that if the bugs got close to them, the only defense would be to run or climb a tree, though they weren't certain that climbing a tree would provide protection. Just because they had never seen the insects climb didn't mean they couldn't do it.

The first order of business was to collect firewood, which they did like Boy Scouts working on a merit badge. While they scrounged for sticks and branches, Antonio Suarez used his machete to chop longer pieces to size. Within a half-hour they had collected enough to last the night. While the younger men did this, Thomas and Duncan selected a site to build the fire, bearing in mind where they speculated the insects would most likely appear. This was based entirely on the direction from which they had run that day. They did not want to believe there were other colonies in the vicinity, nor did they want to believe the insects could cover as much territory as the men had traveled in less than a day. But they knew the symbolic, psychological and physical benefits of a roaring blaze in the middle of nowhere surrounded by the enveloping darkness. At bottom, it would help them feel safe even if they weren't.

Out of compassion, and because Walker could not be moved without raising his discomfort to an intolerable level, they built the fire close enough to him that he could benefit from the warmth. Although Boyd and Duncan carried emergency blankets, the others didn't. They brought them because of their previous experience in the rainforest. It's also why they carried extra batteries for their headlamps.

With the fire casting a semicircle of light away from the outcrop, and having established a watch schedule, they settled down, quiet, contemplative, exhausted, some holding their ears against Walker's periodic screams, all hoping that Murphy had made the right decision.

105

NIGHTFALL CAME SOONER and quicker than Murphy had hoped. As the forest darkened, he egged his colleagues on, another hundred yards, and then another, followed by another. Not too far. The destination was in sight, but it was fluid and until it became apparent they could go no further they stopped where they stood. Had they waited too long? The forest floor was dark even though the sky still held light. Finding firewood was their first priority, but the farther away from their campsite they had to scavenge, the more uncomfortable and isolated they felt. They'd thought that escaping Walker's screams would somehow free them from an intolerable burden, but they discovered new fears in the screeches of unknown animals and movement they could sense but not see. They began to understand why a person might whistle while walking through a graveyard.

Little was said until the fire was going and then they spoke nervously, though they tried to hide their nervousness. Each was frightened by what he didn't know, not the least of which was the location of the insects.

Murphy, the oldest and the boss, struggled to maintain his confidence. With every step he grew less certain they were doing the right thing.

"I, for one, don't mind saying that I'm scared shitless," Bob Mitchell admitted quietly.

Andy Wilson looked at Murphy for a reaction, but could not discern his expression in the fire's jumping light.

"You just gotta let go of that," Murphy said.

"Easy for you to say."

"You're scaring yourself and fear is infectious. Ask yourself, what are you afraid of?"

Mitchell sighed deeply.

"I don't know. Everything. Maybe we shoulda stayed, you know, what they said, safety in numbers. There's only three of us. What can we do?"

"What can we do about what?" Wilson asked.

"Anything. There's things around us and those monkeys or whatever, the screeching, don't you feel it?"

"Sounds like you're afraid of being afraid."

"Exactly. No, wait, that's not what I meant. I'm afraid of what's out there," Mitchell said, pointing into the darkness.

"There's only two things you can do," Murphy said. "Either go crazy with fear, in which case I will personally bash your head in, or you can just do what they do in combat, which is just assume you're a walking dead man and do your job."

"And what's that?"

"What's what?"

"My job."

"Build a bigger fire and try to get some sleep."

106

MITCHELL WAS AWAKENED from a fitful sleep when Andy Wilson whispered into his ear that it was his turn to stand watch. It was about three-thirty and everything around them was engulfed in warm, humid darkness.

"You might want to build up the fire," Wilson said as he tried to find a comfortable position to rest. "The wood around here burns fast."

The three had positioned themselves in a semi-circle near the fire. All around them was open space punctuated by palm trees and clumps of underbrush, which is where they found most of their firewood. Though awake, Mitchell struggled to focus. Whatever sleep he'd had wasn't enough as he stood, rolled his head around his shoulders and took deep breaths. If only they'd had coffee, he thought, as he rubbed his eyes. At least they had water. Dipping the end of his shirt into the bottle, he wiped it across his face, the cool dampness acting as a tonic to his drowsy mind.

"God, what I wouldn't do for an espresso," he mumbled as he stirred the fire with piece of petiole cut from a palm frond.

Most of the wood they'd collected had been burned

and the fire was no longer the blaze it had been when they'd set the watch schedule. The light had diminished to less than twenty feet, and much of that dim. Using his headlamp, Mitchell inched away from the fire and into the darkness. Although he wasn't completely comfortable with the cacophony of sound, he was no longer startled by the high-pitched shrieks emerging from the encircling darkness. What he was most concerned about now was to gather as much wood as he could, as quickly as he could without being injured. Even with his headlamp, he wasn't certain he'd be able to tell the difference between a snake and a piece of twisted wood. Somehow the fear of snakes had pushed the possibility of being swarmed by an army of insects from his mind. Using the palm to poke at the undergrowth, he cautiously grabbed handfuls of small sticks to add to the wood pile. He longed to find just one or two substantial pieces that would burn for an hour but found none. Worse, even as he added wood to the fire, he had to venture farther from the safety of the light until, facing the fire, a dark gap had opened between where the firelight ended and his lamplight began. The dark strip startled him, as if, venturing too far, it was now a barrier that he had to cross to return to safety. His mind was playing tricks—or was it playing games? To prove to himself that he was not afraid, Mitchell boldly stepped through the darkness and back to the fire where he dropped the sticks directly onto the flame, raising a cloud of sparks that rose like sprites in the hot draft.

It was clear to him that he should not have taken the third watch. His companions had already collected the easiest-to-find firewood, leaving him with all the risk. Goddamn it, he thought angrily, upset at himself and at them. Now he was wide awake. The hormones were flowing. He thought about waking them and telling them off. He was the youngest guy and they were taking advantage of him.

"Fuck it," he whispered. I'll know better next time, he told himself as he resumed his search for firewood. Marching forcefully across the dark gap, his shoes stomping into the dry soil like bricks, focused on his task, he didn't hear or see the three shadowy forms as they emerged behind him. What he heard as he bent toward a shrub, his back to the fire, were words in a language he didn't understand. Any chance he had to escape vanished as he turned around to see what was happening, his headlamp marking his position like a beacon. One of the men, holding a shotgun at his waist, stepped toward him.

The man shouted something, motioning with the barrel of his gun for Mitchell to approach him. For an instant he thought of running, but like a fantasy that resolves itself quickly, he could see where it led. He might get away or he might not. The land around him was relatively flat and it was dark. He could turn off his light and if their lights weren't strong enough they wouldn't be able to see him. And sound at night in the forest was hard to pinpoint. But what stopped him wasn't them but *blaberus*. What if he ran into the bugs? What then? He raised his hands and shuffled toward the campsite where the men stood alongside his two companions.

"What the fuck did you do, Andy?" Murphy whispered harshly.

107

HOWARD DUNCAN WATCHED his optimism crumble as Murphy and his companions were led into the small enclosure where he and his group were being held. Their large fire had kept away animals but had attracted several armed men who collected their belongings and led them through the darkness to a camp about an hour's march away. They were fortunate that Antonio Suarez could speak to them in Portuguese. It was through this dialogue that they learned they were being held hostage by a group of criminals who earned their keep through illegal lumbering, theft, extortion and the occasional homicide.

"They are proud of it," Suarez said when reporting to Duncan. "These are bad men."

"I figured that when they killed Walker."

According to Suarez, it was Walker's occasional screams that got the men's attention. The sound carried a long way. It was like nothing they'd ever heard and it made them curious. While they couldn't place it, one of them climbed a palm and saw a distant glow in the darkness. Even though they knew this part of the forest well, they would have found the men simply by following the screams and eventually the blazing fire. Only a couple of the Americans were awake at the time and they were frightened out of their wits when the criminals appeared suddenly from out of the darkness.

The capture was orderly. No resistance was offered. Duncan instructed everyone to follow their orders, which Suarez translated. Walker was the only one who didn't fall in line, because he couldn't. One of the three pointed at the ailing Walker prostrated on the ground, blood dripping ghoulishly from both sides of his mouth, and stammered frightfully, "*vampiro. Ele é um vampiro.*"

As the man stepped back, his companions joined him.

"He's no vampire," Suarez said in Portuguese. "He's sick. He's bleeding inside. He needs a doctor."

The three exchanged glances and laughed.

"He looks like a vampire," one of them said, leaning over Walker for a better look. "*Levantar-se velho.*"

"He can't get up," Suarez said, as the man poked Walker's abdomen, jumping back as the soundman screamed piteously.

The three men briefly conferred.

"Get your men to carry him," one of them commanded, as Suarez translated.

Suarez shook his head, looked helplessly toward Duncan and the others who stood nearby. Duncan was of two minds. With the three men clustered in front of Walker, could he, Boyd and the others overpower them? He scanned his colleague's faces; some looked barely awake, and some were frightened. He tried to whisper to Boyd but Robinson stepped in front of him to help Walker, whose tearful eyes betrayed his pain.

"Someone come help me," Robinson implored as he reached for Walker's shoulder. Walker burst into a screech so hideous that all the other noises of the forest seemed to disappear. One of the thieves held his hands to his ears. This was the moment, Duncan thought. We can take them. Looking back at Boyd and the others, though, he saw that they were so numbed by Walker's suffering that he could not get their attention even if he tried. But what happened next brought the hopelessness of their situation into brutal relief.

Wordlessly, one of the men pointed his shotgun at Walker. One of his companions shook his head.

"Don't waste the ammunition" he said quietly in Portuguese, gently pushing the man aside and, in one swift move, pulled out his machete and plunged it into Walker's chest, once, twice, three times. By the third plunge, all of the Americans were either staring at their feet or looking away.

There was no escape now.

108

SUAREZ TRIED TO remain within earshot of the kidnappers both on the march to their camp and after they were tied to posts in the enclosure. Duncan and Suarez were tied to one post while Thomas, Gruber and Thomas's assistants were tied to another. Robinson and Boyd were tied to a third. Murphy and his cohorts were tied to the fourth. The posts, which supported a hastily built roof covered with palm leaves, were buried in the sandy soil about ten feet apart. Almost immediately, they realized the posts were not buried deeply and wobbled when pressed. It was obviously a temporary encampment, though the men had been there long enough to have set up a small kitchen outfitted with a wood-burning camp stove. There was also a generator and chain saws. The air was heavy with the smell of burned lumber, the ground an amalgam of ash and soil.

While the captives talked quietly, Boyd counted ten captors. The leader appeared to be the man who had killed Walker. Shortly after Murphy's group had arrived, the kidnappers shared a breakfast of coffee, tortillas and beans.

"Wonder if they'll feed us?" Gruber said.

"It does smell appetizing, doesn't it," Thomas said.

"I don't know about y'all but I'm starving," Mitchell said, rubbing his abdomen.

Robinson glared at the young producer and spat.

"What's your problem?"

"You, all of you," Robinson growled. "Jack's dead and you're worried about what you're gonna eat. Show some respect for chrissakes."

Murphy and his two companions clammed up, whispering amongst themselves. Duncan sighed, wondering if he should say something. The last thing he wanted to see was a falling out among hostages. They had to work together. Their survival depended on it, though he had no idea what their captors' intentions were nor any plausible plan of escape.

"There's nothing we could have done about it," Duncan said, finally. "It's not gonna help to focus on what's been done. We have to think about how we're gonna get out of this."

Robinson shrugged and Murphy apologized to Robinson. Duncan leaned toward Suarez. He'd noticed that the kidnappers were ignoring them. When he mentioned this to Suarez, Robinson, who faced the inside of the enclosure, quipped, "That's because they're gonna kill us."

"Shut up with that!" Mitchell scolded. "What's it matter to them what we say? We're tied up in the middle of nowhere and they got guns. Why would they care what we talk about?"

"Stop the arguing," Thomas said. "They don't speak English. Let's conserve our energy and focus on solutions. Howard, what's your guy hearing?"

109

Suarez overheard much of what the gang's leader told his men, relaying what he heard to Duncan. Others in the group were frustrated that Duncan kept what he was told to himself, but he explained later that he didn't want the kidnappers to think that they were listening.

"The leader said they need to decide what to do with us," Suarez whispered. "He said there's too many of us and the fat guy said they should kill all of us."

Duncan listened intently but refrained from asking questions. He could feel his blood pressure rise as he wondered whether the leader had control of his men. What if one of them took it upon himself to start killing? Who would stop him?

"The boss says no. He said something about ransoming us. One of them asked when they were going to get their share of our stuff. That guy said they should vote on what to do with us."

Duncan leaned his head against the post. "Fuck," he muttered. Are these guys pirates or what? Voting was a bad idea, he thought.

"The leader says he needs to think about it," Suarez said. "The fat guy said with so many of us, the policía will come and the boss said they'd come whether we're dead or alive. He said, these gringos are Americans. Now they're all talking at once and, wait, that's it. The boss said to shut up."

Duncan, who was facing the interior of the enclosure stared at his shoes, expecting to hear more from Suarez.

"That's it," Suarez said, "they just dumped our stuff on the ground. They look pretty happy now."

Duncan craned his neck to watch as the leader let his men choose one item in turn until everything had been claimed.

"It's like Christmas," Duncan said.

Duncan finally reported what the kidnappers had discussed. They talked about killing some of us, he told them, and watched for their reaction. Those who had been facing him stiffened while those who had been looking elsewhere suddenly turned to face him.

"Kill us?" Murphy said. "I don't mind being ransomed, but why kill us? Aren't we worth more alive than dead?"

"Some of them think there's too many of us," Duncan said.

"Are they gonna do it?" Jason Gruber asked.

"The leader said he'd think about it. Right, Antonio?"

"Yes," Suarez said, nodding.

"So, what are we going to do?" Robinson asked. "Are we just gonna sit here and wait for them to kill us?"

The discussion grew heated as their vulnerability began to sink in.

"I don't know about you guys, but I'm not going down without a fight," Robinson said boldly. "We could knock this goddamn thing down in no time."

"And then what?" Boyd asked. "Our hands are still tied and they took our knives."

"This is silly," Thomas said. "They've got guns and machetes. What do we have? It would be suicide to resist. No, we won't beat them that way."

"So, how do we beat them?" Robinson asked huffily.

"Out think them, that's how."

"And how we gonna do that?"

"We should be prepared to argue the point," Thomas said. "The leader is smart enough to understand the situation and maybe, if they do decide to kill us, we can talk him out of it."

"They're not gonna debate us," Robinson said. "These guys are killers. You saw what they did to Jack. There were only three of them then. Now there's a lot more. We're fucked if you think we can talk them out of anything."

"So, we're fucked," Gruber said. "You got a better idea, I mean besides knocking down this palapa, or whatever it is?"

Robinson looked for allies among the others but nobody stepped up.

"Maybe we wait until dark. Maybe we spend the day trying to work ourselves out of these ropes. Then we do something."

"Like what?" Boyd asked.

"Like run like hell, for one thing."

"In the dark, in the jungle. How far do you think we'd get?" Duncan asked.

"OK, OK, I don't have it figured out. You guys got a better idea?" Robinson said, whispering to those near him, "Damn, what I wouldn't do for a cigarette right now."

"Well, in that case, it's either fight or flight," Thomas said. "I don't like the odds either way but, depending on how things go tonight, maybe our best chance is to attack them. There's plenty of wood laying around. We could use it like clubs."

"Clubs against shotguns?" Mitchell said. "Seriously?"

"Look, some of us might die no matter what we do," Duncan said. "If we don't do something then we're leaving our fate in the hands of murderers. I don't like the idea of attacking them, but I don't like the idea of being executed either. I think Joe's right. We gotta fight any way we can."

"And we can't take prisoners," Robinson said defiantly. "No prisoners."

WHILE SOME KEPT their eyes on their captors, others worked on loosening their bindings, most of which incorporated constrictor knots, which made it all the more difficult to disentangle the rough sisal rope. Although the rope chafed their wrists, they worked at it through the afternoon, wriggling their hands to stretch it. It was a frustrating and tedious process, which they pursued for five or ten minutes at a time, resting to relieve their fatigue and to avoid drawing their captors' attention.

Boyd and Suarez were the first to free themselves, but they couldn't help the others without alerting the kidnappers, so they did what they could to make it look like they were still bound. Even as they discussed their escape plan, their captors took little notice, satisfied that they posed little risk. They could see them clearly. If they tried anything, their shotguns would do the talking.

As the discussion continued, and as others finally loosened their bonds, they reevaluated their strategy. It was one thing for men who are bound to boost their spirits by visions of overcoming their opponents; it was quite another to set it in motion when they were in a position to do so. It was the difference between the fantasy of taking action and the reality of doing it. As surely as they were in a position to put their plan into action, they began to have doubts. It was not long before they were taking sides.

Robinson was adamant that their best chance at freedom was to overcome their captors, even if it meant that some might die.

"Might die?" Murphy said dubiously. "They got shotguns."

"Not all of them," Robinson said.

"And what about their machetes?" Wilson said. "What do we got?"

"There's scrap lumber everywhere," Robinson said.

"I see a lot of shipping crates," Murphy said.

"Let's not get into an argument," Duncan said. "We can't do anything as long as there's daylight."

"You know, they got a generator," Boyd said. "They got lights strung across the camp."

"Still, if we do something it's better to do it after dark," Duncan said.

"We can attack when they're asleep," Robinson said. "Sure, a couple of them might be on watch but, you know, people fall asleep all the time on watch."

"So, you think they're smart enough to capture us but dumb enough to let us attack them in their sleep, is that it?" Murphy said.

"What else can we do?" Robinson said. "I'll go back to what the doc said before, we gotta fight or die. They're not gonna keep us alive."

Everyone looked at Duncan for a response.

"I don't know what to do," he said.

Robinson eyed Duncan disappointedly and spat bitterly.

"How can you say that? You were all in favor of it before," Robinson said angrily.

"People can change their minds," Nolan Thomas said.

"So, you all just want to wait here and die, is that it? Why the fuck did we bother to untie ourselves, tell me that?"

"So we could have options," Duncan said.

"What options? Running into the jungle at night? How far do you think we'll get before they hunt us down?"

"We could split up," Gruber said. "They can't hunt all of us."

"And then what? You don't even know where you are. You got no food, You got no water. You got nothin'. No, I say we wait until morning, wait for our chance and then bash their heads in or die trying."

The others ruminated. Each had to decide whether he could kill a man.

"I've never been in a fight, I mean, a real fight," Wilson said timidly.

Several of the others admitted the same.

Robinson saw that there was little enthusiasm for his plan. He smiled curtly and lowered his chin to his chest. Duncan saw that the conversation was going nowhere.

"OK, let's settle down here. We don't want to draw their attention or they're gonna come over here and see that our hands are free, that'd be the end of it."

By late afternoon, with nothing resolved, they'd become introspective. Few had faced such a decision, and those that had—Duncan, Boyd, Suarez and Robinson—were divided as well. Only Robinson was adamant, but even he knew the odds were stacked against them. Duncan's mind raced between the two extremes. He was certain he would fight if he had to, but as a choice he preferred somehow escaping into the forest, even if it meant being lost. But would that just be delaying the inevitable? Could they negotiate? No, if they wanted to negotiate, they would already have done it. Still, he didn't know what the kidnappers wanted to do. For all he knew, they were either seeking a ransom, or planning their execution. Or a dozen other things.

Goddamn, he thought. *If only I knew whether they were planning to kill us. That would settle things.*

With no hope, there would be nothing to lose.

Suarez nudged Duncan out of his internal monologue. Sitting alongside each other, he nodded toward a shadowy area between where they were being held and where the camp cook was preparing their supper of beans and rice.

"You think they're gonna feed us?" Duncan asked quietly. "It smells good."

"No, no," Suarez whispered. "On the ground, look."

Duncan wished he could rub his eyes as his eyes were slow to focus. Blinking didn't help.

"What're you seeing?"

"Bugs. Can't you see them?"

Duncan shook his head. Although he hadn't thought it possible, they were now in bigger trouble than he'd imagined.

111

DUNCAN TOOK SUAREZ'S word for what he'd seen and quietly announced it to the others. The response was what one would expect if a snake had been tossed into their midst. They began to move, shifting their weight nervously, staring at the shadowy ground in front of them, as if the insects were already there.

"Don't be obvious," Duncan cautioned. "They're over there somewhere. Don't stare. They'll think something's up. Antonio saw them. They're scouts. No telling where the colony is."

"What do we do now?" someone asked.

"Don't panic. We've got time."

"But what should we do?" Murphy asked anxiously.

"Well, you can try climbing a tree," Boyd said.

"They don't climb trees?"

"We don't know," Duncan said.

"That's just one thing," Boyd said.

"How about we run like hell, like yesterday?"

As darkness swallowed the camp, the generator coughed into operation, powering several strings of bare light bulbs. Some of the bulbs were dead and others were low-wattage, with most of the light concentrated where the kidnappers congregated on makeshift benches near the cook stove. With no light of its own, the enclosure and captives were barely illuminated, which was fine with Duncan and the others. Duncan counted heads. How could eleven men escape if they didn't run before the rest of the scouts, much less the colony, arrived? Given what he'd learned about *blaberus*, there was little doubt that their strategy was to surround their prey before striking, by which time escape was unlikely. And if they ran, could they avoid running into the colony?

He didn't have to listen closely to hear the incipient panic in their voices. As uncertain as they were about how to deal with their captors, it paled in comparison to the fear they had of the insects. They'd all seen what the little killers could do. They were all experts in fear. Unfortunately, fear was getting the better of several, who instinctively stood and tossed their bindings aside.

"What are you doing!" Duncan said urgently but without raising his voice.

"I'm getting outta here," Murphy said, facing Duncan.

"Me, too," one of Thomas's assistants said, looking down at Thomas. "Sorry, boss, but I didn't sign up for this."

"Neither did I," Andy Wilson agreed.

"C'mon," Boyd chided, "we've already been through this. There's nowhere to run. You don't know where the bugs are. You run into them and it's all over. Think about it."

"And please sit down while you're thinking. You're endangering the rest of us," Thomas said.

The three men were agitated as they sat, as if their coach had taken them out of a big game.

"What's next?" Wilson asked.

112

It started with the stamping of feet. The captors were eating their beans and rice when one of them started stepping on what looked like cockroaches scuttling across the dusty, well-trodden soil. Standing, holding his bowl in one hand and staring at the ground beneath him, he did a kind of jig that at first amused his fellows. Then another man, sitting alongside the first, started stamping his feet while the others continued to eat and watch. But it wasn't long before everyone was standing, some of them moving away from where they'd been sitting and others joining in the dance in the dimly lit camp.

It didn't take long for the hostages to realize what was going on. As one or two stood, the others quickly joined them, most tossing their bindings to the ground. There was little time to make decisions. Although it was difficult to make out details, Duncan saw that the insects were casting a wide net as the scouts approached the camp. What he couldn't see because they were concealed by darkness, was what was going on behind them. That became apparent when several of the hostage takers started to move away from the others who were having a difficult time fighting off the increasing number of bugs. It was all well and good as long as the insects were on the ground where they could be stomped, but when they started jumping and flying at them like bats they lost all cohesion, with some running and others grabbing boards and pans, which they swung wildly at the attackers. It didn't help that they were largely shirtless as bugs embedded themselves in their flesh, raising tiny geysers of blood.

"Listen up," Duncan said, "it's every man for himself. Run if you want to, climb a tree, whatever."

The darkness under the palm roof hid the fear on their faces but couldn't disguise the terror in their voices.

"I'm gonna run," Murphy said, "anyone with me?"

Mitchell and Wilson lined up alongside him.

"Like yesterday, we run like hell," he told them. "Nobody stops for anything. Just keep running."

"What are you gonna do?" Mitchell asked Duncan, his heart racing.

Duncan struggled to assess the situation. As dark as it was, he could not tell for certain whether they were surrounded or whether the bugs were conducting a frontal assault. Whatever anyone did, the outcome would be no better than flipping a coin. There was no way to know whether they would be running into or away from the bugs. All he had to go on was what he could see and hear from their captors, who were now either running in circles through the camp, waving boards at the bugs, or waging personal battles against insects that were attacking their eyes, crawling up their legs and chopping at their lips and other soft parts. The noise of the rainforest night was overwhelmed by the screams of the terrified victims.

"Boss, boss," Cody Boyd shouted, pointing at the crates and equipment cases they'd seen earlier. "I'm gonna get under one of those."

"What're you talking about?" Murphy asked frantically.

"Those boxes over there. We can hide under them."

"Are you crazy? The bugs'll get inside."

"And running isn't crazy?"

Duncan was no longer thinking about the others as
he took several deep breaths. There was no time to think.
The bugs were taking over the camp and it was only a
matter of minutes before they would overrun the enclosure. But before he could take his first step, Suarez zipped
past him like a wraith and in seconds was shimmying up a
tall açai palm. As if Suarez had signaled the start of a race,
the others quickly dispersed. Murphy and his group, including one of Thomas's assistants, disappeared into the
darkness. Thomas, Gruber and the remaining assistant,
Robinson, Duncan and Boyd moved quickly toward the
crates and boxes. Even in the lousy light it was clear that
some of them had too many gaps to offer protection.
Rummaging desperately through the potential sanctuar-
ies, they had little time to perform inspections as the bugs
were mere yards away.

Although it had been his idea to hide under the boxes, Boyd thought better of it when it became apparent
that most of the crates were unusable and only the equipment boxes offered protection. Without a word, he bolted to the nearest açai and climbed it like a frightened cat.
The thin trunk swayed under his weight as he clutched
the lower part of the tree's crown, twenty-feet from the
ground. Afraid that moving would cause him to lose his
grip, he stared down at the others as they ran out of time
and the bugs filled the air with the hair-raising whirring
of their wings.

Boyd and Suarez, no more than thirty feet apart, battling fatigue and sleepiness, watched and listened in silence as beneath them hostages and hostage takers alike fought for their lives against waves of advancing insects. For what seemed like hours, they were tortured by the excruciating screams radiating throughout the camp and beyond it. Boyd felt relieved when the noisy generator finally died and the camp was engulfed in total darkness. Although the screams now seemed louder and more tortured, he could no longer see the squirming bodies on the ground. He wanted to cover his ears but there was no way he would let go of the tree and the hope that the bugs weren't climbers.

113

SEVERAL HOURS BEFORE sunrise the screams had mostly stopped, replaced by low, painful moans and the rainforest's normal ensemble of insects and monkeys. As daylight slowly returned, Boyd and Suarez, who prayed through the night, studied the ground intently, looking for insects. Boyd feared that the bugs would remain for days as they consumed their victims and that he would eventually fall out of the tree from lack of sleep. Several fidgeting bodies lay scattered about, but none of them were covered with feasting insects. He wondered how many of his companions had survived and whether Duncan had made it through the night. At the same time he feared the answer. Focusing on what he would do next, he slowly descended from his perch, until about half-way down his fatigued hands lost their grip and he slid the remaining distance to the ground where he nearly fell on one of the captors, whose empty, bloody eye sockets stared at him.

Suarez followed quickly as both of them stood on a bench and surveyed the campsite.

"They're gone," Boyd said quietly. "They just killed these guys and moved on. What the fuck is that about?"

Rather than try to make sense of the insects' behavior, he anxiously approached the boxes and crates where the others had taken refuge. In the back of his mind was the fear that thousands of the bugs were hiding under the containers waiting to launch themselves at him. Almost as bad was the prospect that he would find nothing but bodies under the boxes. He was exhausted and fear was a ferocious opponent.

"You can come out now," he stammered.

114

Duncan was the first to emerge from his stronghold, a rectangular wooden box that originally held tools. It was sturdy and built of heavy plywood. He was grateful that it didn't have a knot hole.

"My God," Duncan said as he pushed himself to his feet. "You're alive."

"So are you," Boyd said, embracing his boss.

Boyd explained that he and Suarez had spent the night in trees. As they talked, others began to emerge from their fortresses. Robinson, Gruber and Thomas' assistant all emerged, tired, hungry and ecstatic about surviving the night.

"Where's Dr. Thomas?" Gruber asked, after getting his bearings.

"I don't know," the assistant said. "Did he run?"

"Dr. Thomas, you can get out now. The insects are gone," Gruber said loudly.

A low groaning came from a longish, narrow crate. Afraid of what they would find, they gently lifted it, revealing Thomas's ravaged body.

"God," Gruber cried, turning away to vomit.

It was fortunate Thomas couldn't see the men as

they leaned over his bloody body, trying to determine the extent of his injuries. His face was an oozing mess. Strands of flesh dangled from his cheeks, and his mouth looked like a macabre Halloween mask where the insects had chopped away enough flesh to reveal portions of his teeth, which were clenched tightly. The fear was that the bugs didn't stop there and that, like Walker, Thomas was undergoing a slow, excruciating death.

At the same time, Duncan took Boyd aside.

"Cody, we can't stay here. I'm surprised the colony isn't here yet. But that's our good fortune. Let's not waste it. See about gathering supplies, water, food, whatever. Make it quick."

Thomas wasn't the only one suffering. Some of the hostage-takers were enduring their own agonizing deaths. Of the kidnappers, only four remained in the camp, the others having fled into the forest like Murphy and his crew. Suarez separated himself from the group gathered around Thomas and, having picked up a machete, approached each of the victims. All clutched at their abdomens as if they'd been slammed with a wrecking ball, their legs folded in a fetal position. Two of them had been blinded, what remained of their shorts saturated in blood, their bodies covered with lacerations. There was little evidence that the insects had done any feeding. The scouts had brought down their quarry and it was up to the colony to digest them.

Standing over the leader, whose one eye stared at him in a fixed gaze, Suarez peered down at him sympathetically, backing away as the man reached toward him with a bloody arm.

"*Me mate,*" he whispered hoarsely. "*Me mate, por favor.*"

Suarez shook his head as Boyd joined him.

"What's he saying?"

"He wants me to kill him."

The young American spat.

"Doesn't matter to me what you do," Boyd said bitterly. "This is the one who killed Walker, right?"

"Yes."

"Let him suffer."

"I can't," Suarez said.

"Can't what?"

"I can't kill him."

"Why not?"

"I feel guilty about what I did to your friend in the flood. I thought I was doing the right thing, but then I was arrested and I've had time to think about it."

"Nobody's gonna care."

"Someone will talk about it," Suarez said solemnly. "That's how I got into trouble. Besides, I broke God's law. God is the judge, not me."

Boyd shrugged and asked Suarez to help him scavenge supplies. The campsite was a mess. Benches were overturned and out of place. The stove and pots were scattered on the ground along with tools and utensils.

"What are we looking for?" Suarez asked as he slowly moved away from the groaning leader.

"Water, food, weapons."

"You think the others will come back?"

"Don't know, but we need to get out of here ASAP."

"ASAP?" Suarez said.

"Right away. The main colony has to be close by. Grab what you can. We need to get outta here pronto."

Boyd took the kidnapper's shotgun, which was loaded, and he and Suarez grabbed several machetes, water bottles and a few snack bars that the thieves had taken from them. While they did this, the others built a stretch-er using a plastic tarp and several boards, two long ones around which they wrapped the tarp and a pair of shorter boards that they wedged between the two long boards so that the stretcher would maintain its shape while carrying Thomas.

While idly watching the men assemble the stretcher, Duncan thought he saw something move under a nearby crate. It was a rough-hewn wood case with large gaps between slats. Moving closer, bending over for a better look, he was startled to see several *blaberus* feasting on what remained of a small lizard. With a sudden rush of antic-ipation, he slowly backed away, afraid that his movement would cause the bugs to scatter. Excited by this opportu-nity to achieve his goal of capturing specimens, he moved about the wreckage hunting for a container to hold them.

"Cody, Cody," he whispered breathlessly, "have you seen any canisters?"

"What?"

Duncan put his hand on Boyd's shoulder and took a deep breath.

"There are live *blaberus* under that crate," he said, pointing. "I need something to hold 'em."

Boyd gave him an incredulous look.

"Shouldn't we be getting out of here?"

"Of course, of course, and we will. But this might be my only chance to get specimens and I'm not gonna let it go. Just tell me, have you seen anything I can use?"

Boyd puffed out his cheeks with air and slowly ex-haled.

"I saw some glass jars over there, by the stove."

Duncan stepped quickly to the overturned stove.

"I don't see them," he said, scanning the ground madly.

"To your right, by that sack of beans."

Rummaging through several jars, some of them broken, he lifted a one-liter bottle with a wide mouth. Inside was a dark red powder. The cover was intact but rusting and removing it took all his strength. Elated when it came off, he sniffed the powder and dumped it on the ground. Using his sweaty bandana, he removed the remaining powder that coated the interior.

"Do you have any water to rinse this out?" he asked Boyd.

"How much you need?"

"Just a half-cup. You can take it out of my share. It smells like, ah, what is that, ah, not chili powder but hotter, ah, like cayenne pepper."

Boyd shook his head but poured a small amount of water into the jar, which Duncan swished around and poured out.

Like a man possessed, he stepped quickly to the crate, relieved to see that the insects were still inside. He knew that he had one shot to capture as many of the creatures as he could and that they would not be cooperative and would likely immediately attack his bare hands. But there weren't any gloves and even if there were he felt rushed and couldn't afford any delay.

"Cody, Cody, come here."

Boyd, whose focus was on gathering supplies and getting away from the campsite, dutifully approached his boss, holding a heavily laden day pack.

"Help me, OK. It'll only take a minute. I'm gonna lift the box and we need to grab as many of these guys as we can and dump 'em into the jar."

Sighing, Boyd knew it was pointless to resist. That would only cause further delay. Positioning themselves on either side of the box, Duncan reached under one side and deftly raised it so that it came to a rest on its opposite side. The insects did not react until both of the scientists had each grabbed two of the insects and without injury dropped them into the jar. All four of them immediately scratched at the glass sides but gained no purchase. As Duncan screwed the top on, the remaining insects scuttled into nearby debris. Duncan stood up triumphantly, holding the jar eye high, smiling with admiration.

"We did it, Cody! We did it."

Boyd smiled faintly.

The men who had assembled the stretcher, watched Duncan with growing impatience. Thomas lay on the blue tarp, issuing muffled moans. They'd done what they could to clean him up but other than patting his mouth with a wet bandana, there was little they could do to relieve his discomfort.

"We need to get going," Robinson said heatedly. "We've been ready to go for five minutes."

"You guys go ahead, I'll catch up. Antonio, Cody, you go too. I just need to find something to carry this jar with."

With Gruber and Thomas's assistant carrying the stretcher, Robinson, Boyd and Suarez made their way from the campsite in the general direction from which they thought they had come. They could not be certain they were retracing their steps since the last mile or two had occurred at night. Meanwhile, Duncan hurriedly scavenged the campsite for a pack to carry the specimen jar, which he'd set on a small wood table used by the camp cook. Having pulled a khaki green daypack from the debris near where the gang's leader lay groaning, he was adjusting the straps when he felt something grab his ankle. Instinctively, he tried to pull his foot free.

"*Agua,*" the dying man stammered hoarsely. "*Agua, por favor.*"

Duncan looked down at the disfigured face, one eye replaced by a bloody crater.

"You want water, is that it," Duncan said softly, as if talking to himself.

Duncan nodded sympathetically at the dying bandit, no longer a threat, and in a single muscular tug, yanked his foot free. Another man lay groaning nearby but he ignored him as he searched for and found several bottles of water. Two of them he stuffed into his pockets and the third he brought to the suffering leader. Keeping his feet beyond the man's reach, he leaned over and brought the bottle to the man's lips and held it securely so that the he could take several sips. He then placed the bottle in the man's hand.

"*Me mate*," the man groaned. "*Me mate, por favor*," he said, letting go of the bottle.

The man repeated his request multiple times, his voice cracking, blood dripping down his chin.

"*Eles estão me matando*."

Duncan wished Suarez was there to translate, but he understood that the man wanted to die. Yesterday, when he posed a threat, Duncan thought he would have granted his request but he no longer felt anger toward him. The man was paying the price for his crimes. Duncan assumed insects were mutilating his esophagus and that it was only a matter of time before he would be dead. Until that happened, he would experience excruciating pain. With one eye ravaged and his cheeks deeply pitted with wounds, he didn't look human.

"Goddamn, you're a mess," Duncan whispered, "but I gotta get going."

As he moved toward the specimen jar, Duncan wondered why he spoke to a man who couldn't understand what he was saying. As he carefully grasped the jar he realized he'd neglected to punch air holes in the lid. It took a minute, but he found a screw driver and began the delicate task of poking holes without breaking the lid or the jar. or injuring the specimens. It took longer than he'd expected and he worried that if he didn't leave soon he might not find the others.

Satisfied that the insects would have plenty of air, he

wrapped the jar in a dirty towel that he pulled from the camp's wreckage and used it to line the interior of the backpack, which he carried on his shoulder. The man screamed as Duncan stepped around his former captor, his hands pounding his abdomen, just as Walker had done.

"*Me mate,*" he screamed several times.

Duncan wasn't sure why he stopped. The scream was primal and raised the hairs on the back of his neck. He knew the man wanted to die and there were several machetes laying about in the dirt. The man reached out with his arm in a sweeping motion, but Duncan was out of reach. Though he'd never killed a man, he picked up one of the machetes by its worn wood handle and inched toward the leader. He wondered how many people the man had killed during his lifetime. Duncan knew of at least one.

Whether he did it in retaliation for his brutal killing of Walker or to relieve the man's suffering, Duncan surprised himself as he raised the blade and plunged it into the leader's chest. Blood sprayed into the air, some of it getting on Duncan's shirt and shorts as he backed away in surprise.

Acutely aware that the insect colony could be nearby, he left the camp at a rapid pace hoping to make up for lost time, afraid that he wouldn't be able to find his colleagues.

116

As it turned out, they followed their own footsteps back to the large rocky outcrop where they'd camped and where Walker had been killed. It had taken them less than two hours to reach the place, where they stopped to rest. It was impossible to ignore Walker's blackening, stinking body. The landscape was flat, with low-growing fields of sparse grasses and brush. For as far as they could see, the sun drenched the ground, interrupted only by the shade of scattered açaí palms.

They knew by the position of the sun that it was mid-morning and that they would be able to retrace their steps back to the village if *blaberus* didn't get in their way. For the first time in several days they felt safe. They were grateful that Boyd had gathered a plentiful supply of water bottles, and wished there were more snack bars to go around but stopping as they did, sitting on the dry, dusty earth, they slowly realized how exhausted they were, having gotten little if any sleep the past two days. Robinson nodded off, unable to resist his weariness.

While Gruber and his colleague joked about the fabulous meals they would eat when they returned to civilization, Boyd climbed the rock to look for Duncan.

He'd thought his boss would have caught up with them shortly after they left and he was worried that something had happened to him. He was relieved when he saw him walking briskly down the trail. Boyd waved his arms and shouted. Duncan waved back and broke into a jog.

They hugged when they met.

"Is that blood?" Boyd said.

"Blood? Where?"

"On your shirt."

Looking down at his wet, unbuttoned shirt, Duncan shrugged, carefully set his backpack aside and sat next to the now snoring Robinson.

"He's got the right idea," Boyd said as he and Suarez sat next to Duncan. "I'm so tired."

"I hear that," Gruber said. Boyd reached over Duncan so he and Gruber could give each other a high five.

Starting with Boyd, an infectious yawn flowed through the group. It would be so easy to fall asleep, he thought.

"You know, boss," he said sleepily, "if I close my eyes I'll be out like a light."

Duncan wanted to sleep, too. Sitting on the soft earth, his back against the cool rock, he struggled to stay awake. He knew that they weren't out of danger. *Blaberus* could be anywhere, but exhaustion was slowly overcoming his fear. Perhaps a cat nap wouldn't be a bad idea. Just long enough to restore the energy that he'd lost. Then, if they encountered trouble, they'd have the strength to escape. Slowly, his mind surrendered to drowsiness. What he wouldn't give for a hot shower and a bed. But there was something wrong. Someone was shouting. Instantly, he sat up.

"Do you hear that?" he said, poking Boyd who was already asleep.

"I do," Suarez said.

The two rose, moving past the rock into the open field where the sound was more distinct. Waving his arms, Duncan shouted, "We're over here. Over here," while Suarez scampered up the rock and peered into the distance.

"I see them," he said, waving his arms excitedly. "I think they see me."

"Who is it, can you tell?"

"I think it's Mister Carl and the army or police, I can't tell."

"Everybody, get up," Duncan shouted. "We're saved."

117

ONCE AGAIN, INSECTS led the news as media swarmed near the entrance to the Manaus Air Force Base where two AS-350 helicopters brought most of the survivors. Nolan Thomas, accompanied by Jason Gruber, was flown by medical chopper directly to a private hospital in the city where he was stabilized. Joined later by Thomas's remaining assistants, the men were subsequently flown by private jet to Texas.

While Carl Murphy and his crew gave interviews outside the military base, Howard Duncan, Cody Boyd and Antonio Suarez, dirty, their clothes tattered, slipped out quietly via taxi, returning to their hotel where they spent the night following showers and dinner at the hotel's restaurant. While Duncan and Boyd had fresh clothing in their suitcases, Suarez had only his shorts. All of their wallets, cards and phones had been taken by the kidnappers and Duncan didn't want to think about the machinations it would take to have everything restored. He was grateful that he'd left his passport and laptop at the hotel. At least he had identification.

Boyd had many questions, ranging from what would happen to the gear they left at the village to how they would get home. Though Suarez was too timid to bring it up, Duncan wondered how he would pay him for his services. He felt that whatever the amount, it wouldn't be enough. How long would it take to get a new credit card sent to Manaus?

"What about your girlfriend?" Boyd suggested.

"Who, Maggie? She's not my girlfriend."

"OK, a friend. I'm sure she'd help."

Getting her number from his laptop, he used the room phone to make a collect call. He hoped she would pick up even though the number wouldn't be familiar. He was surprised that she answered on the third ring.

"Howard, is that you?" she said, excitedly.

"How'd you know it was me?"

"The country code, of course. Who else do I know in Brazil?"

"It's great to hear your voice," he said.

"And yours," she said. "Your expedition is all over the news."

"Really? I haven't talked to anyone."

"Oh, it's not about you. It seems there was this reality crew involved. The story's about them."

Duncan laughed. After answering some of her questions, which she fired off one after another as if reading from a script, he described his situation.

"You need money, don't you, poor thing? No worry, I'll have George take care of it. How much do you need? Will five thousand do? I can send more but, you know, the larger the sum the more scrutiny."

"Five thousand would be great. I'll be able to pay Antonio. You can't know how badly I want to get out of here."

After a brief conversation with George Hamel, Duncan learned that the maximum cash transfer allowed was two thousand nine hundred ninety nine dollars. He would be able to pick it up in a matter of hours from a location near the hotel. He thanked Hamel profusely, after which Cross came on the line.

"You know, you have to come visit me in Chicago when you get back to the states."

"Oh, I will definitely come to Chicago."

"Love and kisses," she said as the call ended.

Duncan felt that he was back in control. He'd showered, ate as much as he wanted, had a good night's sleep, the specimens were doing well in the jar and money was on the way. But as he thought about it, a problem cropped up that threatened to annihilate his plans.

"Goddamnit," he mumbled.

"What is it?" Boyd asked.

"How are we gonna get the bugs through customs?"

"Hmmm. I hadn't thought about that."

"Neither did I, but all of a sudden that's a big deal. It's a deal killer. They're not gonna let these things go through."

"Can we hide 'em?"

"How? No way. Shit."

Duncan's joy suddenly turned dark. His entire expedition was about capturing specimens, but how did he overlook this part of it? He couldn't explain it. Perhaps it was because of all the hurdles they had to jump to even get the expedition off the ground. The court case with Suarez, the difficulty finding equipment and transportation. The rush to beat Nolan Thomas into the field. Normally, the specimens he collected were dead and could be

JOHN KOLOEN

shipped out of the country routinely. But live insects that
might be considered invasive would never be permitted.
There had to be another way.

By noon he had the money in his hand and gave half
of it to Suarez, who at first refused most of it but relented
when Duncan told him that if he didn't take it he would
give it to the maid. Suarez hugged Duncan like a favorite
uncle, mentioned that he would use the money to start a
guide business, and left the hotel with a spring in his step
and more money than he had ever seen in his pocket.

"Well, no matter what happens, at least Antonio is
happy. I wish I could've given him more for all that he
did."

Boyd nodded in agreement.

"I wish it was gonna be that easy for us," he said,
looking at the jar. "I wonder how long those guys will
last?"

Just as Duncan and Boyd were preparing to go out for dinner, and bring back leftovers for the specimens, the phone rang. Duncan thought it was Maggie Cross, whom he wanted to thank for the money.

"Hi, again," he said, "We got the money and I can't thank you enough."

"Pardon me," a man's voice responded.

"Who's this?" Duncan asked suspiciously.

"My name is Haverty, James Haverty. I work for Bio-dynamism and I'm wondering if we could talk."

"What do we have to talk about?"

"I'd rather do it in person, if you don't mind. I'm in the lobby. If it's OK with you, I'd like to take you out to dinner."

Duncan and Boyd were naturally curious about what Haverty would have to say.

"If nothing else, we'll get a free meal out of this," Duncan said as they rode the elevator to meet him.

Haverty, dressed casually in khakis and a short-sleeved, collared shirt, greeted them as they entered the lobby, leading them outside to a limousine parked in front of the hotel.

"I hope you don't mind," Haverty said as they drove, "I've got reservations at Banzeiro. According to TripAdvisor, it's the best restaurant in Manaus. Ever eat there?"

During dinner, Haverty explained that he'd been sent to look after Nolan Thomas's needs and arrange for his medical flight to the states. He learned from Jason Gruber that Duncan had live specimens of Reptilus blaberus.

"When I called the home office, they instructed me to talk to you about what we could do to help you out."

"Really? What kind of help would we need?" Duncan asked.

"Given what you've gone through, you probably want to get back home yesterday. Am I right?"

Boyd and Duncan nodded as they ate.

"Well, we can put you on a private charter and have you back home tomorrow morning. How does that sound?"

"Great," Duncan said, "but why would you do this for us?"

"Yes, cut to the chase, right," Haverty replied. "Well, the company is obviously very interested in your specimens. And we're willing to do whatever it takes to get them safely into a lab where you can pursue your research."

Duncan glanced at Boyd knowingly.

"I don't have a lab," Duncan said. "It's been in all the newspapers. I don't even have a job."

"I know. Your university suspended you, as I recall."

"Since I don't have a lab, I don't see how you can help me."

"The company wants to help in any way it can. We

know the law. We know that you will never get those specimens through customs, not here, not in the United States."

"And you can?" Boyd asked.

"In a word, yes."

"How?"

"The details are unimportant. The company guarantees that we can fly your specimens safely to your lab on our campus."

"My lab?"

"Yes, a world-class lab with as many assistants as you require and whatever else you need to study and breed your specimens."

"Hmmm."

Duncan thought that he must've been dreaming. It sounded too good to be true.

"Can I bring Cody?"

"Of course, anyone you want. We operate like an academic institution, only without sports teams, deans and politics. We're only interested in results."

"What about remuneration?"

"You tell us how much you want."

Duncan was taken aback and had no immediate response. Haverty explained that he could make decisions later but that the company was concerned that the specimens were properly cared for.

"We have a portable habitat for them that I'd like to get them into immediately, if that's OK with you."

"I'm not gonna let them out of my sight," Duncan said.

"I understand that entirely. The habitat is too large to carry into your hotel. We rented a private residence in the Adrianópolis neighborhood. You and your assistant are welcome to stay with us. It's a much better place than where you're staying and you'll be able to keep an eye on your specimens while we take care of everything else. If all goes as planned, we should be in Texas tomorrow."

This is too good to be true, Duncan thought, especially after what he'd been through in the forest. But he had no idea how he could get the specimens out of the country and Biodynamism had a solution that went well beyond his immediate concerns. Boyd seemed happy with it. But so far it was just conversation. He asked how they would formalize their relationship and Haverty said that they would sign a contract in Manaus specifying everything they had discussed and more.

"What do you think, Cody?" Duncan asked as they left the restaurant.

"I don't think you've got a choice. How else can we get the bugs out of here?"

Although Duncan felt anxious about making a decision, the three returned to the hotel where Haverty got his first look at the insects, which were resting at the bottom of the jar.

"So those are the critters," he said. "They look like cockroaches."

"Cockroaches with knives," Boyd said.

"So, Dr. Duncan, are you on board with us?"

Duncan took a deep breath and held out his hand. "Let's shake on it."

THE END

Because reviews are critical in spreading the word about books, please leave a brief review at your online bookseller of choice if you enjoyed this one. Thanks.

Sign-up for the free newsletter (no spam, no BS) to receive updates and exclusive discounts on Insects: Specimens, the final book in the Insects Trilogy:

watchfirepress.com/jk

INSECTS: SPECIMEN - AN EXCERPT

"YOU HAVE TO hear this, boss," Cody Boyd said as he burst into Dr. Howard Duncan's small, sterile office at Biodynamism, Inc.

Duncan, who had been reviewing a spreadsheet on his desktop computer, gave him the annoyed look of someone who had better things to do then engaging in chit-chat.

"Ever hear of knocking?" he asked peevishly.

"Sorry," the young researcher said disingenuously as he slipped into a chair facing Duncan. "This comes from Jason."

Boyd paused as if mentioning the name of Jason Gruber had special magic. Duncan raised his eyes above the black frame of his reading glasses and frowned.

"What is it now?"

"Jason says that Dr. Thomas told his staff to use email if they want to contact him. Can you believe that? No face time."

"What does this have to do with me?"

Boyd's enthusiasm melted quickly.

"Nothing, I suppose," he said, apologetically. "I just thought you might want to know, that's all."

"You know how I hate office politics."

"Technically, this isn't office politics. If you want to know my opinion, which I'm sure you don't but I'm gonna give it anyway, I think he's going nuts."

"You would too if you were him, don't you think?

The man has been through a lot and I don't think it's a good idea to, ah, to report on every foible. Maybe it's his way of coping."

"So you don't think it's weird?" Boyd pressed.

"After what he's been through, no, I don't think it's weird," Duncan said, his annoyance growing. "Anyway, shouldn't you be in the lab working instead of collecting gossip?"

"It's lunch time," Boyd said defensively, rising. "Do you not want me to pass along my intel? We've been here over two months and I'll bet you haven't bothered to learn the names of the people who work for you."

"Of course I know their names," Duncan said. "Even if I didn't, I know your name and you're my senior assistant and you'd know their names."

Boyd was incredulous and told himself as he left the office, carefully closing the door behind him, that he would not let Duncan's attitude bring him down. After all, it was his twenty-seventh birthday. He was still young enough to think it important and worth celebrating and Duncan was forty-five going on sixty, or so it seemed to him. Despite having worked together for three years, the young man didn't fault his boss for not acknowledging his birthday. The man was essentially a computer illiterate and had never bothered to spend the fifteen minutes it would take to manage his own online calendar where he could easily have entered a reminder. Boyd used to maintain it for him when they were in academia but now that he was Duncan's senior research assistant the job fell to Malcolm Desmond, one of the two assistants who reported to him. Desmond was older than Boyd and easy going. In the months said he and Duncan had started working at Biodynamism, Desmond had become Boyd's favorite. They often shared lunch and rode bikes on the company's expansive, wooded campus. It was Desmond who greeted him with "Happy Birthday, boss," when they arrived at the lab that morning. This was Boyd's first supervisory role, and so far he enjoyed it.

Boyd couldn't help but break out into a wide grin as they ate celebratory breakfast tacos at the cafeteria where they often shared gossip and rumors. Even though everyone who worked at Biodynamism signed confidentiality agreements and was instructed at employee orientation not to engage in rumor-mongering or speculation about the work being done there, the employee manual couldn't prohibit human nature.

"I thought I put you in charge of Duncan's calendar," Boyd said with mock disapproval.

"You did, and I do it," Desmond responded guardedly.

"Well, why isn't there a reminder about my birthday?"

"There is," Desmond said. "He just doesn't look at it."

"Is that it?"

"Oh, yeah, I sometimes have to remind him to look at his calendar."

"Really? I didn't know that."

"Oh, yeah. All the time. You want to get his attention, you have to talk to him. Isn't that what you used to do for him when you were working on your master's?"

"Yeah, but I didn't care if he read it. My job was to make sure it was updated."

"Maybe that's the attitude I should have."

"No way," Boyd insisted. "Do as I say, not as I do."

2

"I HATE THE way everything is so compartmentalized in this place," Jason Gruber, senior research assistant to Nolan Thomas, complained to Boyd as they left a lecture hall where company officials chastened senior staff about the failure of staff to properly fill out time records. It was a new system that required employees to record which project they were working on in fifteen-minute increments so the billing department could provide better data to the organizations that sponsored their projects.

"This new system, I hate it," Gruber grumbled.

"I don't like it either," Boyd said. "It's so stupid."

"I know. It's like they expect us to stop whatever we're doing every fifteen minutes to type in a code. Who does that? I mean, we're supposed to be this great research organization and here we are spending more time on accounting than our projects."

Boyd had become friends with Gruber since arriving at Dynamism. They were like two veterans who had shared the terror of the battlefield only to survive with an experience few in the company could relate to. Gruber had unintentionally killed a colleague and it weighed on him whenever he thought about those days in the Brazilian rainforest where the reptilian insect *Reptilus blaberus* had stalked them. Boyd, who had witnessed the death, offered reassurances whenever the dark cloud of guilt came over his friend. He reminded him of how he had risked his life to save one of their group.

"But he died anyway, right? The bugs got him."

"That wasn't your fault."

"I know, I know," Gruber lamented. "I just can't help it."

"How many times do we have to go over this?" Boyd whispered forcefully as they walked down several hallways and out the administrative building to their labs, which were housed in the same two-story building on the western edge of the campus.

"I'm sorry," Gruber said plaintively. "I know I should be able to get past this. but I just can't. My therapist is now thinking I should go on antidepressants for my PTSD. The cognitive therapy isn't working."

"I wish I could help you," Boyd said. "I got over my PTSD pretty quickly after I realized why I was so angry."

"I admire you for that, you know, recognizing your problem and thereby solving it."

"It's not the same. You had it worse. Hell, if I'd killed someone... Aw, shit, I shouldn't have said that."

"No, it's OK. The therapist says talking about it helps me desensitize. And I know, intellectually, if I hadn't done what I did Greg would have died a slow, agonizing death. I just can't work through the emotions, or at least not yet."

"Don't quit trying," Boyd said sympathetically as they entered their secure building.

"Well, you know who's got it worse than me?"

"Who?"

"Dr. Thomas," Gruber said.

3

HOWARD DUNCAN THOUGHT he had everything he needed when he first saw his new lab at Biodynamism. Everything gleamed. The countertops gleamed. The cabinets gleamed. The floors gleamed. Everything was first rate, top of the line. But setting up a lab for the first time was complicated and involved as much accounting as it did science. He had to learn Biodynamism's systems, its administrative software, its human resources department and the organization's rules. Unlike academia, where he was accustomed to discussing and sharing ideas and findings, it seemed that every lab on the campus was compartmentalized from every other lab. As part of his orientation, he visited many of the labs in his building, the first and last time he would set foot in most of them. The lab belonging to Nolan Thomas, the lab he most wanted to see, was off-limits. Something about the contracts he worked under, which he learned later was a subterfuge. It wasn't the contracts that kept others at bay, it was Thomas. It didn't matter at the time because he was still excited about his lab and the chance it offered to study and breed his captive *Reptilus blaberus* specimens.

There were only four specimens, three male and one

female. All were adults and at least four inches long and a little more than an inch in diameter, housed in glass aquaria. He treated them like delicate flowers despite their loathsome appearance and fearsome habits. Anxious to study their behavior in captivity, hoping eventually to understand how they communicated, how they were organized, how long they lived, and a million other things, his primary directive was to have them reproduce. The company CEO impressed this on him at their first meeting.

Galen Mazur was a driven and commanding figure despite his nearly sixty years. Energetic, trim and younger looking than his age, he had always been energized by challenges, such as turning the once moribund bioscience company into a booming operation fueled by a portfolio of corporate and government projects, some of them so highly classified that to even name them would be a violation of federal law.

Mazur spoke grandly but vaguely about the company's work and how far it had come since the days it had been churning out generic medications under contract with big pharmaceutical outfits.

"These are exciting times for us, Dr. Duncan," he said enthusiastically as Duncan admired Mazur's sumptuous office. Sitting in front of the huge, custom-made desk, its top devoid of anything that would interrupt the visual appeal of its highly polished exotic hardwoods, Duncan felt reassured that he had come to the right place. Money was no object here. No longer would he be subservient to funding agencies.

"I realize you've recently arrived and everything is new to you, but your project is extremely important to us. As you know, we went to great lengths to bring you and your specimens here."

"I'm very grateful for that," Duncan said absently, still drinking in details of the impressive office.

Mazur smiled.

"Impressed, aren't you."

"Oh, yeah," Duncan said admiringly. "I've never seen anything like this office. It's like something out of the movies."

"Well, the company rewards success and we've been very successful, as I expect you to be. So, tell me, briefly, what are your plans for your specimens."

Until this point, Duncan had been more attentive to his admiration for the office than the conversation. He snapped out of it quickly, realizing that this meeting was not just about pleasantries.

"The specimens are doing well. They are taking food and so far they seem to be getting along with each other."

"That's good. When do you think you'll start breeding them?"

Duncan was surprised by the question, as if he had the power to make them reproduce. At this point he was happy that the creatures hadn't killed each other, though he had no reason to believe that they would be belligerent toward each other. Everything he'd seen of them in the wild suggested that they were highly cooperative and organized. How they behaved in captivity, however, was a complete unknown.

"That's a good question," Duncan stammered. "What we first have to do is determine whether they will reproduce on their own. As you may know, they are ovoviviparous and what we believe is that they are prolific, but the only person who I know who studied them was unsuccessful at breeding them. Of course, his facilities were primitive compared to ours. But that was before they overcame the limitation that killed off most of the juveniles. That was before what happened in Brazil."

"So, you're starting from scratch."

"Yes," Duncan said, smiling.

"What's your timeline?"

"I don't have one at this time. We're just getting started."

"The reason I ask is because one of Dr. Thomas's projects depends on the success of your breeding program. Your project and his are very important to us, and I will be monitoring both of them closely. You understand, results are important here," Mazur said matter-of-factly.

"Yes, of course," Duncan said, suddenly perplexed. Was the honeymoon over before it started?

Before he could say another word, a large flat screen monitor descended from the ceiling.

"I'm sorry, I have a teleconference coming up. Thanks for coming by," Mazur said, turning his attention to the monitor.

Duncan rose awkwardly and moved slowly toward the double doors that opened into a spacious lobby. On his way, he paused to look at photos and certificates on a wall. Some of them were military decorations and others were photos of Mazur shaking hands with important politicians and others were of him in military gear, his collars emblazoned with silver eagles. Looking back, he saw that the CEO watched him, as if urging him to leave the office before starting his teleconference. Duncan got the hint and moved quickly, not certain whether the meeting had been a success. The place would take some getting used to, he thought.

4

In the time it took Duncan to walk from the administrative building to his lab office, his departmental administrator, Gabriel Cox, wanted to meet with him. The two had met several times since Duncan's start at the company but the meetings had been scheduled. This one was not.

Cox's office was small, windowless, and stocked with medium grade institutional furnishings. The most unusual arrangement was a longish table along one wall with a large computer monitor in the center, flanked by two smaller screens. All of them displayed the Biodynamism logo. His desktop was neat, with an in-out basket on one corner, a large desk pad calendar filled with scribbles and several short stacks of folders.

"I must say that I'm impressed," Cox after exchanging greetings and directing Duncan to sit.

"Pardon me?"

"You've been here a week and already you've had a private meeting with the big boss."

Duncan smiled and shrugged while Cox fidgeted with the folders. In his forties, with neatly trimmed hair turning gray on the sides, open face and high-cheek bones, Duncan thought he looked like a TV newscaster.

"He called me and I came running."

"Hmm."

"Did I do something wrong?"

"No, not really. It's just that as your departmental administrator, you should have told me."

"I'm sorry, I didn't know that."

"Yeah, it's just one of the many things they don't tell you about in orientation. I know you're new here and, really, you're quite the star, or Mr. Mazur wouldn't have called you to his office. That's really quite an honor, you know. I've been here nearly five years and I was invited to his office only once, and even then it was with several others. Of course, I've had other contacts with him, just not in his office."

Duncan looked puzzled.

"So, is that why you called me into your office?"

"Not entirely. I'd like to explain a few things to you about how this place works."

Suddenly, the purpose of the meeting became clear to Duncan. He thought that working at a corporation would be different than working at a university. Apparently, micromanagement could not be evaded. Not good at disguising his feelings, his expression hardened, which Cox noticed immediately. He was well aware of the adversarial relationship that often developed between employees and management and was schooled in how to deal with it. Because of Duncan's status as a scientist and, more importantly, his precious *blaberus* specimens, he needed to keep Duncan happy, but at the same time he didn't want him to ignore the chain of command.

Responding to Cox, Duncan told him that he had gotten a call from the CEO's secretary and that he wanted to meet immediately.

"You see, even if I knew that I'm supposed to tell you about my meetings…"

"Not all of them, just the ones involving people higher than me, especially the big guy. You can appreciate that, right? You would expect the same thing were you in my place. Right?"

"I understand where you're coming from," Duncan said. "I'll definitely keep that in mind. My only interest really is my research."

"Excellent, now tell me what he said."

"Pardon me?"

"Your meeting with Mazur. What did he say, exactly?"

5

Cody Boyd was scanning curriculum vitae that HR had forwarded to him in an email. His job was to choose two from the six on offer. All of them were employed at Dynamism.

"Looks like the company likes to promote from within," he said, as Howard Duncan returned to his office.

"That can be a good thing," Duncan said. "How do they look?"

"I'm not sure I could get a job here, that's how they look."

"You're impressed."

Boyd nodded, swiveling his chair to face his boss.

"What's up? How'd your meeting go?"

Pouring himself a cup of decaf from the office coffee maker, he sat next to Boyd and stared at the screen momentarily.

"I think we could flip a coin on all of them," Boyd said.

"The meeting was kinda strange."

"How so?"

"Oh, he talked about the chain of command—apparently it's a violation for me to talk to the CEO without telling him about it—but then he got into this spiel about how because everything is so compartmentalized here that you have to create your own networks of people to know what's really going on."

"Sort of like at the university?"

"Yeah, but more so. I got the impression he's deathly afraid of being out of the loop."

Boyd nodded knowingly.

"That's what Jason told me. He said it helps to make friends with a lot of people. He said most the managers are paranoid that their bosses will ask them something and they won't have an answer. Kinda weird, isn't it?"

"I take it you're building a network."

"Definitely."

"Good, then I don't have to. Now, why don't you printout the CVs and I'll have a look at them."

6

BECAUSE *REPTILUS BLABERUS* was more than an insect, incorporating traits that normally occur in mammals and reptiles, there were no off-the-shelf breeding kits they could purchase. Duncan's lab had to develop its own approach while at the same time keeping the specimens alive. The scientists worried about the adult males fighting each other over the female so they were isolated from the female in separate aquaria. So little was known about the carnivores' behavior that the scientists feared everything. They feared the female might eat the young. They feared parasites infecting the specimens. Above all, Duncan feared the return of the fungus that had killed most juveniles in the wild.

Throughout the ordeals in Brazil, Duncan felt he knew little about *blaberus*, though in retrospect he could write page after page describing what he had learned about them, some of which he obtained from the research of Professor Fernando Azevedo, whose crowning achievement was identifying the mechanism by which the insects were transformed from tiny, fragile swarms into huge colonies of organized and savage butchers. Azevedo's key finding pointed to the *tabebuia avellanedae*, a tree also known as Pau D'Arco, as the source of a crystal that proved fatal to the fungus. Though he could not determine how *blaberus* had come in contact with the crystal, his research resulted in headlines throughout North America as well as his own gruesome death.

Reproduction was just the starting point for Duncan's lab. He knew the creatures reproduced prolifically in the wild. More important to him was to learn how the invertebrates organized themselves and how they communicated, especially how they foraged for food. In the lab they showed no aversion to consuming bits of irradiated meat that constituted their diet in captivity. In the wild, they hunted, but they did it in groups. He wondered if there was a population threshold beyond which they would engage in foraging. And how was it that thousands of little carnivores, working in groups of several hundred, could scour the rainforest floor for food with all of them converging when a victim was found and somehow reporting to the main colony the location of its next meal? How do they do that? he wondered. How did they do that in such a way that the victim would be incapacitated until the arrival of the main colony, which would reduce it to a skeleton? And how did they develop the tactic of immediately attacking the soft parts of a victim, particularly the eyes and mouth?

"If only we can get our female to reproduce," he told Boyd. "Before she dies of old age."

END OF CHAPTER 6

To receive an email directly to your inbox when
Insects: Specimens is released, please sign up for the free
newsletter at <u>watchfirepress.com/jk</u>.

ABOUT THE AUTHOR

JOHN KOLOEN, a native of Wisconsin, has been a long-shoreman, construction worker, newspaperman, magazine publisher and bureaucrat. He lives in Galveston, TX, with his wife Laura Burns. He is the author of *Insects* and *Insects: The Hunted.*

To receive updates on John's upcoming books, including future titles in the *Insects* series, please signup for the free newsletter at watchfirepress.com/jk.

Made in the USA
San Bernardino, CA
08 November 2016